Praise for

DEAD TO ME

"Simon Canderous is a reformed thief and a psychometrist. By turns despondent over his luck with the ladies (not always living) and his struggle with the hierarchy of his mysterious department (not always truthful), Simon's life veers from crisis to crisis. Following Simon's adventures is like being the pinball in an especially antic game, but it's well worth the wear and tear."

—Charlaine Harris, *New York Times* bestselling author of *From Dead to Worse*

"Part *Ghostbusters*, part *Men in Black*, Strout's debut is both dark and funny, with quirky characters, an eminently likable protagonist, and the comfortable, familiar voice of a close friend. His mix of (mostly) secret bureaucratic bickering and offbeat action shows New York like we've never seen it before. Make room on the shelf, 'cause you're going to want to keep this one!"

—Rachel Vincent, author of *Stray* and *Rogue*

"Urban fantasy with a wink and a nod. Anton Strout has written a good-hearted send-up of the urban-fantasy genre. *Dead to Me* is a genuinely fun book with a fresh and firmly tongue-in-cheek take on the idea of paranormal police. The laughs are frequent, as are the wry smiles. I'm looking forward to seeing what he does next."

—Kelly McCullough, author of *CodeSpell*

"Written with equal parts humor and horror. Strout creates an engaging character . . . clever, fast paced, and a refreshing change in the genre of urban fantasy." —*SFRevu*

continued . . .

"In much the same vein as Mark Del Franco's *Unquiet Dreams* or John Levitt's *Dog Days*, Strout's urban-fantasy debut features plenty of self-deprecating humor, problematic special powers, and a quick pace, with the added twist of overwhelming government bureaucracy. Strout's inventive story line raises the genre's bar with his collection of oddly mismatched, entertaining characters and not-so-secret organizations."
—*Monsters and Critics*

"Imagine if Harry Dresden or Angel had to work in a poorly run office dealing with office politics and red tape. It's a great debut."
—Cameron Hughes, CHUD.com

"A wickedly weird debut from a writer who makes being dead sexier than it's ever been before. And who doesn't love a debonair divination-having, ghost-seducing, cultist-abusing detective in New York? Imagine *Law & Order* but with hot ghostly chicks, rampaging bookcases, and a laugh track."
—Carolyn Turgeon, author of *Rain Village*

"A strong debut . . . Seeing the world through Simon's eyes is a funny, quirky, and occasionally scary experience. Strout's world will be well worth revisiting."
—*Romantic Times*

Ace Books by Anton Strout

DEAD TO ME
DEADER STILL

DEADER STILL

Anton Strout

ACE BOOKS, NEW YORK

THE BERKLEY PUBLISHING GROUP
Published by the Penguin Group
Penguin Group (USA) Inc.
375 Hudson Street, New York, New York 10014, USA
Penguin Group (Canada), 90 Eglinton Avenue East, Suite 700, Toronto, Ontario M4P 2Y3, Canada
(a division of Pearson Penguin Canada Inc.)
Penguin Books Ltd., 80 Strand, London WC2R 0RL, England
Penguin Group Ireland, 25 St. Stephen's Green, Dublin 2, Ireland (a division of Penguin Books Ltd.)
Penguin Group (Australia), 250 Camberwell Road, Camberwell, Victoria 3124, Australia
(a division of Pearson Australia Group Pty. Ltd.)
Penguin Books India Pvt. Ltd., 11 Community Centre, Panchsheel Park, New Delhi—110 017, India
Penguin Group (NZ), 67 Apollo Drive, Rosedale, North Shore 0632, New Zealand
(a division of Pearson New Zealand Ltd.)
Penguin Books (South Africa) (Pty.) Ltd., 24 Sturdee Avenue, Rosebank, Johannesburg 2196,
South Africa

Penguin Books Ltd., Registered Offices: 80 Strand, London WC2R 0RL, England

This is a work of fiction. Names, characters, places, and incidents either are the product of the author's imagination or are used fictitiously, and any resemblance to actual persons, living or dead, business establishments, events, or locales is entirely coincidental. The publisher does not have any control over and does not assume any responsibility for author or third-party websites or their content.

DEADER STILL

An Ace Book / published by arrangement with the author

PRINTING HISTORY
Ace mass-market edition / March 2009

Copyright © 2009 by Anton Strout.
Cover art by Don Sipley.
Cover design by Annette Fiore DeFex.
Interior text design by Laura K. Corless.

ISBN: 978-0-441-01691-4

ACE
Ace Books are published by The Berkley Publishing Group,
a division of Penguin Group (USA) Inc.,
375 Hudson Street, New York, New York 10014.
ACE and the "A" design are trademarks of Penguin Group (USA) Inc.

PRINTED IN THE UNITED STATES OF AMERICA

10   9   8   7   6   5   4   3   2   1

For Donna Marie Strout,
whose sense of humor lives on through me

ACKNOWLEDGMENTS

First and foremost, this book is to you, my readerly little friends. Perhaps you've just picked me up for the first time. Maybe you are part of the Undead Approved, who have already read *Dead to Me*. Whatever way you came to this book, thanks for being here. The adventures of Simon Canderous are nothing without you, and for that you have my sincere and deepest appreciation. Welcome aboard; thanks for joining us. Tell your friends. Say hi to your mother for me.

As for the rest of my hive of scum and villainy? It's time to thank them. Hold your applause to the end, please. My personal kudos are extended to: my wife, Orly, whose patience and love are infinite; my family—those by blood and those by association; Jessica Wade, the editor whose verbosity makes my inanity palatable; superagent Kristine Dahl and Laura Neely at ICM, who put up with my authorly neuroses; copy editor Jessica McDonnell; Annette Fiore DeFex, Judith Murello, and Don Sipley, for another amazing cover; Michelle Kasper; the Dorks of the Round Table—authors Jeanine Cummins and Carolyn Turgeon—for taking time to bruise their eyes on the first draft of this book (support their books, too!); beta reader and cheerleader Missy Sawmiller; beta reader and glamazon Lisa Trevethan; Patrick Rothfuss, my arch nemesis and author of *The Name of the Wind*, who graciously took the time to read a wee baby draft of the manuscript; and the fans, whose snowball effect keeps people coming to the series.

And finally, a special shout-out to all of the various departments at Penguin Group (USA) Inc. that make this book look as pretty as it does, especially my friends and colleagues in the paperback sales department who keep me humble and—more importantly—on bookshelves everywhere. Your names are legion, for you are many.

Revenge is a dish best served . . . erk!

—Anonymous quote found in the Gauntlet archives
attributed to a long-deceased member of
the Fraternal Order of Goodness

1

"Watch out for the elves, Simon," Connor Christos said, tugging at my arm. And since I had come to trust my partner in Other Division, I didn't resist.

He pulled me to my left, allowing me to narrowly avoid two "elves." One wore glasses with black Buddy Holly frames, and the other couldn't have been more than five feet tall.

"Lothlorien sure ain't making 'em like they used to," I said.

"Welcome to New York Comic Con, kid."

"Nerdtacular," I said. All walks of life crowded the hangarlike convention hall. The giant glass structure of the Javits Center on Manhattan's west side looked like it had been conjured straight out of a futuristic fantasy world.

"Would you rather be back at our desks at the Department of Extraordinary Affairs?" Connor asked.

"Lower your voice," I said, looking around.

"Relax," Connor said. "We're the most normal-looking guys in here."

Connor looked like the older and stranger of the two of

us, with a white stripe running through his messy mop of
sandy brown hair. His Bogart-style trench coat hid his
rugged frame, but even that had been no match for the
ghost who had streaked his hair. Comparatively, I was the
picture of youth, with my own hair black, through and
through, still untouched by ghostly harm. Even my knee-
length black leather coat was more fashionable, and did
double duty—both hiding my retractable bat and paying
homage to the one the do-gooder vampire Angel always
wore on television.

"Even so," I said, "I'd prefer it if you kept it down about
the D.E.A."

Connor shook his head. "No one here's even going to bat
an eye at our supersecret government agency." He cupped
his hand over his mouth and shouted, "Paranormal investigators in the house!"

Very few people turned to look at us. A few *woot*s rose
out of the crowd, and when I turned to look we were being
cheered on by a group of guys dressed as Ghostbusters,
pumping the business ends of their proton packs in the
air.

"See?" he said. "Now don't tell me you'd rather be in
the office . . ."

I thought of the pile of paperwork waiting for me—ghost
sightings, zombie infestations, demons rollicking through
hipster bars out in Williamsburg, the usual.

"Actually, this freak show is looking pretty good to me
right now." I held up my writing hand and flexed it, hearing
it pop and crack as I did so. "Besides, if I have to fill out
another form in triplicate, I think my hand will fall off.
And not in the cool, zombie-rotting way, either . . ."

Connor shook his head. "Less than a year in the Department, and you're already burned out on the red tape, huh?"
He pointed at the crowd before us. "Then this place should
take your mind off of all that for a bit. You've got every
type of geekdom out here in full force. Your fans of every-

thing come out for this one, dressed to the nines: superheroes, elves, robots, Jedis, Trekkies. Pirates are really big this year."

"Great," I said. "*That* should help me stay focused today."

"Just relax," he said. "Every agent's been put through the Oubliette."

"And passed it?"

"Well," Connor said, pausing. "No . . ."

"I don't want that to be me," I said, feeling my nerves rising. I'd joined the New York Department of Extraordinary Affairs seven months ago. I was blessed (or cursed) with psychometry, the ability to touch an object and divine information about its past, so getting the job had turned a power that had ruined many a relationship and been a major burden into a highlight of my résumé. Connor had been assigned as my mentor for these past few months, and I appreciated that, but I wanted to pass the Oubliette and earn my stripes as his full-fledged partner. "I don't want to wait another year to retake the test if I fail it."

"Relax," Connor repeated. "You'll do fine."

"Easy to say for someone who passed it years ago and actually got to test on the Oubliette the Department owns."

"Owned," Connor corrected. "With the budget cuts down at City Hall, I don't think the Department's going to be able to afford to fix it. And trust me, from what I've heard, you definitely don't want to be going into *that* Oubliette. Something's living in it now. I don't know exactly what, but Inspectre Quimbley said it was quite unsavory."

"Well, who am I to argue with the director of Other Division?"

"And don't forget he's your superior in the Fraternal Order of Goodness," Connor added. "Not that I'm part of your precious little organization."

I noted the hint of bitterness in Connor's voice.

"Hey," I said. "I was just as surprised as you were when

I got their letter adopting me into their ranks. Their initiation felt like a cross between a toga party and the Skull and Bones society."

Connor started playing the world's tiniest violin between his fingers, so I decided it was best to avoid the subject even though it had only happened a few short months ago. It was like being in high school all over again, except I was in all the advanced-placement classes now. F.O.G. wasn't technically part of the official New York government function of the D.E.A. anyway. I didn't even fully understand where the line between the two was drawn, but I knew that the Fraternal Order of Goodness predated the Department by several hundred years and functioned more like the Freemasons, only they didn't seem to issue cool swords. However, they did have resources the Department didn't have, and they weren't bogged down by nearly as much red tape.

"Still," I said, trying to steer the conversation back to why we had come to Comic Con. "I wouldn't normally think of a comic book convention as a place to rent a magical Oubliette."

Connor shrugged. "But here we are. You'd be surprised at what can pass unnoticed in an environment like this. You ready to go all MacGyver?"

"MacGyver?"

"You know," Connor said. "You ready to improvise on whatever harsh battle conditions the Oubliette decides to put you through?"

I shrugged. "As ready as I can be. I've studied as much as I could over at Tome, Sweet Tome."

"Oh, so Jane helped?" Connor asked. At the mention of my ex-cultist girlfriend, I got a case of the warm fuzzies.

"Director Wesker's been putting her through all this cataloging work while they try to figure out how Mandalay had the place organized before we took it over," I said.

"But even with all that busy work, she found some time to help me go over various Oubliette scenarios. We read up on the two carnival wheels that determine my fate. Then we played out the various combinations of weapons it could give to aid me and what the different challenges thrown at me might be. I'm hoping I get a good combo. I'd love it if the Oubliette gave me a silver-tipped crossbow and matched it up with a werewolf. Fingers crossed!"

"I can't tell which is worse for Jane," Connor said, "having worked for the forces of evil or having to work for Thaddeus Wesker in Greater and Lesser Arcana Division. Still, sounds like she's trying to help you live through this thing. Not bad for an ex-cultist temp."

"Watch it," I said, not really taking him too seriously. "She worked for the Sectarian Defense League more for the benefits package than anything. I think helping me pin their leader to the wall with a sword proves she's turned over a new leaf."

"Fair enough," Connor said, stopping at an intersection to look around. "I'd like to think Jane and I have softened toward each other over the past three months."

As I waited for him to pick a direction, I couldn't help but eye all the tables full of collectibles. I adjusted the well-worn leather gloves I had on. With my psychometric ability, it was hard to keep my hands to myself near all this geeky merchandise. Part of me would love to have touched something and read the past of the object, but now was so not the time for that kind of distraction. While I had gotten better at controlling my powers as of late, I was pretty sure going into the Oubliette after having depleted my blood sugar over a bunch of knickknacks was a surefire way to fail it outright.

"Come on," Connor said, heading off to our right. "I think Inspectre Quimbley and Wesker said it was set up down this way."

"So why *is* Wesker going to be here?" I asked. "Does

the director of Greater and Lesser Arcana have nothing better to do than come ridicule me? We're Other Division. He doesn't even hold any jurisdiction over us."

"But he does hold it over anything magical happening in the tristate area," Connor said, "so Inspectre Quimbley is letting him make sure that the Oubliette rental goes smoothly."

"So Wesker's hope that I fail is just a bonus for him today, is it?"

"Something like that, kid," Connor said.

The traffic of humanity thinned out a little over in this section of the Javits Center. We turned down one aisle and walked until it dead-ended at a hanging blue curtain. Connor pulled it aside.

"After you," he said.

I stepped through into an open space about twenty feet square. The Inspectre and Director Wesker were there, and smack in the center of the curtained-off area was the Oubliette itself. I had only seen pictures of one before, but up close and in person the object that would decide my fate in the Department was a bit underwhelming. Essentially it looked like a prop from a stage show—a round stone well on a wheeled platform. It looked like the kind of well people made wishes on, complete with a little wooden roof and a winch bar running between the beams, with rope coiled around it. Although it didn't look deep enough to even stand in, I knew that once I was lowered inside it, it would open up into the magic and dangerous well I had been studying.

As Connor and I crossed to the Inspectre, a hulking figure rose up from behind the well, a giant of a man who looked like he could be brothers with Penn Gillette.

"Don't tell me I have to fight a giant, as well," I whispered, hoping he couldn't hear me.

"Heavens no," the Inspectre chimed in. He had a booming British accent and a walruslike mustache. "Unless, I suppose, that's one of the options on the challenge wheel for the Oubliette." He waved the huge man over. "Julius, come here."

The giant came over, moving much more nimbly that I would have expected for a man of his size. He held a wooden easel in his hand.

"*This*," the Inspectre said, patting me on the shoulder, "is the young man who'll be testing in the Oubliette today. Simon Canderous."

Julius put down the easel and offered his hand. I took it. With hands that big, he easily could have palmed my entire head like a basketball.

"Julius Heron," he said, sounding like that should mean something to me. He looked hopeful. "Of the Brothers Heron?"

I nodded uncertainly.

"Nothing?" he asked. "You've . . . never heard of us?"

"Sorry," I said, "no."

He looked disappointed. "We're world renowned . . ."

"I'm sure you are," I said, "but I'm kind of new to all this and I don't get out much."

His face brightened. "That's probably it. Anyway, good luck," he said, and headed back over toward the well.

Julius set up two easels and attached the Wheels of Misfortune to them, miniature versions of the one Pat Sajak uses. One Wheel listed the types of equipment I might be given to survive with, while the other listed the challenges, sporting names like Scarifying Scarabs, Sinking Sand Trap, Grievous Guillotine, Watery Grave, Leaping Lizards, and Ravenous Rats. A chill ran down my spine. Although I was a native New Yorker—and therefore rat-familiar by association—the idea of them in particular creeped me out like nobody's business.

As I tried to shake off the heebie-jeebies, the Inspectre turned to Wesker. "Is everything about ready?"

Wesker walked around the well once and checked out the Wheels. He gave the Inspectre a nod.

"Now, then," the Inspectre said, "all that's left is the pat down. If you'll permit me . . . ?"

I held my arms apart and spread my legs farther apart. This felt dangerously similar to my past brushes with the law, but I knew it was simply to make sure I wasn't bringing anything into the Oubliette that would prove helpful in the test.

The Inspectre stopped when he felt the leather holster I usually hung my retractable bat in. It didn't help that I had forgotten to remove the bat from it. He gave me a stern look.

"Sorry," I said, reaching inside my coat and pulling the bat out of it. I handed it over. "Force of habit."

"You mean being a cheater?" Wesker asked, moving closer, no doubt to keep an eye on me.

I ignored him, but after the Inspectre was done with his search, Wesker started looking me over as well.

"What's that?" he said, pointing at a rectangular-shaped item in my front pocket.

"My cell phone," I said, "but if I get to the point where I have to throw it at whatever challenge awaits me down there, I've probably already failed, right?"

"Leave the boy alone now, Thaddeus," the Inspectre said. He turned to me. "Shall we?"

I stepped over to the well and looked down. The shaft plunged into darkness, and I got a sense of disorienting vertigo from the difference of its depth compared to the shallowness of the showroom floor. With little effort, Julius helped lift me up onto the edge of it and then handed me the winch rope to secure around my waist. I pulled off my gloves and tied the rope around myself. Julius gave it a tug.

"Too tight?" he asked.

I shook my head. "It does make me feel like a giant yo-yo, though."

Connor laughed. "No arguments here, kid."

"Would you rather go down there?"

"Been there," he said, backing up, hands raised, "passed that."

The Inspectre stepped forward. "Enough horsing around," he said. His face was serious and he lowered his voice to a whisper. "Listen, my boy. Keep your wits about you and you'll do fine."

"Yes, sir."

"But remember. While many regular Department members have washed out in the Oubliette before, no member of the Fraternal Order of Goodness *ever* has."

Nothing like a little last-minute pressure to get the heart going. Before the Inspectre could say anything further to unnerve me, I pushed myself off the edge of the well and began my descent into the Oubliette.

I focused my mind on everything Jane and I had gone over together. Right now I was in the forty-foot shaft that would eventually open into a large, circular, stone-clad pit. I'd have to watch out for a central hole in the floor, a pit within this pit, the lower one traditionally used for excrement and dead prisoners—at least in nonmagical Oubliettes out there in the world.

After about twenty seconds of being winched slowly downward, I looked back up the stone-walled shaft. Three heads were peering down from above.

"What's the matter, Simon?" Wesker sneered. "Don't care much for small spaces?"

"Leave the kid alone, Thaddeus," Connor said. "I bet you wet yourself when they put you through this."

"Listen, you ungrateful toad . . ."

"Hey," I shouted, "can I have a little quiet? Trying not to die down here!"

"Let the boy concentrate," Inspectre Quimbley said, the ends of his mustache dropping down into the shaft like hairy little stalactites.

"Go get 'em, kid," Connor shouted. "You'll do fine. Besides, I don't want to have to break in a new partner."

"We *do* have safety measures in place, you know," the

Inspectre said, more to Connor than me. He sounded offended.

While the three of them continued watching and talking amongst themselves, I attempted to shut them out. I had to keep my mind focused on the test.

The chattering overhead stopped and I looked up. The Inspectre gave me a hearty thumbs-up.

"Alrighty," he said. "We're spinning the Wheels now."

From the top of the shaft a *click-clack-click*ing began, and I could actually feel energy in the air as the magic started locking in around me. I waited with dread for whatever both Wheels stopped on. I knew I could do this. I *had* to do this, and I would. I was up for any of the challenges presented to me, but what I really dreaded hearing was . . .

"Ravenous Rats," Wesker said, rolling the R's and savoring every evil-sounding syllable of it. It was hard to believe he was one of the good guys sometimes.

"Are you *kidding* me?" I shouted up. "Are you fu—?"

Before I could finish my expletive, the twin blades of one of the other challenges on that Wheel—the Grievous Guillotine—shot out of the wall above me, cutting the rope and dropping me like a sack of seriously screwed Simons. As I fell, I clawed at the sides of the pit, barely slowing the last twenty feet of the fall. I hit the ground hard, but thankfully the leather of my coat cushioned a great deal of the blow. With the wind knocked out of me, lying there and not moving would have been nice. Not that I had that kind of time—the rats would be coming soon.

"What the hell's going on?" I shouted up at them. "Why the hell did the guillotine go off? The challenge Wheel already selected the rats. One peril, that's the rules of the test!"

"Hang on," Connor said, his voice full of uncertainty. "We're experiencing some kind of technical difficulty, kid."

"*You* hang on!" I shouted back. "If something's gone wrong, just get me out of here. Lower the rest of the rope."

"That would fall under the banner of technical difficulty," Connor said. "The winch is jammed."

None of the Oubliette challenge was going according to what I had studied, and now I heard the sound of approaching rats. I rolled onto my side, feeling an ache in my lower back. I positioned my arm on the stone floor to push myself up, but one of my still-gloveless hands came to rest on something, and my mind automatically slipped into psychometric mode.

Given the distractions of pain and trying to orient myself, I didn't even get a chance to think about controlling my power. Suddenly, I was sucked into the past of someone else who had been in this Oubliette. This poor guy was neck-deep in slithering snakes, and thanks to the fact that I was experiencing *everything* he was, I was treated to the sensation of a thousand twisting tails and flicking tongues all over my body. With desperation, I concentrated on pulling myself out of the vision, but found it near impossible with so much sensory input overwhelming me. I closed the eyes of the person I was, blocking out at least the visual of him slowly going under in a sea of snakes. That seemed to help, and as I returned to my own mind I traded the sound of incessant hissing for the squeak and chittering of the approaching rats.

As the first of them came skittering out of holes in the stonework, I quickly pulled my gloves off of my belt and slid them on just in case I came across anything else I might accidentally touch that would trigger my power. I scrambled to my feet and looked up. The opening above was a pinprick of light now, and I could no longer make out the features on the three faces looking down on me. I could, however, still make out the sound of the second Wheel still clacking away.

I yelled up to the opening of the well. "What about the other Wheel, the one that picks my survival equipment?" I asked. "When do I get my equipment?"

"That still seems to be functioning," the Inspectre said with cheer in his voice. Finally, I heard the other Wheel slow to a stop. The Inspectre read off it. "Your equipment is . . . a wooden stake and holy water. Should be conjured up any second, my boy."

Great. Even the equipment being provided wasn't the proper gear for facing this challenge. A torch had been the preferred method of fighting rats that I had studied—even the club option would have been welcomed—but a stake and holy water? If I had been facing vampires, I would have been all set. I doubted either item would have much effect on the rats, unless these were some strange new breed of vampire rats. The holy water would prove useless. The stake, however, at least had a pointy, jabby end, so it still held a hint of promise.

As if on cue, an audible pop of materialization came from directly over my head, and I looked up in time to see the two items in question falling toward me. The thin metal vial of holy water fell first and I caught it deftly with one hand. The stake, however, was falling end over end, and rather than let the pointy end possibly jab into my hand, I opted to let it fall to the ground. Or rather, it would have fallen to the ground if the ground wasn't fully covered with the growing spread of rats. Instead, the stake sank into the sea of rats and disappeared from sight.

What I wouldn't have given to have had my retractable bat right then. I kicked at the rats, but my feet were slow to move through the growing depth of rodents and it was of little use. To find the stake, I was going to have to reach into the mass of rats, no matter how much the idea squicked me out. Thank God I at least had my gloves with me.

The circular room was now calf-deep in rats, and because of their sheer volume they could no longer avoid the guillotine blades popping in and out of the walls. Still-twitching bits of rats started flying through the air. I bent over the spot where I had last seen the stake and thrust my hand down into the writhing mass of still-living rats. As I fished around, I pulled my face as far from the rats as I could. The thought of them clawing and biting at me made me want to scream, but I kept searching. I could feel tiny teeth pulling and working their way through the thick leather of my gloves, and I stood back up.

More rats were climbing up my pant legs, nipping at the denim and digging their claws in. I tried to brush them away, but for every rat I swatted, two more appeared out of the swarm.

I looked up. "Hey, guys. Two perils. Still imperiling me! A little help here," I shouted.

I could see the hands of Inspectre Quimbley and Connor frantically uncoiling what remained of the rope from the jammed winch. Even with the two of them working on it, the end of the rope was still well above me. By my quick calculation, I'd be three feet over my head in rats before they could lower it far enough. There was nothing I could do.

I heard a shrill squeak of pain and looked down. One of the rats had been tearing through the fabric on my jeans but reeled back when it tried to bite me and came across something hard in my pocket. My cell phone. In my panic, I had almost forgotten they had let me keep it. I batted the rodent away and tore my phone free from the gaping hole. I was thrilled to see I had service down here. Maybe it was the magical nature of the Oubliette, but right now I didn't care. I did what I was sure any other guy would do when he was up to his knees in supernaturally generated rats—I called my girlfriend. After all, not every guy had a girlfriend who dabbled in magic.

After I dialed, the phone rang for what felt like forever before Jane answered.

"Tome, Sweet Tome," she said. "You spell it, we sell it. This is Jane speaking."

"Jane," I said, thrilled to hear her voice.

"Hi, hon," she said. "Did you like the catchphrase? I've been trying them out for the store. What do you think?"

"Not now," I screamed. The bites were increasing.

"It wasn't a very good one, was it?" she said. "How about . . . oh, my God, you have the Oubliette today, don't you? Is it over? How did you do?"

"Later," I shouted. "I'm in the Oubliette and kind of in a sitch right now. A knee-deep-in-rats sitch that's about to become a neck-deep-in-rats sitch any second now. And the guillotines are going off as well. I'm fucked, hon. I thought that since you've been working with Arcana for a bit . . ."

That seemed to kill any chatter in her and she went silent. The rustling of paper filled the line.

"Hon . . . ?" I said. "Hello?"

"Be quiet," she said. "I'm looking for something . . ."

"I just wanted to tell you that I love you," I said, wading through the rats. "You know . . . if this doesn't turn itself around fast."

"Just shut *up*," Jane said sternly this time. "I need to concentrate."

"Where *are* you?"

"I'm in the Black Stacks," she said over the sound of more page flipping. "And I'm trying to save your life, so shut it."

"You're in the Stacks? You think looking through Cyrus Mandalay's prized collection of diabolical books is going to help us out?"

"It's not his anymore," Jane reminded me.

I thought of the last time I had seen him, the night he'd escaped from the Metropolitan Museum of Art when the Department had come down on his whole ectoplasmic Ghostsniffing ring. Being trapped down here in the Oubliette with all these rats almost made me miss that chaos-filled night.

I decided to follow Jane's initial advice to "shut it" and I let her concentrate. If I didn't, she might grab the wrong book off the shelves of the Black Stacks and I'd be screwed. Right now she was my only hope.

With the volume of rats reaching waist height now, I figured there had to be a way to at least get above them or on top of them, packed in as they were. I attempted to pull myself up. It felt like I was fighting my way out of a pit of quicksand, only quicksand tended to bite a lot less. At least my upper body was protected by my leather jacket, but my legs were still being scratched to hell.

The writhing rat mass shifted underneath me. My balance gave out and I toppled over. My body immediately sank into the rats, tails and claws flicking against my face as I hurriedly tried to curl myself up into a protective ball. A tail slid into my ear and I pushed it away with my phone, stifling a scream. I didn't want to even think what would happen if I opened my mouth.

"Not to rush you," I said through clenched teeth into the phone, "but right now would be a good time for . . . anything!"

"I'm not sure if this will work," Jane said, "but I think I found something."

Although magic wasn't my thing, I was willing to give it a shot. Dire circumstances made strange bedfellows.

"Lay it on me," I said. "Read it to me."

"No time to explain it," she said. "It's not somatic. Just hold out the phone and put me on speaker."

As much as I didn't want to expose any part of myself, I pushed the speaker button and extended my arm. Instantly I felt tiny noses and heads trying to jam their way up the sleeve of my jacket.

"Okay," I shouted through gritted teeth.

Sound started coming through the phone, but it wasn't speech, or even Jane's voice. If anything, it sounded like the first computer I had ever owned trying to dial into a network, all electronic hisses and whirs. The rats around me became frantic.

A crackle of electricity shot out through the phone and into the sea of rats. Smoke but no flame rose from the mass around me, and I felt myself slowly lowering to the floor of the room as, one by one, the rats turned into gelatinous, rust-colored goo.

Nothing beats the smell of burning rat hair, and although there had been no fire as such, the air was filled with
the charred odor.

Even through my gloves, the phone became unbearably
hot and it started melting in my hand like it was made of
chocolate. I pulled the glove off my free hand, pried off the
back of the phone, and tore my SIM card free. Near-death
experience or no, there was no way I was reprogramming
all the numbers I had stored.

2

As I waited for Connor and the Inspectre to finish lowering the remains of the rope after they disabled the guillotines, I paced back and forth, squicking my way through the rat goo underfoot. My nerves were shot. My clothes were soaked with the rat frappé, but I wouldn't allow myself to freak out right now. I was too concerned about Jane. She must have been out of her mind worried once we had lost communication. If I could have climbed the walls to call her back, I would have.

When the rope finally made its way down, I looped it around my waist, granny-knotted it secure, and let Connor, Wesker, and the Inspectre hoist me up. As I reached the top of the well, I pulled myself up over the edge and collapsed with a sticky squelch onto the hideous red carpeting of the convention hall, the fluorescent lights blinding me as I lay there. I was exhausted and could barely move, but I was able to turn my head and take a look at the well I had just crawled out of. The giant gypsy who had rented it to us knelt beside it, inspecting it.

A shadow fell over me and I turned to see Thaddeus

Wesker standing there, shaking his head. He was holding his phone. I reached my goo-covered hand up for it, feeling the strain in my arm from climbing.

"Phone," I said, opening and closing my hand like a kid wanting a toy.

"*Very* good," Wesker said as if speaking to a child. He pointed at one of the Wheels of Misfortune. "And that's a circle. Now what other simple objects can you identify?"

"Well, I can count to one," I said, flipping him off. "Now give me the phone. I have to call Jane."

I almost couldn't believe I was talking back to Wesker so boldly. I guess after being entombed in living rats, he didn't seem that intimidating in comparison. It was close, though.

"She just called me," he said, sliding the phone back inside his suit coat. "She knows you lived, regrettably."

"Why did she call *you*?" I said, jealousy rearing its ugly head before I could think.

"She works for me, remember? I had told her I was coming down here to supervise," he said, dismissing me with a wave of his hand. "Besides, as the head of Greater and Lesser Arcana, I think she and I have to have a little chat about what just happened."

His ominous tone made it sound like it wasn't going to be a particularly pleasant conversation. Not that any of his conversations were pleasant.

"Is Jane in some kind of trouble?" I asked. Wesker just gave me a wicked smile. I turned to the remainder of my rescuers. Connor shrugged and looked to the Inspectre.

"Not sure, my boy," Quimbley said. "But in all my years I've never seen someone do anything quite like that."

"Liquefy rats?"

"Oh goodness, no," he said with a chuckle. "*That* I've seen countless times. My old partner in the Department used to do it during feeding time at the reptile house out at the Bronx Zoo. Poor snakes didn't know what to do . . . What I mean to say is that I've never seen it done *over the phone*. Technomancy. That's something you don't see every day."

"I'd like to know just what the girl is doing even dabbling in it," Wesker said. "We're not even offering technomancy right now. Not many in-house people can do it."

I really didn't give a rat's ass, liquefied or not, about the magical logistics of it all. If I could get a closer look at the winch, maybe I could figure out just what the hell had gone wrong. The gypsy was still squatting by the well.

"Aren't there supposed to be safety features on this thing?" I asked with righteous anger in my voice. "The rules for the Oubliette state one peril and a set of tools to contend with it. I got the peril of fighting those rats plus guillotines, and I was down there with useless tools. That's not how it's supposed to go. I spent weeks studying it."

Julius Heron was still crouched over, peering intently at the side of the well.

"There *are* safety features," he said. "It seems that all of them failed . . . simultaneously."

"What are the odds of that?" I asked.

Wesker laughed. "About the same as you staying in a relationship with Jane."

I ignored him.

Sudddenly, he shot up. "This Oubliette's been tampered with," Julius said. He leaned down and ran his fingers over a section of the well, but I didn't notice any difference at first. After a few seconds, though, something wavered in the pattern and I could see a spot in the stonework that differed from the rest.

Connor bent down next to it. His hair fell across his eyes. He pushed it out of the way and studied the Oubliette. "Looks like someone has it in for you, kid. Not surprising, given our line of work."

"So who's out to get me this time?" I asked. I turned to look specifically at Wesker. "I can probably spit on one of them from here."

"I don't much care for what you're implying, boy," Wesker said, narrowing his eyes at me.

"You did spend a lot of time working undercover with cultists," I said. "And the only reason I trust you at all is because you helped turn Jane away from them. But that doesn't necessarily mean you've given up their ways. Maybe you had a hand in rigging the Oubliette to fail."

Wesker looked indifferent and shrugged. "Sometimes things break," Wesker said, his voice flat and unapologetic.

"I'm awfully sorry, gentlemen," Julius said. He clasped his hands together. "The Brothers Heron are world renowned for their commitment to quality, and we stand by our equipment. It wasn't our fault. There was outside interference."

"Stand by it?" I said. "Sure, just as long as you don't have to be *in* it. I could have been killed."

"Again, my apologies," Julius said, but his voice was much less apologetic this time. I backed down a bit. "I'll wheel it back to my booth and my brothers and I will try to figure out what exactly happened here."

"I say," the Inspectre said, "I trust there will be some kind of discount, what with your machine almost killing our young charge here."

"*That*," Julius said, "is a matter I will have to discuss with my brothers. If you will excuse me . . ."

Julius took up a thick piece of rope attached to the cart beneath the Oubliette and started to pull it off through the curtains. It would have taken Connor, Wesker, the Inspectre, *and* me to move the cart an inch, but it was no trouble for the giant of a man. Once I had watched him go, I turned back to our group.

"So where were we?" I asked. I stepped toward the director of Greater & Lesser Arcana. "Oh, yes. Wesker was just about to tell us just exactly how he was involved in this . . ."

"Simon!" the Inspectre said with such force I swung around to him. His face was expressionless. "That will be

enough. May I remind you that you are still a member of
F.O.G. and although you are still a fledgling, you will con-
duct yourself in accordance with the Order."

The Inspectre was right. I knew better than to engage
Wesker. Besides, I knew he was always wallowing in a sty
of his own anger over the fact that he had been refused
entry into our elite order. I shut up.

"That's better," the Inspectre continued.

Connor came over and slipped off his shoulder bag,
handing it to me at arm's length.

"What's this?"

"Fresh clothes," he said. He pointed down. A little pud-
dle of rat goo had started to form on the ground where I
was standing. I shivered from where it was still against my
skin.

"Now go get yourself changed," Connor continued. "I've
got a surprise for you."

"Thanks," I said, picking up the bag, careful to hold it
away from my body. "Really? What kind of surprise?"

Connor smiled and shook his head. "If I told you, it
wouldn't be a surprise, now, would it? Just go change, kid."

"Hold on," Wesker called out. "Aren't you going to clean
up your . . . drippings?"

I gave him a look and headed off in search of the restrooms.

"I expect you to clean up this mess, Thaddeus," the Inspectre said as I walked away.

"Me?" Wesker shouted, half laughing. "Make Connor
do it. Or better yet, Simon. Call him back here."

I stopped for a moment, waiting to see if I was going to
get called back. I'd rather have had a rat slither into my
mouth than give Wesker control over me. "Connor and Simon are part of Other Division," the Inspectre said, twirl-
ing the end of his gray handlebar mustache with one hand
and dabbing his other into a small pool of the goo. "This
ichor that used to be rats is technically the result of a magical transformation, which is a matter for someone in *your*

division. And as there is only one representative of Greater and Lesser Arcana here—namely *you*—I'll leave that matter in your capable hands."

I turned away and hurried off. It was hard not to laugh. I just prayed I could control it, though. The thought of accidentally snorting any of the rat goo up my nose wasn't appealing at all.

I gave myself a truck-stop shower in the sink and changed into the clothes Connor had brought for me, then checked my ears one last time for any bits of rat before hitting the show floor. Connor was waiting for me outside the restrooms.

"So, where's my surprise?"

"Follow me, kid," he said and started walking off at a brisk pace into the heart of the convention center.

The crowd was thick and I had to dart through it before I lost him.

"My surprise is in here?"

Connor nodded. "We're gonna be working for a Department recruiting booth for a shift or two."

"Here?"

Connor lowered his voice. "You'd be surprised how many Extraordinary types a convention like this attracts," he said. "Besides, there're a couple of side benefits to working here that I think you'll find interesting."

"Such as . . . ?"

"Well, two things, really," he said. He stopped at one of the booths. Dozens of still-boxed action figures lined the booth. "First, think about the great scores you could find here with your powers."

I had been slacking in using my psychometry to supplement my government salary at the D.E.A., and my SoHo apartment's maintenance fees weren't going to pay for themselves. If I could get some good readings on some of the collectibles here and get them into the hands of the right consumer, I'd be set for a while.

"Brilliant," I said. "Thanks, partner. What's the second?"

Connor stopped and pointed ahead. I looked and saw our booth. There was nothing that suggested the secretive nature of our organization, but there was a table full of pamphlets and reading material . . . and the Inspectre was manning it.

"What's the Inspectre doing over here?" I said. "I thought he was just here to oversee the Oubliette."

Connor shook his head. "He's also here to work the booth."

"Isn't that kind of beneath him, playing booth jockey?"

"You know the Inspectre," he said. "He's a hands-on kind of guy. Likes to take a personal interest in who's coming into the Department. Like you. I thought you'd appreciate the bonding time I bought by volunteering us for this."

I was touched by his thoughtfulness. Before I could think of anything to say, Connor patted me on the shoulder and took off down the aisle toward the Inspectre. I followed him into our booth. Connor took a spot at the back of the space organizing stacks of papers while the Inspectre stood at the front, handing out information. The table was covered with a variety of pamphlets and handouts: *Homebrew Potions: Ask Me How!*, *The Truth About Gated Communities: Ghost Dancing & Ancient Indian Burial Grounds*, *Your Neighbor Might Be Possessed If: Ten Signs It's Time to Move.*

The list went on and on.

"You know," I said, approaching Connor, "for a secret organization, we're sure making quite a spectacle of ourselves."

"Relax, kid," he said. He sounded more curt than usual. "Most of the people just look at us as a marketing ploy for some new line of comics or something. They don't even give us a second glance."

I looked around and noticed what he said was true. A five-hundred-pound guy dressed as Legolas took one of the leaflets the Inspectre handed him and moved on without batting an eye. No one was really paying us any attention.

"So, do you think I passed the Oubliette?" I asked, switching back to my main concern.

Connor paused, silently shuffling the papers in his hand.

"Is something wrong?"

Connor gestured for me to move closer, farther away from the Inspectre.

"What the hell did you do back there?" he asked, not waiting for an answer. "The Oubliette has rules. No outside items. You had your phone on you."

"What was I doing?" I said, angry. "I was surviving . . . because the fucking thing malfunctioned."

"Maybe that was part of the test," he said with an air of superiority. "Did you ever consider *that*?"

I hadn't, but I wasn't going to tell him.

"Well, was it?" I asked. "Was it part of the test?"

"Well . . . no," he said, becoming less heated. "But *you* didn't know that."

"Look," I said. "Before you jump further down my throat, let's talk about what I *did* know. First, the rules stated that no *weapons* could be brought in. I wouldn't have thought my cell phone would be considered a weapon, and since no one's ever done what Jane did before, you wouldn't have considered it a weapon, either."

Connor glared at me, but conceded the point with his silence.

"And second," I continued, "I studied for that damned Oubliette for weeks."

Connor's jaw tightened.

"Not with me, you didn't," he said. And there it was.

"There was nothing personal in my choice of Jane," I said. "It's just that Jane had more access to the books I needed."

Connor didn't look convinced.

"Just make sure you're thinking with the right head when it comes to your girlfriend," he said. "She's working for Wesker now, *and* in the Black Stacks. That's gonna change a girl."

Before I could defend my choice further, the Inspectre appeared at the corner of my eye and put an arm on both of our shoulders.

"Gentlemen," he said, "I'm sure the two of you could go on for hours about the finer points of today's fiasco, but let's call it even, shall we? Given the sabotage, I think Simon did a commendable job. His time with the F.O.G.gies seems to have paid off, and I for one see nothing wrong with being resourceful in dire circumstances. Congratulations, my boy. You passed the Oubliette."

I was thrilled to hear I had passed, and I appreciated the Inspectre coming to my defense, but at the same time his sticking up for me was driving a wedge farther between me and my partner. Lately, anytime Connor attempted to correct me on anything, the Inspectre would intervene, and it was like an annoying Get Out of Jail Free card.

"Thank you, sir," I said with humility. It felt like a bittersweet victory with the unresolved issue of sabotage tainting it.

The Inspectre turned to Connor. "As the two of you will be sitting and manning the booth, this would be a perfect time to get Simon to do his performance appraisal, don't you think?"

At the words "performance appraisal," I withered.

With a final pat on the back, the Inspectre turned and walked off to engage a group of bespectacled cyborgs that had gathered at the front of our booth.

"We could just go cover me with rat goo again instead," I offered.

Connor shook his head. "Sit down, kid. You've been avoiding it for weeks."

"I've been focused on the Oubliette. I forgot about it.

Plus, I don't get why we need them. Isn't being thrown into a pit full of perils performance appraisal enough? I mean, I've never really held a job where I was graded on my performance before, you know, having been a career criminal. The idea of actually reviewing *myself* mystifies me."

Connor pulled out a chair, laid the blank forms down on a table, and handed me a number two pencil.

"What the hell am I supposed to write?" I asked.

Connor shrugged.

"I've got no idea, kid. The Inspectre's still riding me about mine. I'm working on it, but at least he's letting me ride you about yours in the meantime."

"Well, that takes the pressure off," I said.

"Easy," he said. "Wesker will be by in an hour to collect them for the Enchancellors, so be happy you only have me to deal with right now. Just hurry up and finish it."

Finish it? I hadn't even started it. Oh, how I already missed my rat-filled pit!

A man can produce a surprising amount of writing in sixty minutes when the pressure is on. Sadly, I wasn't that man, and I found easy distraction checking out scantily clad "booth babes" and the tantalizing collectibles I couldn't wait to get my hands on. Before I knew it, forty-five minutes had passed and I was staring at the still-blank pages before me when I was interrupted by the sound of the Inspectre's phone ringing. He motioned Connor over to him and they conferred, leaving me to a final fifteen minutes of staring.

"Wrap it up, kid," Connor said, patting me on the shoulder. "We've got a case to check out."

I shied the pages away from him, hiding the fact that they were still blank. Great. Wesker would be back any minute, and now I had to leave.

"Stop hanging over my shoulder, would ya?" I said. "Give me a second to finish up."

"Simon . . ." Connor said impatiently and, at the sound

of my name, I decided the least I could do was write it
down on the sheet.

NAME: *Simon Canderous*
DIVISION: *Other*

Then I scanned down the first page until I hit the only
essay question:

HOW DO YOU FEEL YOU PERFORMED THE DU-
TIES ASSIGNED TO YOU WITHIN THE CAPAC-
ITY OF YOUR DIVISION?

I stared at it for a moment longer, then hastily scrawled:

Didn't die.

I snapped the number two pencil in half, stood up, and
headed off toward Connor. He handed me back my retractable bat and we pushed through a crowd of Sand People as
we headed for the door. I resisted the urge to take my bat to
them.

3

We stopped at a deli to fill my pockets with Life Savers, Connor's treat. The guy behind the counter didn't even blink an eye, but this was no surprise. We were only a block away from the Javits Center, and with two Spider-Men, one Conan, and three cross-dressing Buffy's in line behind us, buying eighteen packs of Life Savers looked pretty normal.

When we were done, we headed west toward the water, the cool wind of the river intensifying as we got closer.

"You sure I'm going to need all these?" I asked. I looked down at my bulging pockets. I felt like a squirrel storing up nuts for the long winter.

"Not sure, kid," he said, darkness in his voice. "Just want you to be ready. We don't want you sending your body into hypoglycemic shock."

If Connor was stocking me up with this much life-savery sugar, we were probably heading for something big.

"You mind telling me what's going on?" I asked.

Connor shook his head.

"I'd rather you see for yourself. I don't want to put any

ideas in your head before you get a chance to check out the scene."

We crossed the West Side Highway and headed north toward Pier 84. Police tape ran across the entrance to the pier and a few cops were lingering nearby, but none of them would make any sort of direct eye contact with either of us, which was unusual. More often than not, the regular cops regarded the Department of Extraordinary Affairs as a bullshit operation, and we were constantly the butt of their derisive jokes. This time, however, there was a cloud of quiet hanging over the cops that I liked even less than their usual disdain.

Luckily, David Davidson, our liaison with City Hall, was waiting for us outside a small office complex farther along the pier. He was politics personified, but with one foot in our paranormal world, he was also the best friend we had when we wanted to get anything done in this city—when he wasn't busy being just as helpful to a million other (and often evil) interests.

After showing our badges to the cops manning the police tape line, we ducked under it and headed toward Davidson. The wind blew his tan trench coat out behind him like a superhero cape, making me wonder if he might be heading over to the Javits Center later to hang with that crowd.

"Gentlemen," he said, forcing a practiced smile. He shook hands with both of us, but the smile disappeared in a grim flash.

Connor seemed unfazed by it all. "Still aiding and abetting the enemy, Davidson?" he said. "The Office of Plausible Deniability keeping you busy?"

"Listen," Davidson answered with smoothness in his voice. "The mayor has the interests of all his constituents to consider. Politics is a slippery slope. You *know* that, Connor. And when we took up the clarion call of the Sectarians Rights Movement, well . . . Even we make missteps sometimes."

I looked back over my shoulder at the somber faces of cops.

"What's got everyone so spooked?" I asked.

Davidson cleared his throat and looked at me with eyes that often held a hypnotic quality, but didn't today. "Harbor patrol dragged one of those booze cruise boats in today after the boating company reported that it hadn't returned to port last night. Party boarded at six thirty; ship left at seven and should have been back around ten after circling Manhattan."

"A three-hour tour," Connor said, trying to sound like Thurston Howell but failing on every level. "Were the Professor and Mary Ann on board?"

Davidson gave him a look that shut him down. I reminded myself to thank him later. If I had to hear Connor call me "Lovey" one more time . . .

The sound of footsteps coming from farther down the dock made me turn, and I saw a familiar figure from the D.E.A. heading toward us. Godfrey Candella was in a suit, as usual, with his dark hair neatly parted but threatening to fall down over his black horn-rims.

"Godfrey?"

"Hello, Simon . . . Connor," he said, fidgeting with a notebook in his hands. His face looked grave.

"You get what you need?" Davidson called out to him.

Godfrey nodded. "For now," he said, and looked at Connor and me. "I'll need to talk to you both back at the office when you're done checking out the scene. For the Gauntlet archives, of course."

"You okay?" I said, noticing how green around the gills he was. Not that he wasn't normally a little sickly looking, but today he somehow looked worse.

"I'll be fine," he said. "I'm just not used to such gruesomeness."

Connor turned to Davidson. "Since when do you call the Gauntlet in before the investigators get a look at the scene?

I'm all for the paper hounds getting things down for historical records, for future generations and all. Hell, I'll even nominate Godfrey for sainthood just for archiving Simon's rambling oral history of the whole Sectarians Surrealist Underground thing at the Met, but there's a protocol for an investigation. Members of the Gauntlet do not do field investigation, only reporting."

Davidson held up his hands. "Whoa, now. *I* didn't call him."

"Bullshit."

"Suit yourself," Davidson said, giving up.

Connor was clearly gearing up to lay into him, but Godfrey cleared his throat.

"Actually," he said, "I just happened to be in the neighborhood. I was following up on some leads we have in the archives on old ghost-pirate sightings on the river and one of them led to an old boathouse nearby. That's when I spotted Davidson and his officers and I came over." He gave a grim smile. "I'm lucky like that, I guess. Anyway, I thought I'd just get down some reporting notes since I was here. I know my job as an archivist is to observe and nothing more. I didn't even touch the crime scene, I swear."

"I told you," Davidson interrupted, the impatience thick in his voice. He walked farther out onto the pier, leaving the three of us behind.

"You'll stop by after you've had a look?" Godfrey asked. "I should get back to the Gauntlet."

I nodded. Godfrey gave a quick smile and headed toward the city.

"Are you two going to check this out or not?" Davidson called out.

"Keep yer panties on," Connor said. We started toward the end of the dock, where a boat was moored.

"I'll warn you," Davidson said, "you may want to strengthen your resolve before stepping on board."

The party boat had two short decks and was the length

of maybe four city buses. Long windows for sightseeing lined both levels, but from the outside they looked dark, and I couldn't see through the tempered glass. We boarded at the back of the boat and I stopped dead in my tracks. Inside the main section of the boat there were bodies all over the place, pale limbs sticking up from a sea of colorful suit coats and party dresses.

The deck of the boat was thick with the dead. As we picked our way toward the doors to the interior, I had to step with caution. Unfortunately, my eyes settled on those of a lifeless dark-haired woman in a green, swirly-patterned dress and my balance faltered. I grabbed for the railing and steadied myself before I could peel my eyes away from the blank glare of hers. Her sheer stillness creeped me out to the nth degree. It was surreal, like being in some sort of macabre fever-dream. I had never seen so many dead bodies in one place before.

Connor and I pushed through the first set of doors, with Davidson following behind us. The main level of the ship's interior was a large oval dance floor surrounded by a second-story balcony overlooking it. Bodies were draped haphazardly over the railing, and the faint copper stench of blood was in the air. I fought back the urge to throw up.

"Jesus," I said.

Connor shook his head. "I don't think Jesus had jack to do with this, kid."

I crossed to the one thing left standing along the edge of the dance floor, the spot where a DJ had set up his sound system. A young man in a skewed trucker's cap, most likely the DJ himself, was slumped over the console, as lifeless as everything else on the ship. I positioned my hands to examine him and then looked to Davidson.

"May I?" I asked.

He nodded. "None of those cops out there could make heads or tails of it. Be my guest."

Connor stepped up next to me. A dried spot of blood

was on the mixing board below, and it lined up with a tear of chewed-up skin at the base of the man's neck.

"You know," Connor said, "for the number of bodies at this crime scene, doesn't the place seem sorta bloodless to you?"

I checked the floor for blood. Connor was right—there was very little. With this many bodies, the place should have been slick with it.

"Vampires?" Connor said, sounding slightly hopeful despite the fact that we were standing in the middle of a slaughterhouse.

Even though the Department had government tedium written all over it, at its heart we were all closet cryptozoological nerds eager to spot any number of oddities. While the motto of the NYPD was "To Serve and Protect," I had always thought our motto should be "To Gawk and Appreciate."

"I don't want to jump to any conclusions," Connor continued, "but everyone from the Inspectre on down has been chomping at the bit for any sign of vampiric activity."

I nodded and thought of the dry-erase board mounted high over the bull pen in our office. It read: "It has been 736 days since our last vampire incursion."

"I don't want to go all Code Bela over all this," I said, "but it's a possibility." I turned to David Davidson. "Are there any witnesses?"

He shook his head. "Not anyone who survived," Davidson said. "They even fished a few people out of the water who looked like they had jumped to escape whatever did this. They weren't bitten, though. They simply drowned."

"I doubt there's anything simple about drowning," Connor said, and his face went dark. I remembered that his own brother had gone missing from a beach when they were kids, and it was likely he had drowned.

Connor squatted next to the DJ's equipment and examined two women who looked like they had been clutching each other for dear life before they had died. He pulled a vial from one of his pockets and flipped the lid on it, releasing the scent of patchouli into the air.

"What the hell is he doing?" Davidson asked, covering his nose. "Trying to attract hippies?"

"Quiet," I whispered. "He's attempting to bait any lingering spirits."

I waited as long as I could before speaking again.

"You getting anything?"

He shook his head, scanning the roomful of bodies. "Nothing. Not a soul in the room right now. Don't know how I'm supposed to talk to the dead if they've scattered off already . . ."

Davidson stood there watching the two of us, making me self-conscious on top of already being creeped out.

Finally, Connor looked up. "You ready to dig in, kid?"

"Not really," I said. I pulled out a roll of Life Savers, unwrapped it, and crunched the whole thing down in three bites. "But we owe it to these people to get to the bottom of it, so . . . let's find out why this whole mess has landed in the hands of Other Division, shall we?"

With my gloves on, I gently lifted the DJ off his array of turntables and lowered him to the floor with care. There were a lot of things that Connor and I had yet to try in my training, but I wasn't about to start taking psychometric readings off corpses. I couldn't read clothes, anyway. Objects had always been the trigger for me, so I pulled off my gloves and started with one of the turntables.

I willed my power into action without a problem. The turntable was ripe with fresh information. I could feel it arcing into me as the electric hum of connection to the object hit the center of my mind's eye. As I popped into the vision, I found myself standing in the exact same spot; the only exception was that, in my vision, all of these dead bodies were still alive and dancing. My heart ached at how full of life, movement, and sound the room was.

I was the DJ in this scenario, feeling whatever he felt

last night. At the moment, he was charged with the energy of the deep bass he was pumping out and I found myself caught up in his sensations, his heart rushing in time with the music.

I looked down and caught his reflection off one of the CD cases lying on the edge of his equipment tower. I wore headphones, each the size of a cinnamon bun, giving the DJ a Princess Leia–like quality as he worked his sound equipment. While one song played out over the crowd, he was busy cuing the next with the use of the headphones. His concentration was so fixed on his job that it was no wonder he didn't notice much of what was happening around him.

Although I was a passive passenger in the DJ's body, I was able to look around the rest of the room even though his focus was on the turntable. Faster than I could follow, the dance floor was turning into a sea of panic, people screaming and running for their lives. I wanted to scream out for him to lift his goddamned head and see what was going on, but by the time he looked up from his turntable, half the room was writhing around on the floor as the rest of the crowd trampled over them in their attempts to get away. But from what? Looking around, the DJ couldn't see whatever caused the commotion, which only meant . . .

He spun around in time to catch a flash of glowing red eyes as a humanoid shape lunged at his neck, the sharp tear of fangs puncturing his jugular. Trapped in his body as I was, I could feel him dying as his blood was being drained. His chest tightened, a scream of horror catching in his throat as his heart started to slow. Caught up in the DJ's fear, I felt helpless to pull myself out of the vision. I'd never been trapped inside someone in the throes of death before, and I wondered if there was any chance that I would die myself if I stayed in that moment long enough. It seemed I was about to find out—I couldn't pull myself out of it and my world went dark.

I snapped out of the vision only to hear the tail end of my own scream echoing in the now-still room. I was laid

out on the floor with Connor standing over me, one fist
balled like he had just punched someone—which made a
lot of sense because my jaw hurt like a son of a bitch. I sat
up, touching my face to assess the damage.

"You okay, kid?" Connor said. "Sorry about decking
you. You went all white and you were screaming."

I stood up on shaking legs, leaning against a nearby
column for support.

"I . . . I . . ." I started, but couldn't finish. My face hurt,
and my blood sugar felt abnormally low. How long had I
been in the vision and how much energy had it sapped
from me? My body shook with the dizziness of hypoglyce-
mia. The faint smell of blood mixed with the overpowering fruitiness of the Life Savers I had eaten minutes ago. I
felt my stomach clench. I was going to be sick.

I fought back the urge as I staggered for the doors at the
far end of the room. My feet slammed into several of the
bodies as I went, repulsing me even further, but by the time I
ran out onto the back deck of the ship my only concern was
not throwing up all over them. I jumped over the railing
and onto the pier, fell to my knees, and emptied the con-
tents of my stomach into the Hudson River.

I felt better the moment I was done, except for the shaking. I collapsed on my side. Although the idea of eating
anything right now seemed impossible, I fished out another
roll of Life Savers.

"You okay, honey?" a voice said from behind me. I
rolled over. A woman in her fifties stood there in a white,
button-down shirt and blue sailor pants that rose a good
two inches above her navel. A tiny gold badge from the
cruise line proclaimed that I should "Come Sail Away
with . . . Maggie!" Her blond hair was done up in a fifties
beehive, making her look like an ancient version of the
cruise director from *The Love Boat.*

I nodded and rolled to my knees. The sugar replen-
ished itself in my body, and I eventually stopped shaking.

By the time I was on my feet, Connor and Davidson had joined me.

"This," Davidson said, "is Maggie, the woman who called in the missing boat last night."

"Our condolences," Connor said. "To your guests and your crew."

She pursed her lips and shook her head, on the verge of tears. "Thank you."

"Is there anything you can tell us?" Connor continued. "Anything you saw that might have been out of the ordinary?"

Maggie thought a moment. "It was very late," she said, "and when they towed the ship back to dock, there was a heavy fog. When it pulled in, I could hear some of the stray dogs we get down here on the dock going wild. I just assumed they sensed death or whatever . . . whatever had happened to all those people. Then they went silent and when I caught sight of them, there was a strange one I had never seen before, just standing there menacing the whole crowd of them until they all shied away. Then it ran off toward the city. And then I realized everyone on the boat was dead. Who could have done something like this?"

The woman burst into hysterical sobs. There was nothing I could say. Davidson put an arm around her. I gave Connor a look and moved him away from them to talk.

"Are we talking werewolves here?" I asked. I had read at least three of our pamphlets on lycanthropy, and thanks to one *Five O' Clock Shadow or Something More?* I knew how rare they were in an urban environment.

Connor shook his head. "I don't think so, kid. If that boat was the work of werewolves, those bodies would have been half-eaten and there'd be blood everywhere. What did you see in your vision?"

"Not much," I said, "but enough to freak me out—that's for sure. Everybody was panicking, so it was hard to focus on just what the hell was going on. I caught a glimpse of

what killed the DJ, though. Red eyes, fangs, went straight
for his throat. Drained him almost completely. This gives
us enough to call it in, right?"

"As long as you're sure, kid."

I nodded. "When we get back to the office, we'll call it
in as a vampire."

"*A* vampire?" Connor said. "A single vampire couldn't
have drunk all that blood. We're talking about a good-sized
nest of them."

I nodded, just a little excited by the prospect, despite the
tragedy I had witnessed. Being part of Other Division, you
had to get off a little on the extraordinary things you ended
up dealing with. Vampires were certainly high on the list.

Davidson walked off with Maggie, escorting her back
to the boating company's office.

"Are they going to do anything for her?" I asked.

"For her?"

"I think she might be a little traumatized by all this," I
said. "I know I am."

"It's New York City," Connor said with a shrug. "She'll
write it off mentally. Weird shit happens. Most people ignore it."

I stared at him. "That's it? We're just going to leave her
mental stability to chance?"

Connor stared at me a minute, but I refused to look
away.

"Fine," he finally said. "I'll put a Shadower team on her.
If there's any signs she's flipping out, we'll bring her in and
put her through counseling. Happy?"

I nodded. Davidson returned from the offices alone.

"She's okay," Davidson said, his smile returning as
he joined us. "I was testing out some of the spin I'm going
to have to use with the media on this one. She seemed to
be buying the 'bad shrimp' story I was planning on going
with."

"Deadly shrimp-poisoning?" I said. "People are going
to buy that?"

Davidson nodded. "It seems a lot easier to buy than, say, vampires, doesn't it?"

He had a point.

"Don't worry about it," he said. "That's for the Office of Plausible Deniability to contend with. Besides, on the plus side of this case, at least we got lucky in one respect . . ."

I felt my anger twitch in. "What the hell's lucky about a boatload of people dying?" I asked.

"It could have been worse, gentlemen," he said. "This could have been far more tragic. Luckily, the cruise was booked as an office party for a bunch of litigators. Mostly legal counsel for oil companies."

"Wait a minute," I said. "We've got a boatful of dead *lawyers*?"

Connor actually grinned. "So one set of bloodsuckers took out another set of bloodsuckers?"

"Exactly," Davidson said.

The three of us started back up the dock. All things considered, I suddenly didn't feel as bad as I had. Still, whoever or whatever had done this had to be stopped. Connor and I parted ways with Davidson at the end of the pier, grabbed a cab, and headed downtown toward the office.

4

The cab dropped us off in the East Village on Eleventh Street in front of the Lovecraft Café.

Up front was our cover operation—a coffee shop, its exposed brick walls covered with a variety of old movie posters. The furniture was a mishmash that ranged from hideous to vomitous, but there was a soothing charm to the room. A mix of regular customers and Departmental agents filled the room, and, as usual, Mrs. Teasley was reading someone's fortune using a soggy pile of coffee grounds.

"You okay, kid?" Connor asked. I looked down and noticed that my gloved hands were shaking.

"I guess not," I said. "I'm guess I'm still bothered by what I saw."

"Good," Connor said, sounding almost cheerful.

"Good?" I said. "What the hell is good about that?"

He put his arm around my shoulder conspiratorially and steered me toward the coffee bar that ran along the entire right side of the room.

"It's good," he said, lowering his voice, "because the second you see something like what we saw on that boat and it *doesn't* affect you, it's time to get out of this business. You remember that."

"You don't look so spooked," I countered.

"I've got years of practice at hiding it, kid. Believe me, there's nothing I saw there that doesn't have me shaking on the inside."

Connor stepped to the counter and bought two iced mochas. He slipped one over to me. I wondered how the caffeine and sugar was supposed to reduce my shaking, but it seemed to work. We headed toward the back of the coffeehouse and entered the curtained-off movie theater that lay behind it. The old-world style of the 1930s architecture always took my breath away, and this time was no exception. The enormous and ornate chandelier high overhead sparkled as light from the movie projector danced among its many crystals. On the screen, Sigourney Weaver was sneaking around a metallic Gigeresque spaceship in a tank top and undies.

Connor and I continued down the movie theater aisle and keycarded our way through a door marked "H.P.," heading into the Department proper. The general bull pen area of the front offices of the Department of Extraordinary Affairs was a spacious cubicle farm. The far wall was carved with arcane runes of warding and below them was a series of doors. I had no idea where most of them went, but with new divisions springing up every month, it was no wonder. Connor and I moved past the general bull pen and headed farther back to another section, where our improvised partners desk sat.

I say "improvised" because in reality it was just two desks pushed together so we could face each other. It seemed to help out when we were bouncing ideas off each other on a case. We dropped our stuff off at our desks, and I slipped my bat off of its holster and slid it into my top-left desk drawer.

I looked over at Connor and then we both turned to check out the whiteboard that hung higher up on the wall and overlooked the entire room. Behind it, arcane glyphs

like the ones in the bull pen scrolled along the entire wall
and radiated power. But the board, while not magic, had a
power of a different kind.

It now read: "It has been <u>737</u> days since our last vampire incursion."

I turned back to Connor. He nodded, then gestured toward the board. I crossed through the bustling activity of
cube dwellers and investigators scurrying back and forth.
Against the wall was a ladder that led up to the whiteboard. I started up it, only to have someone tug on my pant
leg when I was about four rungs up.

"Someone already changed it today, Simon," a familiar
voice said. I turned to see Godfrey Candella standing below me, looking the same as he had at the dock, the neat
part of his black hair matching the perfect knot of his tie
and his black horn-rim glasses.

"Someone already did that today," he repeated. "The
number's already been switched."

I smiled at him.

"I'm sure they did, God, but I don't think they were
about to do this," I said, and continued up the ladder, my
nerves tingling.

When I was twenty feet up, one by one, everyone in the
room fell silent, until the only sound was that of my shoes
against the rungs of the ladder. I reached the top and from
the thin lip at the bottom of the whiteboard, I grabbed the
eraser and ran it through the 737. A collective gasp rose
from the rest of the agents. I picked up the marker and
wrote a large zero in its place.

A nervous cheer from the crowd broke the silence. It felt
strange, given the dark implication of it, but part of me was
also beaming with pride for being the one to have discovered the first sign of vampires in Manhattan in over two
years. Divisional leaders and members of the Enchancellors Board came streaming out of doors and down the stairs,
genuine concern on their faces. By the time I climbed

down, Inspectre Quimbley stood waiting for me at the foot of the ladder along with Godfrey and Connor.

"Are you sure, boy?" the Inspectre asked, serious as can be. "I trust you have three points of collaboration?"

I nodded. Although I had only attended the afternoon seminar "Pains in the Neck" on the subject of vampires, the one thing I remembered was that we were required to have at least three solid signs of vampirism before calling for a Department-wide warning.

"We didn't have a direct sighting of the vampire," I said, "but everything else seems to match up."

"Let's hear them, then," the Inspectre said, his eyes widening.

Godfrey pulled out a Moleskine notebook and started writing like mad.

"The event took place at night," I said, "so that makes it a possibly nocturnal creature. Second, the victims exhibited blood loss accompanied by the puncture wounds on their necks, but there was very little blood at the scene. Third, it was a foggy night and the woman at the docks said she had seen several dogs at the site. Animal familiars of the creature or shape-shifting into wolf form, perhaps?"

"Well," the Inspectre said, "your last point seems a bit of a stretch, but I think we can count the blood loss and puncture wounds as two separate things, so you still have three points."

I took a brief minute to tell him what Davidson, Connor, and I had discovered on the boat while the rest of the agents and higher-ups gathered closer. I felt like I was sitting around a campfire telling ghost stories, only this was a lot more intimidating.

When I finished, there was a moment of office-wide silence.

"So," I said, trying to hide the nervousness in my voice, "do we gear up? Is there some roomful of vampire-slaying equipment that we get to break out?"

Connor came over and clapped me on the shoulder. "Easy, kid."

The Inspectre said, "The Department of Extraordinary Affairs takes an alert like this very seriously, but there's a lot of red tape and paperwork to put in downtown. We haven't mobilized something like this in well over two years."

"Paperwork?" I spluttered. "With all due respect, sir, people are going to die if we don't move on this quickly."

"The kid's right, Inspectre," Connor added.

The Inspectre looked at Connor for a second, then turned back to me, staring straight at me and speaking in a deliberate tone.

"Perhaps the two of us should take this off the office floor," he said. It wasn't a question, but an order barely veiled in politeness. Before I had a chance to respond, he turned away from me and headed back toward the stairs leading up to his office. The crowd parted before him like the Red Sea. He stopped for a moment without turning and said, "I believe you all have assignments you were working on . . . ?"

The spell of silence broke and everyone scattered to the four corners of the office—everyone except Director Wesker, who took the time to shake his head at me in disappointment before heading off to Greater & Lesser Arcana. No one stopped to ask me questions. A few of the White Stripes—the agents whose exposure to paranormal activity had left them with skunklike stripes in their hair—stopped to whisper with Connor for a second, but then they left and the two of us were alone at the base of the ladder.

"Well, that was anticlimactic," I said. "I guess we should be getting upstairs."

Connor shook his head. "Not me, kid. The Inspectre's invitation, in case you didn't notice, was very pointedly for one."

My heart leapt into my throat. "But we're both on this case. You've got more experience with these things . . ."

"Tell me something I don't know," he said with bitterness. I watched his face close off from me, and I wished I had something to say that might help, but I was at a loss. "Somehow I think this has something to do with your special little club . . ."

The Fraternal Order of Goodness. I should have thought of that myself. No wonder Connor seemed upset. He was far less bitter than Thaddeus Wesker about being passed over for F.O.G., but it was a minor point of contention between us.

"Whatever," I said, and headed upstairs to find the Inspectre. He stood behind his dark oak monster of a desk, his hands resting lightly on top of two stacks of paperwork.

"Close the door behind you, please?" he said, his voice concentrated yet quiet.

As I shut the door, I couldn't help but get that whole summoned-to-the-principal's-office vibe. By the time Inspectre Quimbley gestured for me to have a seat in one of the big leather chairs opposite him, I felt like a third-grader.

"I suppose you're feeling like I dressed you down a little there," the Inspectre said. He sat down himself and shifted one of the piles of paper crowding his desk out of the way so I could see him better.

"A little, sir, yes."

"Perhaps you think I acted a little less enthused than you would have liked?" he asked.

"The thought had struck me."

"I'll let you do the mental legwork on this, son," he said. He folded his hands on top of his desk. "Why do you think I reacted the way I did?"

Away from the crowd, I hoped a cooler head would prevail, so I set my mind to putting myself in the Inspectre's shoes. How would I have reacted if one of my agents had just made a bold and possibly terrifying accusation that would affect every other division in the Department?

"Because . . . of the mixed company we were in?" I asked, piecing my thoughts together as they came.

The Inspectre grinned. "Continue . . ."

"Well," I said after a slight hesitation, "there were members of every division on hand down there, including the Enchancellors. If you had blown your cool in front of all them . . . Well, I'm sure there was a lot at stake politically, all dependent on your handling of the situation."

He nodded in agreement. "I meant what I said in front of all them, Simon. The wheels of change and progress are indeed slow around here. We *will* be investigating this matter, but most likely it won't be at the pace that either of us want."

"So we're just supposed to sit here and wait it out while the Enchancellors send out interoffice memos and get all the right signatures lined up?"

"I didn't say that, either," the Inspectre said, raising a finger. He gave me a wry smile mixed with a look of what I hoped was infinite patience. "If we're dealing with vampires, it's a big thing to mobilize troops and equipment for dealing with them. The Enchancellors answer to the city of New York and err on the side of being obsessively careful in these matters. You forget, though—you're part of the Fraternal Order of Goodness. We have been around much longer than the Department and we answer only to ourselves. The Department rose up around us only because there was a need for us to interface with modern government, but F.O.G. allows you to work above and beyond the constraints of the Department in some capacities. In some cases, while the governmental red tape of the Department will take forever, the secret nature of F.O.G. will allow us to start moving forward more quickly. I believe that something of this caliber would be such a case. If vampires don't count, frankly, I shudder to think what would."

"So is there something I can do to get the ball rolling on this?" I said, feeling a bit overwhelmed at the prospect.

The Inspectre nodded. "Until the Enchancellors say the rest of the i's are dotted, yes. I want you and Connor to continue looking into this on the sly, but *do not*, under any circumstances, put yourself in serious harm's way."

I wanted to ask if it was okay to put myself in minor harm's way, but stopped myself. I wasn't about to get into what constituted the fine line between the two. Frankly, coming in to work at Other Division every day was, by definition, putting myself in harm's way.

"Now," the Inspectre continued, "since this is technically Fraternal Order business, I'm putting you in charge of this."

"Over Connor?" I said, not wanting to outrank my mentor. It didn't feel right.

"He's not part of the Order, son. He can assist you on this, but you have to be careful to keep Order business out of his ears. It's a fine line between the D.E.A. and F.O.G., I know, but it's up to you to walk it."

"Wait," I said, raising my hands like I was waving back the idea. "Inspectre, please, you can't. My partnership with him is already strained . . ."

The Inspectre dropped his fatherly tone, dead serious.

"Dammit, boy. When I first told you that you'd face severe challenges by being part of the Order, I wasn't merely talking about the Things That Go Bump in the Night variety. Part of your responsibility is learning to handle others."

I sat silently, not wanting to say anything to exacerbate the situation.

"Is this going to be an issue, son?" he asked.

Of *course* it was going to be an issue. "No, sir."

"Good," the Inspectre said, returning to his usual self. He began rummaging through one of the file folders on his desk. "I need you to keep the Order's eye on things in this investigation, Simon, until the Enchancellors are ready to make a move. I'll try to hurry along the process, but you can well imagine how long that might take."

After my three months of paperwork settling the case of the ghost of Irene Blatt and the whole Metropolitan Museum of Art debacle that came with it, I imagined it might take roughly an eon or two to light a fire under the right people in the Department. At the moment, though, I was powerless to do anything about it. Maybe I could talk to Davidson to speed things up downtown. That was, if Connor didn't kill me for being put in charge of him on this.

The Inspectre looked lost in thought as he went through the file in front of him. I realized he had moved on from our conversation.

I backed toward the door, showing myself out. Just as I was about to close it gently behind me, the Inspectre spoke up again.

"Oh, my boy," he said, looking up from his paperwork.

I pushed the door back open.

"Sir?"

The Inspectre raised his hand and stroked his handlebar mustache. "I think we should step up your combat training to meet Fraternal Order levels, you know, with all this vampiric activity going on. For now, I want to see you every day for Unorthodox Fighting Techniques. I'll see to it personally, of course, so put aside some time starting later today, won't you?"

A ball of dread filled my stomach, but I nodded. More training most likely meant more danger in my near future, and that never filled me with the warm fuzzies. I gave a weak smile and closed the Inspectre's door.

I headed for the stairs, wondering how much I couldn't tell Connor while moving forward with all this. If a scrub like me tried to pull rank on a mentor like him, I suspected he wouldn't take it well, even if passing the Oubliette meant I was technically now his equal in the Department.

5

Fate, it seemed, had cut me some slack. When I returned to my desk, Connor wasn't at his, so it looked like I was momentarily spared figuring out how to implement my new orders. Tension in my shoulders, which I hadn't even realized was there, melted away, and I dropped into my seat feeling exhausted.

The rest of the office had returned to normal, and the buzz of the hive activity was soothing to my ears. I hated being in this position. It was one thing to have been chosen for the Fraternal Order—that was beyond the scope of the work Connor and I did together. Holding sway over Connor in an official capacity after only six months with Other Division, though, would be an entirely different situation.

For now I made the decision to keep Connor in the dark. Maybe I could handle the situation so that he never realized I was in charge. I was new to the art of deception, and the guilt was already eating at me. To compensate, I started thinking of ways to make it up to him.

Then it hit me: his brother. When we had first started testing my power of psychometry, a beat-up Spider-Man

PEZ Dispenser led to the tale of how his brother had vanished one summer at Cape Cod back when they were kids. Unfortunately, any follow-up had been pushed aside when the craziness with cultist-rights leader Faisal Bane and occult bookstore owner turned paranormal drug czar Cyrus Mandalay ensued.

But now I finally had a chance to get back on the ball with helping Connor, even if it was to ease my own guilty conscience. No time like the present for starting on the brother stuff.

I glanced around the office before standing up and heading over to Connor's side of the partners desk. It was marginally neater than mine. Instead of three-foot-high stacks of casework, he had only one-foot-high stacks. I could only aspire to such streamlined paper-stacking skills, but until I had Connor's many years' experience under my belt, I'd have to contend with my larger Leaning Towers of Paper.

We had used the Spidey PEZ Dispenser several times since that early training session, and I knew he kept it in the desk somewhere. I sat down at it, excited at the prospect of helping out Connor with his missing brother, and not for a second feeling guilty about going through his desk. In the past six months, I had been over there hundreds of times to get forms, Post-its, and whatnot from him.

I slid the desk drawers open, one by one. The usual assortment of crap was in them—Post-its, pens, a microcassette recorder, an assortment of half-empty vials, presumably for that ghost-capturing mixture he always had on him. In the bottom-left drawer, a clipped bundle of papers caught my eye and I pulled them out. Some of them were Xeroxes from the historical archives, but others were simply newspaper clippings or memos. The top article came from in-house and showed the archives' heading. Underneath the heading was an article detailing the night I had dressed as Zorro at the Sectarians' museum bust. I flipped to the next page. This copy of a file described the night I had assisted Connor with that rogue spirit in an alley near Washington

Square, the very night Connor had become a White Stripe. I skipped all the way to the bottom of the pile and found that even the first entry was also about me—a welcome mention in the Department's HR newsletter. Connor had kept all of it. Having found this emotional treasure trove made me feel a little awkward about going through his desk, even though my intentions were good. I stood up and shut the drawer. I couldn't do this right now.

I was both warmed by the discovery and ashamed by my behavior. Only when someone nearby spoke up did I snap out of it.

"Lost?" Connor asked, half joking and half suspicious. I looked up and there he was, standing in the main aisle by our desks, still in his trench coat.

"Umm, I was looking for a requisition form for getting myself a new cell phone," I lied, patting his stacks of case-work as if I had only been giving a cursory look at what was visible. "What with the old one melting in the Oubli-ette . . . I thought you might have a form."

Connor shrugged. "Not sure, kid. I'd check with the sup-ply room. I think they have a twenty-pager you have to fill out, one of the kinds that still uses carbon paper, so your fingers should be good and purple by the time you're done. And remember to press down firmly. I think it's a 21-10, if I remember correctly. And you'll have to get Jane's signa-ture on it as well."

"Jane?" I said, startled. "What for?"

As if we were two sumo wrestlers sizing each other up, Connor territorially circled to his side of the desk and I went back to mine.

"Well," Connor said, slipping off his coat and sitting down, "technically, she's the official offending witch for melting your cell phone, and the Department likes to keep records on that sort of thing."

Even though Jane had been taken under Wesker's wing in Greater & Lesser Arcana, I hadn't really thought of her as a witch. Until she had turned my phone into a smoldering mess, I hadn't even known she had the ability to do such a thing. Now I knew differently. She was clearly dabbling in something powerful.

"Where'd you run off to?" I asked, wanting to change the subject.

Connor grabbed about an inch of paperwork from the top of the pile in his in-box. He winced in faux pain and dropped the paperwork on his desk, flexing his hand.

He sighed and said, "Couple of Faisal's old followers were brought in and some of the White Stripes needed a hand getting them down to booking. Got a little rough."

I was shocked to hear the mention of Faisal Bane. "You mean the Sectarians are still operating?" I asked. "I had hoped we'd put them out of business."

Connor laughed and looked up at me.

"Cultists don't just go away because their public funding does, kid. The Department will be chasing down Sectarians long after you and I are both gone; that's for sure."

I stood at my desk, feeling somewhat defeated.

"So any victory we gain will always be undermined by a second, third, or even fourth wave of evil washing over this city. It never ends."

"Pretty much," Connor said. "We'd be out of a day job if it did."

What it really meant was that the piles of paperwork sitting on my desk would just keep growing with each and every encounter.

I decided to get out of there. If I went down to Supply, got the forms, and then headed over to Tome, Sweet Tome for Jane's signature, I could at least start the requisitioning process for my new phone. With a day as shit-filled as this one, I'd take the small victories wherever I could get them.

And then, of course, there were the vampires to find . . .

6

The guys down in Supply were thrilled for once I was only coming for a phone requisition and not for the usual assortment of odd equipment requests I had made over the past several months. Once I had the form in hand, I headed to the Upper West Side to Tome, Sweet Tome. After the day I'd had—almost dying in the Oubliette, working the convention show floor, confronting a shipful of bodies, everything back at the office—seeing Jane would be a welcome relief.

Or so I thought. The front section of the store was unattended except for a few kids checking out the child-friendly section. Happy painted wizards and witches on the wall seemed to follow me with their eyes as I looked around the front of the store. I knew Jane had been doing a lot of exploratory work back in the Black Stacks, so I weaved my way through the shelves and teetering piles of books until I found the Stacks. As I approached the copper caged area, I could hear Jane's voice. She was laughing. It was good to hear a little happiness for a change, and my mood brightened.

Until I actually saw her.

I had learned to be cautious when entering the Stacks, so I pushed the gate open all the way and entered slowly. Many of the books here had a mind all their own, but luckily none of them came flying off the shelves to attack me like they had when we chased Cyrus through here months ago. I found Jane two rows in—with Wesker. She was poring over a book with a smile on her face while Wesker looked over her shoulder, leaning too close for my liking and touching the small of her back. My heart always leapt when I saw her long blond hair, her beautiful features, and, of course, the low riders she was wearing, but not this time. I cleared my throat and the two of them turned in unison. Wesker, I noticed, dropped his hand from her back in a heartbeat. Jane's eyes lit up and she snapped the book shut before running over to me. Her ponytail bobbed as she ran, and she barreled into me with such force that her hair flipped up on top of my head when she hugged me. I hugged her back, relishing the affection despite my discomfort.

"Simon," she said. "You're okay!"

"I *told* you he was alive," Wesker said, sounding disappointed. He looked at me. "Could you please not hug the help?"

"I'm here on official business," I said. I reached into my coat pocket and pulled out the form. "Jane has to sign off on whatever she did that melted my phone earlier today. They can't replace it until I have all the signatures."

"Oh, by all means," Wesker said, losing all traces of the good humor he had been in before I had interrupted his alone time with Jane. "Don't let me stop you."

Jane grabbed the form and smoothed it out. She pulled a pen out from behind her ear and leaned up against the nearest bookcase.

"Oh!" she said. "I hear congratulations are in order on passing the Oubliette."

"Only on a technicality," Wesker added.

I looked at him and said, "If the damn thing hadn't been tampered with . . ."

"I bet that's why they passed you," Jane said. "Improvising under *real* danger like that!"

"Not everyone who voted on it was in agreement," Wesker added. "Calling Jane was cheating."

"Was not," I said.

"I wish I knew exactly what I did over the phone," Jane said, taking a moment to sign the form I had brought.

"Yes," Wesker added. "So do I. I've been meaning to talk to you about that. Since when are you a technomancer? You're not authorized to be doing Greater Arcana yet."

"Don't you have some children to scare?" I asked.

"Watch it," he said. "I still have seniority over you."

Unlike at the convention center, I didn't have Connor or the Inspectre here to back my bravado just now. Plus, Jane still had to answer him, so it was in my best interest to not sound too much like a smart-ass.

"I wasn't being snarky, *sir*," I lied. It was getting easier after almost being caught rummaging through Connor's desk. "I just thought I saw some of the kids in the Young Adult section acting suspiciously, and since no one's up front, God knows what they're up to . . ."

Wesker didn't look like he believed me fully, but I knew he wouldn't abide any potential shoplifting under his watch. He excused himself from the Stacks and headed off toward the front of the store.

Jane pushed me up against one of the bookshelves and kissed me. I kissed her back with equal fervor until I became self-conscious. We were, after all, making out in a roomful of evil—or at least enchanted—books, and I couldn't shake the feeling that we were being watched. I pulled away, though it pained me to do so.

"So . . . what was up with that rat-blendering spell?" I asked.

Jane looked surprised. "Arcana hasn't let me start working

with greater magic in an official capacity yet, but Thaddeus has authorized me for some Lesser Arcana practice."

Thaddeus? I bristled at her familiarity. Since when had Divisional Director Wesker become Thaddeus to her? I tried to swallow the ridiculous schoolboy jealousy that I found had sprung up inside me. My relationship with Jane was the first one that had lasted more than a few weeks—now that I had learned to control my powers somewhat—but it also meant that I had to start learning how to control the teenlike jealousy that came with the unfamiliar territory of something long-term.

"What other magic can you do?" I asked, trying to get back on track.

Jane shrugged and shied her eyes toward her feet. "Just little things. I can light a match, change the temperature of water, make milk go sour . . . April Fool's Day–level stuff, really."

"Well, that's great," I said with as much encouragement as I could muster. "So the rat thing . . . ?"

She reached over and squeezed my hands, passing her excitement over to me. "I don't know. I've been spending a lot of time filing things away in the Stacks and when you called, I guess I just let my fingers do the walking. I found what I hoped would work on maybe a *few* of the rats in the second book I opened."

"It didn't just take out a few, Jane. It was like a Cuisinart had been taken to *all* of them to make one big rat smoothie . . ."

Her eyes widened. "Really?"

"Don't get too excited," I said. "I don't like the idea of you delving into the spells that fill the books of the Black Stacks here."

"Why? Because I'm a girl?" Jane gave a little pout. "No offense, hon, but that comes off as kinda sexist. Am I going to have to call HR?"

I shook my head and held up my hands. "I don't mean it like that. I was just surprised to hear that you were dabbling a little bit with black magic. I dunno . . . I just thought that's something you would have told me about." I suppressed the urge to ask what *else* she might have neglected to tell me about, specifically just how she had become so chummy with her boss, "Thaddeus." I took a deep breath until the feeling passed before changing tactics. "It's just that you're not a field agent. You're a researcher for now, and I don't want you to get mixed up in practicing anything from all this dark source material back here."

"That practical application *did* save your life, you know," she said, striking a he-man pose and flexing her muscles.

"Fair point," I said, relaxing a little and kissing her on the nose. "I just worry; that's all."

"I know," she said, and hugged me. I grabbed her head and kissed the top of it, which gave me an idea.

"Speaking of worrying," I said. "I suppose I could give you a little field agent expertise, like how to fight zombies. I've already been through "Shufflers and Shamblers," so this will give you a leg up."

"Okay," she said.

"First off, never let them get as close to your skull as I just did."

Jane gave me a thumbs-up. "Check."

"And your best bet is to try to outrun them. You're faster than ninety percent of the zombie variants out there, but if you're cornered and have to fight, blunt trauma to the head still seems to be the best way to take them down."

Jane went a little gray. "You really are worried, aren't you?"

I nodded. "Yeah," I said. "About a lot of things, but zombies are on the rise and just this afternoon we came across this boatful of dead people that might have been killed by vampires. I haven't really been schooled so much on them yet or else I'd be teaching you about them, too. There's only so much vampire slaying I can learn from watching the *Buffy* boxed set. Then, on top of all that,

somebody messed with the Oubliette . . . so I just want to
make sure that you're prepared."

"Vamps? For real?" she asked, practically bouncing up
and down with a morbid excitement. I took a moment to
observe how all the right parts on her shifted with the
movement. It was hard not to.

"You might want to rethink the low riders," I said,
pointing at her pants.

She looked at me with a mask of confusion.

"Do zombies or vampires have something against fashion?" she asked.

"No," I said, before I could stop myself, "but maybe you
could not wear them while working with Director Wesker."

It was juvenile, but I couldn't help it. Being with Jane
brought out something protective in me.

She tugged them up a little higher to cover the hint of
her zebra-stiped underwear that was sticking out. "Simon,"
she said, a little perturbed, "don't be silly."

"I'm just saying," I said, trying to sound disarming, but
failing completely. I didn't quite know how to deal with
this feeling welling up inside me, and although I had held
my tongue at first, I could feel myself slipping.

"I'm just saying," I repeated, "you don't see me calling
Inspectre Quimbley 'Argyle.' "

Jane rolled her eyes. "Can we not get into this now?" she
asked. She lowered her voice. "I'm kinda at work here . . ."

Do not get into this with her, especially not here, I thought
to myself. Just leave before you say something stupid.

"Sure," I said. I picked up the requisition she had signed,
folded it, and slipped it in my pocket. "Thanks."

I turned toward the gate.

"Simon, don't go away mad," she pleaded.

"Just go away, right?" I couldn't stop myself.

"Jeesh," Jane said. "Do I crawl up your butt when you've
got a case you're working on? I'm making real progress
here. They've got me researching like crazy in total Willow-

mode here, and I think I have the Stacks actually playing nice with me."

I paused. Truthfully, I *was* impressed, but with the horrible day I'd had, this wasn't the way I wanted to end it. She was the one good thing I had going for me right now, but I couldn't control the schoolboy jealousy.

"Can we discuss this later, then?" I asked, hoping I didn't sound as cranky as I felt. Jane nodded, wrapping her arms around the book she held, but she didn't move. "Just come on over after you're done here. I'll be home. I hope you and Thaddeus have a great time researching."

I wish I hadn't said it, but it was too late. I walked away before I could make it any worse that it already was, but Jane let out a heavy sigh as I went. I never would have thought the hardest thing to deal with back in the Black Stacks would be my girlfriend.

7

I headed back downtown for my appointment with the Inspectre, going over what had just happened and wondering
why my inner alpha male had flared up so much over Wesker. How had a little light instruction on combating the
undead turned into a fit of jealousy?

Things with Jane had been going great. Well, as great
as they could be for an ex-cultist and a psychometric detective with little experience in long-term dating, anyway. I
cursed the years I hadn't been able to control my power.
They had kept me from ever having a relationship success-
ful enough to get to this stage of emotional irrationality.

Now that I was confused and full of steam to blow off,
it was the perfect time to head back to the D.E.A. for that
Fraternal Order of Goodness–level Unorthodox Fighting
Techniques the Inspectre had mentioned. When I got there,
I wove my way through an area upstairs that was a labyrinth of musty old offices but with slightly emptier corri-
dors because of the restrictive exclusivity of F.O.G. The
furniture was ancient, as if the minds of ages had been bat-
tling evil here for centuries, and after several wrong turns,

I found Inspectre Quimbley in one of the training areas, suiting up in elbow pads that he was slipping on over his tweed coat.

The Inspectre looked up and gave me a fatherly smile.

"Almost ready," he said.

He slipped on his protective headgear, the kind a boxer wears, and over his chest he pulled on an umpire's padded vest with a large red heart painted where one would expect the actual heart to be, only it had a target on it. The padding made him appear even more walruslike than his mustache did, but I knew all too well that was only in appearance. Looks could be deceiving with Inspectre Quimbley. You didn't live to be his age in his field unless you had serious skills.

"You F.O.G.gies don't mess around when it comes to fighting," I said.

The Inspectre was still giving me that paternal look when he stood up. "The forces of Darkness certainly don't mess around when it comes to attacking us, so why should we hold back? Especially vampires. I'd rather have you prepared, my boy, than dead. Now, then . . ."

He pulled a long black cape off the back of the chair he had been sitting in. As he tied it on, I almost laughed. I was pretty much looking at a walruslike version of Count Dracula. He scooped up an enchanted coatrack in both his hands and brandished it like it was a staff. The little metal coat hooks at the top of it snaked to life like tiny metal pincers. All of this certainly helped dissipate the patriarchal mood and any humor.

I looked around the general clutter of the room for something weapon-y of my own.

"That's your first mistake," the Inspectre said.

"Sir?"

"Unorthodox Fighting Techniques at this level provides very little in the way of conventional weaponry. Open your mind to the art of improvisation during conflict. Few fights ever go as smoothly as they look in the movies, do they?

You never know under what circumstance you might be called upon to defend yourself. Or with what."

I missed the lower levels of this class. In those, I had fought with weapons like carnivorous sofa cushions, fire stokers that kept blowing soot into my face, potted trees that screamed when you hit them, pool cues, fountain pens, living lawn gnomes, and once, purely by accident, normal swords.

This time, however, nothing really jumped out to me and I was at a loss.

"You've already got the best weapon," I said, backing away. Even the length of the coatrack gave it a considerable advantage. I was unsure of what to do, but I was still in the mood for a good fight. I had so much pent-up anger and frustration over the whole Jane situation.

"Use your head, boy," the Inspectre said, smiling and moving cautiously toward me, "for more than just a place to hang your hat."

His smile betrayed him. Even in a fight, the Inspectre couldn't help throwing encouraging clues at me. A place to hang your hat, I thought to myself . . . would be at the top of *another* coatrack. I glanced quickly around the room and there it was, another coatrack blending in to the wall on the opposite side of the room. The Inspectre moved into swinging range. I had to act.

I turned and dashed across the room, feeling my hair stir as the air from the Inspectre's swing blew by me. Ever the gentleman, the Inspectre waited until I got my hands on the other coatrack before charging me. The hooks on the rack sprang to life and I relished the chance to finally let my growing aggression out. All of it—the discovery of the people on the booze cruise, my troubles with Jane, the fact that someone had tried to sabotage the Oubliette—all of it came flooding out in quick, vicious attacks, all of which the Inspectre was trying his best to counter. On the plus side, he had landed very few strikes against me, so I considered our score pretty even by my count.

The old man spent the better part of an hour putting me through the wringer.

As fatigue started to set in, our coatracks clashed together as we struggled across the floor of the fight studio. For once, I realized I had the Inspectre on the defensive and pressed my advantage. I lunged toward him with the business end of the coatrack. The hooks waved like tentacles as they sought to disarm Inspectre Quimbley. I thought for sure I had him, but he sidestepped and parried. My weapon smacked harmlessly against the wall, and one of the hooks latched on to a light fixture, forcing me to stop while I untangled it.

"Good form," the Inspectre said, "good form."

I was too caught up in freeing my weapon, and the Inspectre knew it. He swung his own rack low and caught me behind the knees before I could turn back to him. They buckled, causing me to fall flat on my back, and I stayed there, the wind knocked out of me.

"The hardest part to mastering the coatrack," he said as he triumphantly planted his on the floor, "is forgetting that it is *not* a staff. Most apprentices treat it like they're sixteenth-century warrior monks from a Hong Kong action movie. Well, who ever heard of a monk using a coatrack to fight? Staff forms are the totally wrong fighting technique for them to practice . . . when what they should master is the tricky art of the rack."

He offered his hand and helped me up.

"Of course," he continued, his breathing a little labored, "if you were using this combat technique and a vampire was involved, the smart thing to do would be to snap off the end of it to make a stake to impale him with, but, bless my heart, these coatracks are so bloody cute with their hooks. They're like little baby fingers."

I pulled at my own tangled coatrack, which was now swinging playfully from the light fixture. It grumbled as I tugged it free, and I turned, readying myself. The Inspectre, however, looked winded and was leaning heavily on his own rack. The hooks seemed to be petting his shoulder.

"Sir . . . ?"

"No worries, my boy." He looked up and smiled. "That last parry simply took a lot out of this old man. Guess it *is* best that we're training a new generation. The hand that rocks the cradle rules the world, after all."

I hobbled to the table at one side of the room and helped myself to a fresh donut there.

"Ahh, the spoils of victory," the Inspectre said.

Putting in the extra hours being part of F.O.G. added to my already overloaded work schedule, but at least there were snacks.

"You keep this up," I said, "and you're going to have to roll me out of here. Remind me to hit the gym more often. Or maybe at all."

"You might want to look into that, son. It's just one of the perks of being a F.O.G.gie, you know. It's free. I wouldn't want you to put on the 'Fraternal Fifteen' on my account."

"Sure it's free," I said. "You want to get me on a treadmill so I can get better at running from even nastier things than I'm already used to running from."

The Inspectre nodded.

"I think I'm starting to learn that 'more perks' really means I stand a greater chance of dying. The more access I have around the Department, the shorter my life expectancy, right?"

"Well, don't beat around the bush," the Inspectre said, letting out a hearty laugh. "Perks aside, 'doing good' is supposed to be its own reward, but it certainly doesn't hurt to have free donuts and an elliptical machine. Ready?"

"Do you mind if I ask you more about the Fraternal Order of Goodness?" I asked. The Inspectre shook his head. "We're the most-talked-about secret society I've ever heard of. Divisional managers like Wesker call the order a bunch of snobby do-gooders."

" 'Dangerously underqualified' is what we call blokes

like him," he said, then paused. "My boy, you don't get to
be Inspectre without learning to read people over the years.
I can sense some kind of trouble with you, and I know
what turmoil can do to a young agent."

I looked up, drawn in by the kindness in his voice.

"I still don't feel right about being in charge of Connor,"
I said. "I mean, he is my mentor, after all. I just don't know
if I'm ready for this. And frankly, he's touchy on a good
day. Then there's the responsibility of calling the shots . . .
What if I make the wrong call and do something rash?"

I expected the Inspectre to try to reason with me, to
quell my nerves or tell me to stop acting like such a child,
possibly even a no-nonsense chiding.

"Well," he said. He put down his towel and grinned.
"There's rash and then there's *rash*, isn't there?"

I cocked my head. "I don't think I follow you, sir."

"Well," he said, "there are distinctions in the details,
aren't there? There is *stupid* rash and there is *noble* rash.
Both can make you dead, I suppose, but one at least stands
a chance of causing great heroics, yes? For instance, and
this is all hypothetical, mind you . . . If I were in a position
where I had a chance to take down something as dangerous as a vampire before the local government could even
get through all the red tape, some might think it incredibly
foolish of me to act upon that."

I nodded. "Connor's always telling me to keep an even
head about things," I said, "to not let my emotions get in
the way, and to think clearly. But now I've got to worry
about putting him in harm's way as well."

"Yes, well, Connor's right in one sense when he talks
about absolute clearheadedness. That is what works for
Connor." He poured himself a glass of water and began
drinking. He leaned over, drawing conspiratorially close.

"You and I are men of *action*, Simon. So are the rest of
the F.O.G.gies. Most people don't understand that. Most
people never will. Sometimes all we have to go with *are*
our emotions. That may be the one thing that gives us an

edge, the one thing that saves us all in the battle between good and evil, especially in the face of bureaucracy."

I swallowed hard. I felt the pressure of failing coming on once again. I had vampires to deal with. The Inspectre clapped me on the back.

"Don't worry yourself about it too much," he said cheerfully. "If you die, at least you'll die spectacularly. That's the mark of a true hero." He clapped me on the back. "Same time tomorrow?"

I nodded, thinking, And the day after and the day after . . . until I either become the most expert vampire slayer since Buffy or die trying.

8

I cleaned myself up after my training session and headed back down to the main floor. With the graveyard shift arriving, the offices were dead and of *course* Supply was closed, so after making a quick copy of the form I'd had Jane sign, I slid it under their door. Then I headed back out through the movie theater and into the coffee shop up front. With its bare brick walls, classic movie posters, and big, comfy, secondhand chairs, I thought it would be the perfect place to brood. I had seen many a dark literary writer gravitate to this place with their laptops, and once I had my coffee, I navigated through a sea of them until I found an unoccupied large purple chair to curl up in. I set my coffee down on a table in the center of a few other chairs, one of them occupied by Godfrey Candella. He was furiously writing away in one of his notebooks.

"You know, a laptop would be faster," I said.

Godfrey looked up from his writing.

"Excuse me?" he said, somewhat distracted.

"A laptop," I repeated. I gestured toward his pen and notebook. "It would be faster."

"Ah," he said, and his face lit up, "*but* would it be as reliable?" He held up his notebook like he was displaying it on QVC. "The Moleskine notebook is a near-legendary form of record keeping, used by great minds for well over two centuries. Hemingway, Picasso, even Van Gogh . . ."

"My apologies," I said, cutting off his little nerdgasm on the history of notebooks. I raised my coffee mug in salute. He did the same and we drank in silence for a moment, but it didn't last long. Godfrey started flipping back through his notebook until he found whatever he was looking for.

"Do you mind if I ask you a few follow-up questions about what happened earlier today?" he asked. "The incident involving the Oubliette? I just wanted to clarify a few things."

I sighed. Maybe helping Godfrey clarify his historical documents would help me with my own, or at the very least provide some form of distraction. Besides, I liked Godfrey, despite the quiet loneliness that radiated from him—or maybe because of it. I knew a thing or two about loneliness.

"Go ahead," I said, settling back in my chair. "Shoot."

"Great. Thanks." Godfrey smiled and looked down at his notes. "So, earlier the Inspectre mentioned something about the Oubliette and you . . . ? Unfortunately, Director Wesker yelled about it so much at the time, I kind of missed what exactly happened."

"It's a wonder we ever get anything done around here with Wesker shouting," I said. I couldn't shake the image of his hand resting against Jane's lower back. I tried to push it out of my mind by telling Godfrey Candella all the details I could remember about the incident at the Javits Center. It seemed to help. When I finished, I was no longer thinking about Jane and Wesker together, but instead about being swallowed up by a sea of rats and then being knee-deep in rat goo. Believe it or not, the nostalgia of being knee-deep in rat goo was a mental step-up.

Godfrey wrote frantically to keep up, and about a minute after I stopped speaking, he finally looked up. He pulled the pen out of his hand and flexed his fingers.

"So," he said, "you think it was sabotage?"

I nodded.

"If you had to make a guess," he continued, "who do you think tried to kill you?"

He said it so earnestly, I laughed.

"I'm sorry," I said, and then thought about it. "Well, I've only been here half a year, so I haven't had a ton of time to make that many enemies, I hope." I thought for a moment. "I'd say the Sectarians, for a start. But their leader is locked up in jail."

"The Sectarians," he said. Godfrey's eyes rolled up into his head as if he were a computer accessing some archived file. "Oh, right. That whole pincushioning their leader to the wall of the Met thing . . ."

Yeah," I said, "*that*." I couldn't help but have a little bitterness in my tone.

"Did I say something wrong?" Godfrey said. He looked genuinely concerned that he might have somehow offended me. He worried the notebook back and forth in his hands.

I shook my head.

"I just thought things would be different; that's all," I said.

"Different how?" he asked, looking enrapt.

"I don't want to trouble you with any of this," I said, starting to stand.

"No, please," he said. He wasn't moving and his eyes were eager like a starving man coveting someone's sandwich.

I sat back down.

"After that night at the museum," I said, "when you caught me just outside on the steps almost immediately after it went down . . ."

Godfrey nodded. He tapped the side of his temple. "I remember."

I was sure the Computer Who Wore Horn-Rims did. I continued.

"I was on cloud nine . . . cloud ten, even. Everyone was patting me on the back, congratulating me. I had been in hog heaven with all that attention, plus with Jane on my arm. The Fraternal Order had just taken me in . . ."

I couldn't put words to it.

"You're lamenting your success," Godfrey offered.

"That's exactly it," I exclaimed, almost physically relieved to hear him say it.

"I hear that a lot, actually," he said.

"Really?"

Godfrey nodded. "A lot of agents bring it up when they're recounting stuff for the Gauntlet. Let me guess. Right now you're experiencing a bout of depression, especially after the day you've had . . ."

"Yes," I said. It was invigorating to get this kind of validation. "I spent three months after the whole Met incident doing the paperwork on it. *Three months.* And then I have days where I almost die on an hourly basis and everything goes wrong around here. Then I have to file a twenty-page form to get a new cell phone from Supply. With all these swings between the mundane and the fantastical, I feel like I'm losing my mind."

Godfrey gave me a kind smile. "You *do* realize you work for the Department of *Extra*ordinary Affairs, don't you? Try not to confuse things. It's the affairs that are extraordinary, not us. *We* still have to be ordinary in the face of it. Sure, some of us might do extraordinary things, but we can't live our lives at that heightened level."

I did feel better having heard it, but it still nagged at me. "It feels so crazy and thankless."

"Welcome to civil service," Godfrey said, and he laughed. "Good deeds are supposed to be their own reward, are they not?"

I nodded and started to laugh as well, hearing the Inspectre's words echoed. "Yeah, well, a little reward every now and then wouldn't hurt. Do you know what I came up with when they finally forced me to do my own performance appraisal? I wrote 'Didn't die.' "

Godfrey laughed harder, the two of us now cackling like witches around a cauldron. A few of the norms who hung out in the Lovecraft Café gave us the evil eye, but I didn't care. Something pleasant in me had bubbled up to the surface, and I embraced it.

Godfrey reached into a messenger bag sitting on the floor next to his chair and pulled out a stack of paper. "This is mine," he said. "Forty-three pages so far, and still counting . . ."

I raised my mug to him once again.

"You, sir, have given me a sense of perspective," I said, the laughter starting to calm. "Not to mention the best laugh I've had all day."

He clinked his mug against mine.

I was somewhat exhausted from my day, but at least my mind was in better spirits. Too bad I was about to spoil it by heading home to deal with the fallout from my tiff with Jane earlier this afternoon.

9

A calm washed over me as I embraced the nighttime quiet of the SoHo streets. By the time I clambered into the wrought-iron cage of my building's elevator, I was practically asleep. I was also full of regret, remembering how I had conducted myself at the bookstore with Jane earlier. Now all I wanted was a chance to apologize, *if* Jane was even going to stop by now.

When the elevator hit my floor, I slid the accordion doors open and stumbled down the hall, barely awake. My apartment door wasn't locked, but with my brain shutting down for the day, I didn't think much of it. I *was* expecting Jane, after all, and besides, if I had afforded myself any luxury in this world, it was that I lived in a pretty nice and secure building. But I'd been wrong before. I woke right the hell up when a fist shot out from behind my door and popped me in the jaw. The hook of the swing made the left side of my head smack hard against the solid oak of the door itself.

Part of my special training from the D.E.A. kicked in as one of the lessons I'd learned in the first session came to

me. *He who turns and runs away, lives to live another day.*
I wasn't about to get ambushed in my own apartment, and
since the punch had spun me to face my door and potential
freedom, I gladly started off in that direction . . . until an
arm snaked around my neck from behind and dragged me
back into the apartment. My legs were sprawled out in
front of me as I was pulled backward toward the couch in
the center of the room. Whoever was attacking me was
strong as hell. There was no way I was going to overpower
him from this position.

I waited for him to stop dragging me. My training was
more than just how to fight; it was how to fight dirty if
need be. I vividly remembered the unfortunate day when
our instructor had said, "When you're not sure what you're
dealing with—be it humanoid, lycanthropic, or other—go
for the breadbasket." I did just that. I put all my weight on
my right leg and threw the rest of it into the heel of my left
foot, raising it high and hard into my attacker's crotch. My
attacker let out a grunt but didn't release the hold around
my neck. Just then, it dawned on me with rising horror just
what type of creature could withstand a kick to the groin. I
was being sleeperholded by a woman.

Jane couldn't be that pissed, could she?

"I apologize," I croaked out, but it was lost in the commotion.

"Apology accepted," a woman who was most definitely
not Jane said from right behind my ear. Panic set in, but
before I was able to free myself, the weight of my body was
used against me and I was thrown down onto my couch.
Luckily I landed in an upright position, almost perfectly
sitting, but before I could get up my attacker straddled me
and pushed me back against the leather. I caught a flash of
steel in the darkness and felt a cold blade against my neck.
Just like that, the fight went out of me.

The figure leaned forward, crossing into a stream of
moonlight coming in through the ceiling-high bay windows that covered one whole wall of my living room. The

woman's hair was dark red and shoulder length, cut so she sported Bettie Page bangs. Her eyes showed a hint of devilish delight in manhandling—womanhandling—me. Her lips were pressed thin as she slid the knife against my throat, but there was something familiar about her.

Recognition hit me.

"Liza Saria?" I said.

"It's Mina now, remember? Took you long enough, Sherlock," she said. "Miss the old crew?" She relaxed a little, then put her left hand—the one *not* brandishing a knife—on my forehead, stroking my hair back hard.

This was worse than I thought, actually.

"Long time, no want to see," I said, afraid to speak too loud for fear of moving my throat against the blade. "And no, I don't miss the old crew. That was back when I was a cocky young con artist hell bent on fucking my life up. Can't say I really miss that, 'Mina.' Still have the unhealthy obsession with the victimhood of Dracula's paramour, I see."

"You didn't miss me?" Mina said, pouting her lips. "Not even a little?"

I shook my head carefully under the blade. "Sorry. I'm not terribly proud of myself or the people I used to associate with back in the day. How the hell did you find me?"

"If you didn't want to be found," she said, loving every minute of controlling me, "maybe you shouldn't have left the name Canderous on the mailbox downstairs."

I looked over at my open door, and now I could see where part of the doorjamb had been torn away. She had flat-out broken her way in. I really needed to talk to the co-op board about beefing up security around here.

"So you were just wandering by and happened to see it?"

Mina laughed. "What the hell do you care, Candy?" she asked. "Isn't it enough that I found you?"

I winced at the nickname. "Can we not call me that? I know you coined it and all . . ."

Mina laughed again. "Despite all the terrible illegal shit you've done—the crimes, the thefts, conning people out of their money—it's the nickname that bothers you most?"

Illegal though it all had been, Mina and the rest of the crew never had an idea that I had any special powers that made it all possible. They had simply assumed I was a crack thief with a good eye. The paranormal didn't figure into their world.

"You shouldn't be here," I said, giving up on the name and trying to be logical with her. "There's a reason I haven't kept in contact, you know. Some ties should remain broken."

Mina gave me a firm pat like I was her dog. Worse, she was messing up my hair.

"Why did you leave all of us?" she said, her eyes full of crazy. "We were like family. Things were just getting interesting when you ran out on us."

"Is that how you see it?" I asked. It was hard not to laugh in her face. "I ran out on all of you? Mina, I barely escaped getting arrested when you switched to robbing museums. And that last one, well . . . I read about the debacle you went through, barely pulling it off."

Mina laughed. The blade pressed harder against me.

"But we *did* pull it off, and that's the important thing," she said, writhing around on top of me. There was nothing sexy about it to me, but she seemed pleased. "God, don't you remember the rush from those days?"

"I know the museum eventually got *The Scream* back again . . ."

"But they won't have it for long." Mina's laughter turned into a schoolgirl giggle. Despite the knife at my throat, it dawned on me what she had come here for. I was getting angry and my body was cramped from our position on the couch.

"I'm not going to help you steal *The Scream* again, Mina," I shouted.

"I need your lock-picking skills," she pleaded, letting the knife fall from my neck. "It's just me this time; none of the old crew."

I relaxed, but only by the tiniest margin. With crazy, there's never much room for relaxation.

"You know you want to," she said, and she jumped off me, walking like a cat in the dark, heading straight for my galley kitchen. She tucked the knife into her belt and started rooting through my refrigerator. "*The Scream* is on loan to the Museum of Modern Art. It's closed right now, so it looks like I'll have to check it out tomorrow night before it closes. Then you and I will hit it the following night. Three days. That's all I'm asking for."

My retractable bat was still hanging at my side and I wondered if I should use it. I could imagine pulling it free, hitting the button, and watching it telescope out to full size. The metaphor for restoring my masculinity was not lost on me. I stood up. Mina was a little bat-shit crazy, but I doubted she would really kill me. She had come here, after all, to enlist my help.

"I don't do that sort of thing anymore, Mina," I said. I flicked on the lights and looked with pride around the main area of my apartment. Handpicked leather couches, floor-to-ceiling windows, and an entire wall of ownerless books and antiques that I sold for a profit when I had the time to go through them psychometrically. I had an existence I had worked hard at salvaging. "Look around you. I've got a real life going on here now. I've moved on."

Mina pulled a beer from the fridge, twisted off the top, and drank half of it down. She wandered around my gentleman's club setup in the main room.

"You seem to be doing well for yourself," she agreed. I couldn't ignore the bitter bite in her voice as she said it. She stopped in front of my bookshelves, which also ran from floor to ceiling. They were full of dozens of items I had gathered over the years. "What is all this?"

"I work with antiques now," I said, bending the truth a

little. "I have an eye for things; that's all. I'm a collector, either for myself or sometimes I sell to dealers or track down the previous owners and sell them back to them."

Mina perused the shelves. She could have picked up any number of classy items. She ran her hand over an ornate stone incense censer, then moved on to an art deco clock I had been holding on to for far too long, before she picked up a plastic replica of the shark from *Jaws*. It was attached to a game board, the shark's mouth full of tiny plastic garbage pieces. My powers had told me that the piece once belonged to a CEO at Chase Manhattan, and I had been meaning to make some bank off it. I had been slow to return it to its owner. What can I say? The game was fun.

"Pay well, does it?" she said. "Playing *Sanford and Son?*"

"I make my rent," I said with a dismissive shrug.

"*This* allows you to pay rent?" she said, not believing me. She shook the shark as she spoke and the tiny plastic garbage fell out of its mouth. Its jaws snapped shut.

"Please put that down," I requested, not wanting to sound too desperate.

"Sure, Candy," she said, all rainbows and sunshine now. I wondered if I had been this bipolar back then as well. "No problem."

"Thanks," I said. Why was it that I had felt less threatened with a knife at my throat than when she was messing with my stuff? Something told me I had to get my priorities straight sometime in the near future.

Mina turned to face me, the knife once again in her hand.

"You *are* going to help me, though, Simon."

This time I pulled my bat free, hit the switch on it, and watched it spring out to its full length.

"That's where I think we have a problem," I said. I rested it on my shoulder in a nonthreatening manner. "Look, I'm glad we had time for a lovely, touchy-feely reunion. Glad we had a chance to reminisce about the old days. But I'm so not going to help you."

She smiled sweetly at me, shaking her head, her eyes going all Glenn Close.

"We're doing this," she said, the smile slowly fading. There was desperation in her eyes. Mina was in some kind of serious trouble.

"We are doing this," she repeated in a slow, deliberate manner, "and you're going to help me. You think Krueger or Myers can pick a fucking lock to save their lives? I need your talented little hands on it."

I didn't say a word. Little did she know that my hands held a talent greater than picking locks.

When I didn't respond, Mina looked more and more pissed. "Wouldn't it just be the worst luck if Krueger or Myers got wind of where you're living now? Think of what they'd do to you if they got their psychotic little paws on you. You'd probably live, but I'm sure it would take you quite some time to heal, and you'd probably walk with a permanent limp."

She stopped by the sofa and picked up a picture of Jane and me from the D.E.A. ice cream social a few months back.

"And I shudder to think what they'd do to this cute little number of yours," she said. "Or perhaps *I'll* just hurt the girl. Jane Clayton-Forrester, right? Lives on West Twenti-eth Street?"

I felt an intense wave of panic. "What synapse in your brain isn't firing, Mina?" I said, tightening my grip on my bat. I couldn't allow any of those sociopaths back into my life, and certainly not near Jane.

Was I really willing to strike down someone who wasn't an actual monster or undead? Creatures were one thing, but raising my weapon against another person . . .

I wasn't sure what I would do if Mina pressed the issue, but I also doubted I could talk her out of this heist, given the desperation in her voice. She was unpredictable on a good day, and I wanted her to get the hell out of my life as fast as possible.

"Don't threaten me or Jane with those goons," I said. "If I help you—and it's a mighty big *if*, Mina—you've got to swear I'll never see you or them again. I don't know what the hell you've gotten yourself into, and maybe it's better I don't know, but I mean it. I help you this once and we're through. And you certainly can't tell Jane."

Before Mina had a chance to answer, the door creaked open behind me.

"Can't tell Jane what?" Jane chimed in.

I didn't dare turn around. I looked at the clock on the wall. It was only a few minutes before midnight. If I was lucky, the shittiest day of my life was almost over. If I wasn't, maybe my life would be. Either way, I was just looking forward to an end to it all.

10

I just couldn't turn around to face Jane yet. Instead, I simply stared at Mina, who peered over my shoulder to check out my girlfriend. She slid her knife into her jacket. I didn't think Jane could see it from her angle. At least, I hoped she couldn't. Explaining why I had a choke hold on my bat in front of this strange woman in my apartment was going to be tough enough.

Before I could think what to do, Mina's face melted from psychotic to a big, cheery smile. Chalk one up for the mood swings of a sociopath, I thought. She brushed past me and offered her hand to Jane. I turned around. Jane had a metric ton of books in a shoulder bag. She lowered it to the floor to take Mina's hand in hers.

"You must be Jane," Mina said, sounding like the mom on *Leave It to Beaver* as she faked being charming. "I'm Mina. Simon's told me so much about you."

Jane shook her hand and smiled back, but there was still a little of that darkness from back in the bookstore in her eyes.

"He has?" she said, and looked to me.

"Yup," I said, not skipping a beat.

Jane looked at the bat resting on my shoulder.

"Is everything alright here?"

"I was just showing her my bat," I said lamely, realizing how innuendo laden that must have sounded.

Jane's eyes narrowed. "Is that some sort of euphemism?"

"Boys and their toys," Mina said with a pleasant laugh. Hadn't she been threatening my life just five minutes ago?

Jane rolled her eyes and stepped toward me, but not before looking Mina up and down. There was no denying the fact that Mina was physically hot; most of her ugliness was hidden in that messed-up little brain of hers.

"I didn't realize you were going to have *company* tonight," Jane said. I knew that tone. "Company" came out like it was a dirty word.

"I didn't either," I said. I lowered my bat, but didn't let go of it just yet. I wasn't sure what Mina was up to, and I didn't want to get caught unaware if she suddenly changed tack in the middle of all this.

"Simon and I are old friends," Mina said, circling behind the couch. "We used to work together."

"Oh, really?" said Jane, relaxing a little. She gave me a mischievous grin and sat down on the couch. "He doesn't really talk all that much about his past with me. I'd be curious to hear all about it."

There was an undeniable hot side to Jane when the little bits of her old darkness came out, the same ones that no doubt had made her a valued asset when temping for the cultists, but the idea of Jane chumming it up with this truly evil psycho from my past was a bit overwhelming.

"Um . . . how about not?" I said, trying not to sound too defensive, and failing completely.

Mina put on an apologetic face and circled behind Jane on the couch.

"When I came into town, I had plans with friends, but they bailed on me," Mina said. She gave me a pointed look. "You know how unreliable *friends* can be."

She started pantomiming strangling Jane and slitting her throat so only I could see. "I know it was very last minute, but I had nowhere else to turn, and Simon was gentleman enough to give me his sofa to crash on for a couple of nights."

I could see Jane's face fall, but I wasn't about to contradict Mina. I needed to get Jane out of here safely.

I turned to Jane.

"Hope you don't mind," I said, giving her a weak smile. I didn't know what else to say. *I'm sorry one of the psychos from my past is extorting me into helping her and I'm just trying to keep her from killing you* didn't seem to fit. Plus, I hadn't told Jane much at all about my criminal past, and now didn't seem like the time to start.

"You can stay," Mina said with a sweet smile. "I don't want to be an intrusion. Don't mind me."

Jane stood up, gathered up her bag of books, and moved toward the door before turning to face us. She looped the bag over her shoulder, cradling the books protectively close to her chest.

"No, thanks," she said, her face showing signs of agitation. "I've got a lot of reading to do, and it sounds like you two have some catching up in store."

It didn't surprise me that she wasn't taking it so well. I put the shoe on the other foot. If I had shown up at her apartment to find a hunky old coworker of hers, I didn't think I'd be taking it so well either. Still, a relationship like ours was new to me and I found myself at a real loss as to what to do.

"Nice meeting you," Mina said with a sweet smile, waving.

Jane nodded. "Same to you." She walked over to me and gave me deep, territorial-marking kind of kiss. When she pulled away, her eyes were cold. "Talk to you tomorrow?"

"Sure," I said, nodding.

Jane headed out the door, closing it behind her as she went. None of this sat right with me. The monkey wrench that was Mina just added to my problems with Jane. I had to do something.

"Give me a second," I said to Mina. "I'll be right back."

I headed for the door.

Mina cleared her throat and I looked at her. She put a finger to her lips.

Shhh.

She lowered her finger away from her mouth and waggled it at me slowly.

Don't tell Jane anything, it said.

As I ran out into the hall, I watched Mina slide herself behind the door and I heard the sound of the knife coming out of her jacket again.

"Janey, wait," I called out.

I caught up with her halfway to the elevator.

She turned and her face was a blank slate. I couldn't get a read off her about this whole situation, and if I couldn't warn her about the dangerous woman I was dealing with, I at least wanted a chance to apologize for Mina being here. The demons of my past were mine to bear, and I couldn't hold Jane responsible for having a negative reaction to them.

"I just want to say I'm sorry," I said, trying to take her hands in mine. She reluctantly let go of the bag of books and gave me her hands. I lowered my voice. "You know, about earlier, at the bookshop . . ."

I was trying to avoid specifics, just in case Mina could hear us.

"Okay," Jane said, and then just stood there. I squeezed her hand, but she didn't really squeeze back.

"You okay?" I asked.

"Yeah," she said. She let go of one of my hands and rubbed her eyes. She looked over my shoulder to make sure we were alone, but lowered her voice as well. "Just worn down from doing that . . . rat thing . . . over the phone earlier. Wesker wants me to stop inventorying the Stacks and read more about . . . technomancy."

"But you're not mad?" I asked suspiciously.

Jane smiled and shook her head, the darkness on her face vanishing in an instant.

"Just go and make sure your friend is okay," she said with sincerity. "I know what it's like to be in this city and not have anyone to turn to. It's okay."

Jane and I still had our issues to iron out after the fight earlier, but this was probably the best answer I was going to get from her under the circumstances. I kissed her on the forehead and watched her until she closed the accordion doors of the elevator and it started down.

I walked back down the hall and into my apartment, mulling over our exchange as I went.

When I entered, Mina was in the kitchen going through my cabinets. She had already stripped down to a white wifebeater that left little to the imagination. Even after all these years, Mina was in amazing shape, without an ounce of fat on her upper body.

I sat down on the other side of the galley counter as Mina continued poking around.

"So, she's what passes as interesting to you these days, eh, Simon?"

"Watch it," I said.

Mina grinned at me. "I thought you like them a bit more adventurous and less . . . bookish?"

I ignored her dig at Jane. I could have told her about Jane's past temping for the forces of evil, or how she had tried to kill me, or even how we had fought side by side at the Met. I could have told Mina all that, but I didn't. To bring it up would be to bring up the Department in its entirety and that was a part of my life I didn't want Mina to have anything to do with.

"I don't really know this Jane of yours, Simon," Mina said, throwing a skillet down on the stove and drizzling olive oil into it, "but don't you think her reaction to having a gorgeous woman like me here was a little . . . odd?"

"How so?" I asked, looking up at her as something in my chest tightened up.

"Well, first of all, you were looking a little guilty when you were not so suavely trying to cover up why I'm really here. Maybe Jane knew you're hiding something . . . maybe the past you've had with me, or maybe she thinks we're hooking up. But maybe she doesn't really care. She didn't seem angry enough. Maybe because she has something of her own to hide."

Mina's words set something off in me. What if she had a point? What if Jane was really the guilty party here? That would explain all the QT with Wesker, and I definitely didn't put it past Wesker to try it on. My heart raced as I really started to give it serious consideration, until I realized I was taking relationship advice from a seriously screwed-up mind like Mina's.

"Jesus," I said. "Don't put stuff like that in my head. I've got barely enough hamsters in their wheels up there to handle my regular level of paranoia."

"Something to eat?" Mina asked. Gone was the threatening bitch from before, replaced by this younger, hipper, but equally mentally unbalanced Rachael Ray.

I ignored her question and headed off to the back of my apartment toward my bedroom.

"Clean up after yourself," I said. "There are blankets and a pillow in the bottom of the closet in the bathroom. Enjoy the guest room and try not to kill me in my sleep."

As I left her, I thought about my performance appraisal again. *Didn't die.* Felt like I wanted to, though. Part of me would have loved nothing better. But I didn't. And, lucky me, tomorrow *was* another day.

11

Once Mina left the next morning, I headed up to the Javits Center. After fighting my way across the convention floor through a line of either dark elves or Smurfs—I wasn't sure what look they were going for—I made my way back to our D.E.A. booth. Connor was nowhere to be seen, but the Inspectre was already busy arranging the piles of brochures and aptitude tests.

"Anyone try to kill you yet today, my boy?" the Inspectre asked with cheer in his voice.

"Not unless you count crosstown traffic," I said, "but I don't think I can blame that on cultists."

We were interrupted by a short, balding man in a hideous tweed suit approaching our booth. "Good day, gentlemen," he said with a flourish of his arm and a deep bow. I figured him to be dressed as a character from *Doctor Who*.

"Pamphlet?" I offered, holding up a copy of *Ask Not What Your Country Can Do for Ghoul*.

The man shook his head. "Perhaps another time. We, like you, are fellow vendors."

I wondered who this "we" he referred to was, as he was

standing there alone. I looked down at his color-coded badge and saw it was the same jaundiced yellow as ours. I put the pamphlet down.

Short & Balding had an accent that hinted at Middle American mixed with something exotic. Whatever it was, it was enough to confuse me.

"I trust you are having a good show so far?" he asked, the model of politeness.

The Inspectre nodded, but didn't say anything. I kept my mouth shut, taking his lead.

"Excellent, excellent," he said, sounding a little like a pitchman. I suspected he was here to set up some kind of vendor exchange, which was popular among so many of the non-paranormal vendors here.

"I'm Marten Heron," he continued with another, more formal bow. Was this guy for real? He looked like he'd be more at home chatting it up back at the Lovecraft Café than here. "Of the Brothers Heron, Booth 1601-A. Perhaps you've heard of us?"

There was a twinkle of expectancy in his eye.

"You're one of the Heron Brothers?" I said. "Julius is your brother? We rented the Oubliette from you yesterday. You know, the Oubliette that tried to kill me?"

The twinkle burned out in his eyes, but was back in a flash. "Yes, unfortunately," he said. He wrung his hands together. "Julius told me about that. Rest assured, we're looking into what happened." He paused, then lowered his voice. "You didn't happen to notice anything particularly unusual around here today, did you?"

"Unusual how?" I asked, curiosity getting the better of me. "Nothing's tried to kill me today, if that's what you're hinting at."

Marten paused, his hands clenched together like he might burst into a choral number any second.

"Oh, nothing in particular, really," he said. "Just wanted to make sure the show is going well for you, after the Oubliette and all."

I went to speak, but I felt the Inspectre's foot come to rest on mine and stopped. Instead, the Inspectre extended his hand and spoke up.

"Argyle Quimbley," he said. "A pleasure. I've only met your brother."

Marten Heron grabbed his hand and pumped it with great enthusiasm.

"Ah, yes, Julius. There is a third brother as well, Lanford, but he hasn't had much time away from the booth. Not one for the socialization, you see."

Marten continued shaking hands. This went on for several moments before the Inspectre broke it off.

"If I'm not mistaken," the Inspectre said, "you're one of the Romnichal, are you not?"

"Romni-what?" I said, unable to contain myself. This time the Inspectre slammed his heel down on my foot, and I stifled a cry of pain.

"*Romnichal*, actually," Marten corrected, smiling. "We're Romany, from Downers Grove. You have a good ear."

"It was your last name that tipped me off, actually," the Inspectre said. "Fairly common among the nomadic tribes in America."

"I've never met any gypsies before," I piped in. "Downers Grove sounds very exotic."

Marten shrugged. "If you consider Illinois exotic, sure."

I scrunched my face. "Illinois gypsies?"

"For part of the year anyway," he said. "But as your friend so astutely points out, we are nomadic, so my brothers and I do get around."

He reached into his pocket, pulled out a handful of business cards, and started sorting through them. Halfway through the pile, he stopped and pulled one free.

"If you hear of anything out of the ordinary happening at the show, please, give me a call," he said, trying to hand it to me. I kept my hands at my side, not wanting to explain my gloves. The Inspectre reached for it instead.

I read the card over the Inspectre's shoulder.

The Brothers Heron

Purveyors of Modern Miracles, Cure-Alls,
and All Manner of Items Fantastical

Marten Heron

I noticed there was no address, but it did list a phone number.

As if he anticipated my thoughts, Marten pulled a cell phone from his pocket and waved it at me like it was doing a little dance.

"It makes being nomadic a little easier," he said. He checked the clock on the face of his cell phone. "If you'll excuse me, I have to be returning to my brothers now. A pleasure to make your acquaintance. Come on by if you're looking for anything special—charms, potions, whatnot." He started to turn, then spun back around. "And again, sorry about the almost-killing-you thing."

Marten Heron walked off into a sea of Wookiees, elves, and samurai, leaving the Inspectre and me alone once again.

"Tell me, boy," the Inspectre said once he was gone. "Did anything seem suspicious about all that?"

A few young men drifted toward the table, picking through what we had to offer them.

"Other than him owning the device that tried to kill me?" I asked, trying to control my snark. "He seemed a little jumpy, like he was nervous about something. It makes me wonder what he's trying to hide and if it might have anything to do with our problem at the dock yesterday. I mean, how much suspicious activity can go on in this neighborhood, right?"

I spied Connor hustling through the crowd, coming down the aisle in front of us.

"It certainly warrants a little bit of investigation," the Inspectre said.

Connor came into our booth and threw his trench coat and bag underneath the back table. Inspectre Quimbley pointedly checked his pocket watch.

"Sorry I'm late," he said. "There was another zombie scare downtown, so traffic was a bitch. Small outbreak, it looks like, but they're getting more and more frequent lately."

The Inspectre nodded. He turned back to me. "Why don't you take Connor with you and see what you can find out?" he said. The stone-serious look he gave me left no doubt he was giving me Fraternal Order–level orders, putting me in charge. "I'll man the booth by myself for a while."

"Sure," I said, hoping Connor wasn't really paying attention.

I grabbed Connor and headed out in search of the short man's booth.

"What the hell was up with that, kid?" he asked. He sounded good and pissed.

"Up with what?" I said, feigning ignorance as I dodged a pack of Live-Action Role Players dressed in fairy costumes.

"Why's the Inspectre giving you our orders instead of me?"

"Oh," I said, pausing to think up something. "That. It's nothing. You were late so we just started discussing one of the Illinois gypsies who stopped by the booth."

Somehow this seemed to mollify Connor, and he relaxed. "What did I miss?"

As we searched for the Brothers Heron booth, I explained the conversation we had had with Marten Heron. By the time I was done, Connor had spotted the sign at their booth, and the two of us walked over.

The Brothers Heron booth looked like a movie-set medicine show. Their setup consisted of an actual gypsy wagon, the kind I'd seen either in cartoons or on television shows where snake-oil salesmen would try to pawn their wares off on unsuspecting townies.

"Well, color me Romany," Connor said with a whistle. "A bit theatric, don't you think?"

Unfortunately, the Brothers Heron themselves were nowhere to be seen. As we approached the wagon, however, the incoherent sounds of arguing in a language I didn't understand were coming from behind the wagon curtain, making it apparent where they were. I turned to Connor.

"Stay here," I said.

"Excuse me?" he said, with a little bite to it.

"I just need you to distract them for a few minutes while I take a look back behind the scenes of their wagon."

"Whoa," Connor said. "I think we're going to have to clear that with Enchancellors."

"We don't have to clear shit," I said, feeling a little bold with power. "We don't have time to fill out a bunch of forms or make some calls. I'm doing this under the authority of the Fraternal Order of Goodness, and that's that."

"And that's what you'll say if we get called out on breaking with Departmental procedure?"

I nodded. Connor shrugged, but I could tell that he was only feigning indifference. "Good enough for me. I'll defer to your F.O.G.gie authority . . . this time."

"Thanks," I said, uncomfortable with the strange power play that had just happened. "I'll be right back. Shop their table. Pretend you're interested in their wares."

Connor looked down at the table. It was covered with stoppered bottles, vials, totems, and fetishes. "But I *am* interested in their wares."

"Good," I said, walking off. "Then it shouldn't be such a stretch for you. I'll be back."

I disappeared around the corner of the booth without giving Connor a chance to speak again.

I had to see what the hell was going on. I inched my way along the blue-curtained section behind the wagon as

I followed the sound of the voices. I found the nearest seam and pulled it aside slowly, praying to God that I didn't find someone staring back out at me.

The area behind the Brothers Heron's shop held the Oubliette and also a clutter of various-sized packing crates. Three men stood around a broken crate that reached chest height, and none of them looked happy. The balding one called Marten was there, and across from him stood two others: one was Julius, the dark-haired Penn Gillette look-alike, and the other was a man in his early twenties who looked just shy of being a total Ichabod, with the same dark hair. I thought Marten had said his name was Lanford.

Even though I might have been able to read their lips while they argued, the language they spoke was still impenetrable. My best guess was that it was probably some sort of gypsy Cant.

"Excuse me?" I heard Connor call from out in front of their wagon. "Hello?"

Marten spoke and the three of them acted as one, slipping a tarp over the broken crate before stepping into the wagon. I prayed that Connor could keep them distracted long enough, and then I darted inside the curtain toward the crates, carefully sidestepping the Oubliette. I had to see what they were so eager to hide.

As I approached the tarp, I reached in my pocket for a roll of Life Savers and began scarfing them down. I didn't know what to expect when I read the crate, but I didn't want to pass out only to have the gypsies find me sprawled on the floor of their booth later. I wasn't sure how threatening Illinois gypsies could be, but Julius had looked pretty imposing, so why take chances with a guy who could probably crush my head like a rotten pumpkin?

I slipped off my gloves and lifted the tarp along one side, exposing the shattered section of the wooden crate. It looked empty, but it was too hard to tell for sure from the shadows inside of it. I moved my head closer, but all that did was block the light and make it darker inside. There was a definite odd and unpleasant smell coming from it, though. I covered my mouth and nose, and stepped back. Maybe more light getting into the box might help before I dared take a reading off it. That was when I heard the gentle scratching of claws against wood coming from somewhere behind me.

I turned to find a stack of smaller crates. The one nearest the top rocked slightly and had air holes in it. I moved my face closer, hoping to catch a glimpse through one of the holes, but I jumped back as a wild chittering rose from the crate. The rest of the crates beneath it also sprang to life, producing unique noises that bordered on sounds that I could only imagine would be found in Lovecraft's Cthulhu mythos.

"No, wait," Connor shouted from out in front of the booth, no doubt for my benefit. "I'm very interested in these exorcism ear candles."

"Dammit," I hissed.

There was no time to take a reading from the crate. The Brothers Heron would be steamrolling back through their wagon any second. I threw the tarp over the broken crate and dove for the seam of the curtain I had come through. I darted back around the corner and down along the blind side of the gypsies' booth before slowing down to turn the next corner in my approach to where I had left Connor.

Connor stood there with Julius while the other two brothers had disappeared, no doubt to check out the commotion from the back of their booth. Connor clutched two long, hollow candles in one of his hands, reminding me a little bit of the Statue of Liberty. His eyes bored into me questioningly, and I gave the slightest shake of my head *no* in response.

"Look," Connor said, feigning enthusiasm, "I found those exorcism ear candles you were looking for."

"Oh," I said, throwing my gloves back on. "Great."

I took one from Connor and pretended to examine it, turning it this way and that. I wasn't even sure what an exorcism ear candle was. It looked like a red corncob made out of wax with a wick sticking out of the end of it.

"Oh, no," I said. I realized that we probably had to get out of there, and fast. "These are all wrong." I smiled up at Julius. "Thanks, anyway."

I put the candle down on the table and hurried off. Connor followed in my wake.

"Find anything, kid?" Connor asked.

I shook my head.

"Just a broken packing crate that smelled like an animal," I said. "Well, more like an animal that had eaten another animal and then threw it back up. There were also a bunch more crates that contained some other creatures, but I didn't get a chance to check out what any of them were."

Connor sighed.

"If any of those animals can be proven to be of paranormal origin, we could get them shut down for trafficking," Connor said, "but until we know for sure, there's nothing we can do. We'd better talk to the Inspectre. And we need to get back down to the docks and go over them again. There's got to be something there."

When we approached the booth, however, and saw the grim expression on the Inspectre's face, all thoughts of talking about the Brothers Heron or the docks left us.

"Sir?" I said as we entered the area behind the booth. "Are you okay?"

He turned to face us, his cell phone still clutched open in his hand.

"That was Dave Davidson just now," he said, slowly folding it shut. "I need you two to check something out in Central Park."

"Not the park," Connor muttered, more to himself than either of us.

"What is it?" I asked.

"He didn't want to discuss it over the phone," the Inspectre said, "but he *did* ask for you two specifically."

A sense of dread started to build in me, and I tried to push it aside. I had always wanted to be one of the popular kids. Just not in this way.

12

As we traversed Central Park's Great Lawn, I prayed we weren't headed for another crime scene. Connor looked unusually nervous. Whenever my mentor started looking a bit mental around the edges, I started to worry. But maybe he was just pissy about me ordering him around back at the gypsy booth. He was generally the calm, cool, and collected one, thanks to all those Bogart movies he loved. Right now he looked more Peter Lorre than Bogie.

"You okay?" I asked.

Connor's head twitched in my direction for a second, but he kept walking, his eyes darting around.

"I'm fine, kid," he said. "This place just gives me the creeps."

I looked around. It was a gorgeous, sunshiny day. Young couples were lying out on blankets, kids were throwing Frisbees, and the more health conscious were busy biking or Rollerblading.

"Yeah," I said. "It's, umm . . . terrifying."

Connor scoffed. "Didn't the Inspectre make you read *Trail of Breadcrumbs: Into the Woods and Beyond* yet?"

I shook my head.

Connor looked cheesed off. "Probably the budget cuts . . . Anyway, Central Park is ranked as one of the most dangerous places in our line of work."

"Really?"

"This place is old," Connor said, "though not as old as you'd expect. We're talking only back to the 1850s. Most of this was landscaped, but a lot of the area was residential. There was a lot of life and humanity here before it became a wilderness, and now it's been taken over by nature. That type of change just invites all types of Extraordinary Affairs. Man-made or not, these woods call out to all manner of creatures."

It was odd to think of Central Park having been fabricated like that. I had always assumed that it had been an untamed part of the city that had been set aside as some sort of nature preserve.

We rounded a bend in the path, following a paved section of road that led toward a set of stone stairs. Several police officers were blocking the way, but when we flashed our IDs, they let us up the stairs without a word. At the top was a small circle of benches about one hundred feet across, and at the center of it stood a tall stone spire that rose at least eighty feet. Standing by its base, waiting for us, stood Dave Davidson. At his feet was a body covered by a sheet.

"Things must be slow at City Hall if they can afford to keep you hanging around here waiting for us," Connor said, giving him a polite nod.

Davidson smiled, all polish.

"Believe me, they can afford to keep me standing here when things of this nature keep turning up," he said. He motioned for us to come closer. Davidson reached down and pulled back the sheet. On the ground was the body of a man in his early forties with a typical wreath of baldness going on. He wore running shorts, track shoes, and a T-shirt that read "Sherlock Ohms." Beneath him a small pool of blood coated the bricks and stones.

" 'Sherlock Ohms' . . . ?" I asked.

"We believe it's some sort of electrical joke," Davidson said. "We think he's a scientist. Name's Dr. Richard Kolb."

"Or a yoga nerd," Connor suggested.

"Let's compromise," I said, "and go with science nerd."

Our usual manner of bantering away our discomfort wasn't working, so the three of us stood in silence, taking in the scene for a few moments.

"People get killed in the park all the time," Connor said by way of dismissal, sounding rather heartless. "What makes this guy so special?"

Davidson reached down and turned the dead man's head, revealing a savage tear wound to his neck. "As you can see," he said, "there's a little bit of blood around the bite mark, but that's about all that's left of it." Davidson stepped back. "The coroner's already been by and said he's drained. Feel free to take a closer look."

Connor and I stepped to either side of the body. Already I was thinking about the people on the boat. I looked at Connor.

He placed his pinkie and index finger against his mouth, making fangs with them.

"The vamps from the dock by the Javits Center," I continued. "Great. While we wait on the goddamned paperwork to go through, more people are dying."

Connor turned from the body and was already stepping away as Davidson laid the cloth back down over the dead jogger. I stood.

"We're putting it through as fast as we can," Davidson reassured, but I was already getting pissed and couldn't hold back my frustration.

"How many people are going to have to die before City Hall picks up the pace? Don't you have any feelings?"

Davidson held his hands up disarmingly.

"I'm just a political liaison. It's not in my job description that I have to have feelings. Sorry."

He was so cold about it all that I wanted to pull my bat on him. I turned to Connor, who was looking back down the stairs and off into the park.

"Do something," I said. "Say something."

"Sure, I'll say something," he said, distracted by whatever was catching his eye. "You want to get some answers? Turn around and take a look."

I did, and started scanning the park.

Connor specialized in dealing with ghosts, so that was what I was looking for, but in broad daylight it was near impossible for me. I didn't notice anything unusual, and I threw up my arms in frustration.

"What am I supposed to be looking at?" I said. "I don't have your power. I don't do your thing . . ."

"Just shut up, kid," Connor said. He raised his arm and pointed off to a specific section of the park. "Shut up and concentrate."

I gave up trying to argue with him and stared down the trajectory of his finger, putting more effort into really observing the crowd.

There were people everywhere, very few of them paying attention to us or to Davidson's regular cops nearby. Two couples were walking hand in hand, three Rollerbladers, a line of passing bicyclists, and one jogger.

Bald and wearing a "Sherlock Ohms" shirt. It was the ghost of Dr. Richard Kolb.

"Son of a bitch," I marveled, but before I could get anything else out, Connor shoved past me, jumping down the stairs. I fell in behind him, the cops scattering as the two of us pushed past them all.

By the time Connor and I hit the middle of the Great Lawn, I was a mess, winded and already aching in my calf muscles. I must have run through at least seven different picnic setups, angering the people trying to have a pleasant afternoon in the park.

"Why couldn't he have been some big old fat guy?" I

shouted ahead to Connor, who was still sprinting like the
dickens after our jogger. My foot came down in a wicker
picnic basket and I heard a plastic crunch.

"Sorry!"

"Don't let it get away, kid," Connor shouted back to me,
and poured on the steam. I wasn't about to be shown up,
and despite my aches and pains, I started running to catch
up, gaining on Connor little by little. We were just about at
the crosstown road that connected Eighty-sixth Street on
both sides of the park when I overtook him. I was wheez-
ing by this point, but I kept pushing myself. The jogger
dashed down the embankment and out onto the two-lane
road without a glance either way, and although the cars
passing by almost hit him, not one of them sounded a horn
or moved to swerve. They clearly didn't see him, and I remembered that I hadn't seen him either, until Connor had
pointed him out to me.

I slid down the embankment and tried to keep my pace
while I crossed the road with caution. Horns blared, but I
was almost all the way across when I felt a tug on my jacket
that spun me around like a top. I heard the sound of it tearing. My coattail must have caught on a passing car because
the speed at which I spun reminded me of the old Wonder
Woman quick-change on TV. I was no superhero, though,
and although my coat luckily tore free from whatever car
had snagged it, I was dizzy and stumbled around as I regained my footing.

Connor came down the hill and across the street at a
slower pace, and by the time he reached me, I was ready to
fall back into pursuit mode. The jogger was already halfway
down the next embankment, headed toward the reservoir.
There wasn't anywhere for him to go without having to circle the reservoir. My blood was up and I was pissed about
almost dying, not to mention the tear in my jacket. I charged
down the second hill after our elusive dead athlete.

The jogger still didn't seem to notice that he was being
chased, but he was quite fast for a dead science nerd.

"Don't make me drown you," I shouted after him, hoping to get his attention. He was almost at the reservoir now. I pulled my bat free from the holster on my belt and flicked off its safety before telescoping it to full length. I wasn't sure what the jogger would do once cornered at water's edge—or what damage my bat could do to a ghost—but I wanted to be prepared for anything. I slid the rest of the way down the embankment with Connor right behind me.

"Be careful, kid," he shouted. I came in swinging low, hoping to take the jogger right below his knees. I didn't, however, expect him to just keep on running—not into the water but *along the top of it*. Without breaking stride, the jogger continued his pace across the top of the reservoir.

Connor slid into position next to me. "Well, that was a bit biblical."

In my frustration, I made one last attempt to stop the jogger by chucking my bat at him. I couldn't help myself. My aim was perfect, but unfortunately the bat sailed through the jogger's body and fell into the water with a splash.

"Simon—" Connor started, but I interrupted him.

"Right," I said, slapping my forehead. "Ghost."

We watched the jogger disappear off into the distance. Even if we made our way around the reservoir, he'd be long gone by then.

"That," Connor said, huffing and puffing from the run like he was going to die, "ends that. Let's head back to the scene, kid."

I sat down at the edge of the water and pulled my shoes off.

"Kid?"

"It's already killing me that I'm waiting for a replacement phone from Supply," I said, rolling up my pants above the knee. "I'll be damned if I'm going to wait on a new telescopic bat. It'll take months, because even after I churn through all the paperwork, they'll still have to have it custom-made. If I have to wait on it, I'll be long dead before the order ever comes through."

"Suit yourself," Connor said, starting up the embankment, showering me with little bits of dirt and pebbles as he climbed. "I'll be waiting up by the road."

I stepped into the freezing water. My foot hit the slime-coated reservoir bed and I fought back the urge to throw up. Was being a do-gooder really a better life than the one of crime that I had left behind—a world of Mina's and other assorted psychotics? As something slithered its way over my toes, I really wasn't sure.

13

My luck held true to form and my bat was much deeper in the water than I'd expected. By the time I got it, I was soaked through to the middle of my thighs. On the bright side, being wet was a step up from being covered in lique-fied rats.

The chase had taken a lot out of us, and as Connor and I hobbled back to the crime scene, I asked, "You think our vampires did this?"

Connor shrugged as he limped.

"The cause of death seems to be the same as the one for the people on the boat," he said.

"Do you think the vampires knew the jogger? Or was it something random?"

Connor shrugged again. "Maybe they simply hated bad science jokes."

"Eh?"

"The jogger's shirt," Connor reminded me. "'Sherlock Ohms.' If I were of the evil persuasion, I might kill some guy just for wearing that shirt."

"That doesn't seem very likely," I said.

"Always consider the unlikely, kid," Connor said. "We're Other Division. Unlikely is our bread and butter."

When we returned to the little park surrounding the spire, the Metropolitan Museum of Art rose into sight through the trees like a scenic backdrop, and in the foreground I could make out the figure of David Davidson pacing near the body. Connor and I headed straight for him.

"What was that all about?" Davidson asked when we were within earshot. He shooed away several of the cops meandering near the crime scene.

"Nothing," Connor said.

"That chase was for nothing?" Davidson raised his eyebrows.

"Did *you* see anything?" Connor asked, sounding a little sharper this time.

Davidson shook his head.

"Okay, then," Connor continued. "Well, that's that, and until I have something more concrete to say on the matter, keep considering it nothing. I don't want you reporting guesswork back to the people downtown."

"Just have them push through the paperwork on the *you know what*," I added.

The cops were still lingering too close for my liking.

"Vampire?" Davidson whispered under his breath.

I nodded as I checked to make sure no one had heard us.

"Easy there," Connor said. "I don't know if this is the same thing, kid. Look at the body. There're an awful lot of tears in the jogger's shirt. Those could be claw marks."

"I'd try clawing, too, if someone sank their teeth into my neck," I said. "Unless we're talking about Jane, of course."

Connor rolled his eyes. "You want to take a reading off him?"

I shook my head. "I don't do the dead. Well, not off the body, anyway. At least the DJ had equipment with him on the boat. Remember?" Connor nodded. "But let's see what he has on him. Maybe I can read that."

As I reached for the body, Connor stopped my hand. "Don't bother. With jogging short-shorts like those, he's not hiding anything."

"Besides, we already checked," Davidson added. "No keys. No wallet. Nothing. The only way we ID'd him was because he matched the description of a missing-person call that came in."

I stepped away from the body, frustrated. "Jesus. You'd think he'd at least be wearing an iPod or something." I turned to the spire at the center of our little park. "What is this thing anyway?"

Davidson and Connor both looked up at it, but it was Davidson who spoke.

"That, my friends, is Cleopatra's Needle."

"That's some big needle," I said.

"It was a gift to the United States," Davidson said, "from Egypt, in the hopes of establishing good trade relations. I believe there are three of them."

"Three?" Connor perked up. "A triumvirate . . . a power number."

"Maybe we're approaching this investigation in the wrong way," I offered.

"Meaning what, exactly?" Davidson said with a bit of venom.

"Don't take it personally," I said. "I'm not blaming anyone, but rather than wondering if this specific dead jogger was an actual target of the vampire, maybe we should be looking at the things around us for answers. Things that, say, stand out."

"You mean something like an ancient Egyptian artifact in the middle of Central Park?" Davidson said.

I nodded.

"Gee," Connor said, "where would we go about finding one of those?"

"I know, right?"

"Well, then," Davidson said. "I trust your little Indiana Jonesing around the spire here means that I can finally

attend to my corpse. You two enjoy your giant phallus investigation. The boys in blue and I have a body to drop
off."

Davidson gestured to his men and two of the cops laid a
long black bag out on the ground next to the body before
moving the dead jogger into it.

"I'll trust you two to let me know if you come across
anything of any significance?" Davidson asked. Neither of
us answered. We were too caught up taking in the impressive sight of the giant needle.

When the cops were done packing up the victim, they
headed down the path and Davidson started off after them.

"One last thing," Connor said. "Is there a time of death
on the victim?"

David Davidson turned back to us. "We won't know
for sure until we get him to the forensics lab, but the on-
site medical examiner guessed between four and six this
morning."

Connor started circling around Cleopatra's Needle with
a hint of a smile in his eyes and a look of awe on his face.
Up close to the spire, it was hard not to marvel at the sight.

Cleopatra's Needle was surrounded by a short, decora-
tive railing to keep people from getting too close to it. The
monolith itself was set upon three white stone steps that
surrounded a ten-foot-high block of rock that acted as the
spire's base. Little indentations just below the main shaft
housed four bronze crabs about the size of medium-sized
dogs, one sitting at each corner.

"Impressive," I said, giving a whistle. "What's it made
of?"

"Red granite," Connor said. I turned to him, impressed.
He shrugged. "If I had to guess."

"Thanks, Dr. Jones," I said, moving closer. "It looks
like a miniature version of the Washington Monument."

As I approached, I noticed it was covered with inscriptions all up and down the sides. I climbed over the low railing and approached it. "Are those hieroglyphics?" I asked,

reaching out. Connor came dashing around from the other side of the needle and grabbed my arm before I could touch the structure.

"Yeah, kid, all of it is in ancient Egyptian," he said, lowering my arm. "I don't really think you should be touching it, though."

"My powers," I said, getting it. It was foolhardy for me to even reach for it, especially not knowing what psychometric flashes it might have in store for me.

Connor pointed down at a large gray slab of rock at the base of the steps. The words "Translation of Hieroglyphics" were written across the top of the slab. It talked about the history of Horus and Ramses, but I couldn't make any direct correlation to our case out of it. I stared back up at the statue.

"If this doesn't serve some arcane purpose in this town," I said, "I don't know what does."

"Let's not jump to conclusions, kid. Our vampires may not even be linked to this thing, whatever it is. This is something better left to Greater and Lesser Arcana. You ask Janey about it when we get back to the offices, okay?"

At the mention of her name, I felt my heart twinge a little.

Connor pulled out his phone. He flipped it open and started taking pictures of each face of the Needle. He circled to the far side of it.

"This side's mostly blank," he said, taking a picture anyway. "Probably weathered away over the years by wind. I'll send these to the Department if you want to head back there and see if you can decipher any of it after blowing them up."

"Or I can just check this marvelous thing called the Internet," I said.

Connor gave me a stern look. "Yeah, well, maybe these will show something the others don't," he said. "The Internet doesn't solve all, especially when it comes to the occult. Just get going."

I hesitated. I didn't necessarily want to go back down-town to the offices, but Connor was clearly trying to reas-sert his authority over me after the lead I had been given by the Inspectre.

"What, kid?" he said, but it wasn't just his normal short-ness with me. He looked pissed off. Was it just the job, or was it something more? Connor walked over, meeting me eye to eye.

"Is that a problem?" he asked.

I shook my head no immediately. I didn't like being put in my new role of responsibility, especially if it meant this type of confrontation came with it. Connor must have seen the look of fear and concern in my eyes. He backed off.

"Sorry, kid," he said. There was a weariness on his face I had never seen before. "There's just a lot going on right now."

"You wanna talk about it?" I offered.

Immediately, the anger returned to his face. Anger and fear. "No. Just drop it, okay?"

This was a new attitude for Connor, and he didn't wear it well. Back when we had been testing my skills, he had started to trust me as a partner. That trust meant a lot, es-pecially since it had partly concerned the disappearance of his brother. Now it seemed gone, and I made a decision not to push it for now. I had already pushed my luck by going through his desk. I changed the subject.

"What about the booth back at Comic Con?" I said. "Won't Inspectre Quimbley need me there?"

"Don't worry," Connor said, relaxing with the switch to more mundane subject matter. "I can cover the booth with the Inspectre."

The thought didn't exactly thrill me. If I wasn't there to monitor the situation, what might the Inspectre possibly tell my partner about the case? Would the fact that I out-rank Connor on this investigation come up?

I didn't think so. Orders given under the confidence of

the Fraternal Order of Goodness were usually not discussed with outsiders. At least, I hoped that was the case.

Handling the actual investigation of Cleopatra's Needle all by myself back at the Lovecraft Café would give me a chance to find out if it meant anything to the case at all.

"Sure," I said, resigning myself to his orders. It was just easier to let Connor think he was in control, especially because he didn't look like he wanted to be crossed at the moment. Besides, his instincts in this investigation seemed to be leading us in the right direction, so no harm, no foul.

"I'll log what I know with Godfrey or one of the other archivists once I get a better idea what arcane connections this thing might have," I said.

Connor nodded and I started up the path leading to the park's Fifth Avenue exit.

"Oh, and kid?" he shouted after me. I turned. Connor was staring down at the base of the spire where the jogger had been found. "Don't make any plans for tomorrow morning. Davidson said the time of death was sometime between four and six."

"Let's hope this ghost jogger is a repeater, then," I said. I didn't relish the idea of waiting for this ghost to appear again, but the likelihood of it showing up was stronger during the hours it had originally died. "So what time are we talking?" My body already ached from our chase, and without an early bedtime, I knew it would be as stiff as a board come morning. I wasn't looking forward to it.

Connor checked his watch.

"On second thought," he said. "Maybe you just better meet me here at three a.m."

"You sure it's wise to be here that late at night?" I shouted back down the hill. "You're wary of the park in daylight hours."

"Kid, the idea of being here at night terrifies me," he said, looking around, "but I'm sick of playing catch-up on this case. If we go back to the docks now, we'd simply be wasting time. We need to catch this ghost if we're going to get some answers. We've got a job to do, and even though I'm not happy about being out here at three a.m., at least I can take comfort that I won't be alone in my misery."

Connor smiled and turned back to the spire just in time to miss me flipping him off, which, all in all, was probably a good thing. I didn't need to give him any excuses when we met up later tonight to push me into the path of any creepy crawlies or boogeymen we might run into.

14

By the time I got back to the office, I was thankful that my pants had finally dried from their dip in the reservoir to retrieve my bat. As I walked through the coffee shop, I noticed that Godfrey Candella was scribbling furiously in one of his notebooks. He barely looked up.

I pushed my way through the theater curtain and headed down the aisle toward the offices. *Nosferatu* played on-screen, and an army of young gothsicles was crowding the theater for it. I continued on, swiping through the office door and then shutting it against the stench of clove cigarettes coming from the theater.

The main office area was pretty busy this time of day, and I couldn't find signs of Jane anywhere. I stopped by my desk, hoping to remember where I had scrawled her phone number at some point. Since I only had it programmed onto the SIM card of my now-melted phone, I didn't know it off the top of my head. Who the hell memorizes phone numbers these days anyway?

After several minutes of looking, I shifted a growing pile of my casework into my in-box, and found the number scrawled on the corner of my desk blotter. I also noticed that someone had already printed out black-and-white copies of the obelisk photos Connor had taken and left them on his desk.

I sat down and flipped through the photos while dialing Jane's cell phone number from the phone at my desk. It felt strange to be using a regular phone, and I wondered if I had ever actually used it before at all.

"Tome, Sweet Tome," I heard Jane say when she finally answered. "Everything from abracadabra to zoology for the cryptozoologist. How may I help you?"

"Jane," I said. "It's me." I checked the number on the caller ID. I hadn't dialed the bookstore, had I? "I'm sorry . . . Did I call the store by mistake?"

"Shoot," she said. "No, you got my cell. I'm back in the Stacks, and I forgot what line I was answering. I'm a bit distracted right now. Sorry."

The sounds of her shifting books around came over the line.

"It's okay," I said. "I'm just happy to hear your voice."

"Oh," Jane exclaimed. "Did you get your new phone from Supply yet?"

"No. I'm at my desk. I was hoping to get a little investigative work done, hoping you were here."

"I'm not," she said.

"We've established that."

"Right . . . duh!"

She was back to her normal self, not a trace of the ol' darkness. There was something so cute about the way she sounded that all of the paranoia that Mina had planted in me last night started melting away.

"I could probably swing by the store," I said. "I have to log some time back in the Black Stacks anyway. We came across this Egyptian monolith thing in Central Park when Connor and I were called in to check out a dead jogger at the base of it. I have to head back out to the park at some ungodly hour of the morning tomorrow, but I need to check the Stacks in the meantime to see if there's anything listed about Cleopatra's Needle in them."

In the background, I heard a male voice, and the cadence of it seemed distinctly like Director Wesker. His words gave way to laughter and Jane started laughing as well.

"Thaddeus, shh!" she said on the line. "I'm sorry, Simon. What were you saying?"

Last night's paranoia quickly seeped back into my heart. I cleared my throat.

"The Stacks," I repeated. "I need to use them."

"Oh," she said. Jane sounded distracted. I tried to imagine what she could possibly be doing there that was so damned important. *Maybe she's doing Wesker,* Mina chirped up in my head. I tried to shake that image loose, but couldn't.

"I'll be there soon," I said, and hung up.

Was I crazy and just simply the victim of an overactive imagination? Or was I right on the mark about there being something going on between the two of them? I grabbed my shoulder bag and stuffed the printouts of the photos into it. I headed back toward the exit, trying not to break into a full sprint across the office as I did so. The entire office didn't need to get caught up in my private life. As it stood, there was ample material for them to ridicule me about.

In the cab heading uptown to Tome, Sweet Tome, I reminded myself to give Mina a swift kick in the ass later for causing all this doubt in me with her evil, twisted whispers last night. Not to mention the fact that because of her, I might be committing a felony tomorrow night, and that was weighing heavily on my shoulders.

The cab pulled up to the curb. After I paid the driver, I hurried toward the bookstore and swung open the front door, but no one was up by the registers. Of course not. Why would there be? Why would either of them hang out up there when they could be all alone hidden away at the back of the store? I wandered through the towering piles of books, careful not to knock any of them over, although lashing out at something felt like a pretty good idea right about now.

I entered the gated Black Stacks and was relieved to find Jane seated alone cross-legged in the middle of one of the aisles. She made notes on a PDA, but she wasn't actually using a stylus to enter information. Jane was staring at the screen while that now-familiar sound of old-school dial-up came from her mouth and words magically appeared on the screen in front of her.

"Well, that's new, isn't it?" I asked.

She looked up, startled. She didn't smile.

"That was rude," she said, and turned back to the PDA. "What was?"

Jane finished whatever she was working on and then set the machine down. "Hanging up on me like that before," she said. "What was *that* all about?"

I looked down the aisle toward the back of the store. "Is Wesker around?"

Jane shook her head. "One of the books tried to escape again. I think they really miss having Cyrus as their owner. I know he was evil and responsible for the whole Ghost-sniffing operation, but they really seem like they were attached to him."

It had been a while since I had heard anyone say his name. Just hearing it mentioned was enough to bring back horrifying memories of the several times I had been attacked by the Black Stacks at Cyrus's command.

"Anyway, Thaddeus went chasing off after it somewhere," she continued, still looking somewhat disconnected. "I suggested we start chaining the more aggressive ones to the shelves but he said no."

"Can you please not call him that?" I said, losing patience. "He's your boss. You *should* call him Director Wesker. That's just good business"

Jane rose from the floor with a sinister look in her eyes. She slammed the book she had been working with back on the shelf, then gave it a soothing pat. "I'm sorry if Other Division is so formal."

"Don't tell me you're now part of the Departmental in-fighting, too? Are you telling me that you and *Thaddeus* are thick as thieves? Ask anyone in Greater and Lesser Arcana about him, Jane. Do you think they all live in fear of him because it's some kind of joke?"

"If you remember," Jane said, defensive, "Director Wesker saved us from the Sectarians. He's the one who clocked Faisal Bane when we were cornered in my old office . . . with your own bat even."

"That doesn't mean I'm just going to blindly trust him."

"And I'm not either," Jane said, getting angry now. "But I do work for the man, and I have to take how he treats me at face value. So far he's been nothing but kind, which is more than I can say about you lately."

I felt slapped in the face by that. "Meaning what?"

"How's Mina?" Jane asked with acid in her voice, and there we had it.

Now I felt slammed in the stomach, feeling shady once again for having to even deal with Mina. I wasn't cheating on Jane with her, I reminded myself, but I still felt shady hiding our criminal past together.

"You said you were okay with her staying for a few days," I said.

"Well, thanks to you getting all suspicious about me, I just became un-okay with Mina staying in your apartment," Jane said. She stormed past me toward the gates. "I'll be up at the front of the store. Try not to agitate the books, will you?"

"Wait," I said. "How am I going to find what I need?"

"Find it yourself," she said, and I watched as she walked out the gates toward the registers.

Maybe it had been a blessing when my powers used to be out of control. Sure, I couldn't really stay with a woman too long because of my inability to harness my psychometry, but at least it kept me from having to deal with these

petty jealousy issues that came with a long-term relationship. It was enough to drive me mad, but I pushed it from
my mind as best I could.

I turned my attention to the Black Stacks and started
walking up and down the aisles, gloves on and careful not
to touch any of the books that might take offense. I didn't
want a repeat of the time Connor had had to rescue me
from a rampaging shelving unit.

I needed something that might give me more information on Cleopatra's Needle and what arcane purpose it
served. After a few minutes of pacing the aisles, I found a
stretch of books that was a section on local historical phe-
nomena, and I perused the titles until I came across one
that looked the most promising: *The Rough Guide to Supernatural New York City.*

I reached for it, then stopped myself before actually coming in contact with it. I looked up at the bookcase it sat in.

"Umm, hello," I said, feeling somewhat foolish. "I don't
know if you're friends with that other bookcase that had a
gripe with me that other time I was here, but I was hoping
to take one of the books off your shelves."

The bookcase, as I expected, didn't react.

"Okay," I said. I raised my hand to the book. "Well, I
promise I'll read it right here and then return it in the same
condition. No harm done. No need to attack me or anything like that."

Still no reaction. With one hand I reached for the book
and with the other, I thumbed off the leather safety strap
on my bat holster. I grabbed the book and pulled it slowly
from the shelf, ready to put it back at the slightest hint of
movement on the part of the bookshelf.

I let out a sigh of relief when nothing happened.

"Thanks," I said. I wasn't sure if this particular bookcase was even like the other, more homicidal one, but it
didn't hurt to be polite anyway.

I sat down on the floor just as Jane had, put the book on
my lap, and flipped it open.

Only to have it slam shut on both my hands. Well, it wasn't a slamming shut so much as it was a biting down. With teeth. Hard. I let out a scream of pain and instantly reached for my bat, pulling it out by using the open palms of both hands. I had to push the button to telescope it out against my knee, but I was still screwed. In order to use the bat against the book, I needed to have one hand free to swipe at it. The pain in my fingers grew stronger, even through the gloves, but luckily there didn't seem to be any blood seeping through the gloves.

I dropped the bat and started slamming the book against the floor. It didn't release, but it did increase its pressure on my hands. My fingers were screaming with pain now. Movement at the end of the aisle struck panic into my heart. I prayed it wasn't another bookcase coming to kill me. I looked up and saw Director Wesker running down the aisle toward me. It wasn't a vision that inspired much relief.

He shouted something I stood no chance of understanding, and instantly the book let go and fell to the floor, harmless.

I flexed my hands, checking my purple little fingers for any breaks in the skin. Luckily there were none, but both hands now felt like they were asleep with pins and needles.

"What the *hell* was that?" I said, hissing with pain.

"That," Wesker said with disdain in his voice, "would be just another reason green agents should never be left alone in the Black Stacks."

"You left Jane back here," I reminded him.

"While she may be new," he said, "she's a quick study, unlike *some* people. Besides, I wasn't very far away. I would never leave her unattended back here."

"I bet you wouldn't."

"Do I detect something accusatory in your voice, Agent Canderous?" he said. "If so, let's hear it."

"Funny," I said, "I don't hear you laughing it up and having a grand old time when it's just you and me back here in the Stacks."

"That's because Jane doesn't do ridiculous, dangerous things," he said. He bent over and picked up the book, closing it and placing it back on the shelf. He pointed to the title on the spine on the book. "It's called a 'Rough Guide' for a reason, nitwit."

15

I left Tome, Sweet Tome in a state of complete frustration, without even saying good-bye to Jane. Empty-handed, I stormed out of the bookstore past her and headed back downtown to the Department. I had another option for answers. I'd seen him sitting in the Lovecraft Café a few hours ago.

Godfrey Candella was exactly where I had left him, with his head down in one of his notebooks, scribbling away.

"Busy day?" I asked. Godfrey finished the line he was writing before he looked up.

"Actually," he said, pushing his horn-rims back into place on the bridge of his nose. "It's a slow business day. I'm catching up on my records for the Gauntlet."

"Slow day, huh? I wish someone had told me," I said, and recounted the story of the dead jogger we'd found in the park as well as our failed chase after his ghost. When I was done, I pulled out the printouts of Cleopatra's Needle and showed them to Godfrey. He looked through them carefully.

"We should bring these down to the Gauntlet," he said, standing up. I didn't move. "Have you ever been?"

I shook my head.

"Come with me," he said. We headed back through the movie theater and straight to the D.E.A. offices. Past the cubicles and beyond the red velvet curtain that separated the front office from the back, he led me down a set of stairs that I had never noticed before. They went down forever and my knees actually started to hurt from the walk. At the bottom was an office door much older than the ones I was used to upstairs. Godfrey swiped a different colored keycard than the one I had against an electronic plate and the heavy door swung open. Immediately, a wave of musty air hit my face and I coughed.

"It's a little bit stuffy down here," he said, giving a small cough of his own, "but you get used to it."

"That's what I'm afraid of," I said, but followed him anyway . . . down *more* stairs. These were far older than anything in the building above and were actually carved into the very rock itself. "We're off the grid, aren't we?"

Godfrey gave a little laugh. "Yes, I suppose so. The Gauntlet predates the construction of the Department of Extraordinary Affairs by a few hundred years or so." He pointed up at a line of cables hanging from hooks along the chiseled ceiling. "We've slowly been bringing computers into the picture and backup systems for archiving purposes, but it will take years to deal with all the historical data. The team and I are up to the year 1820 right now. Did you know that Benjamin Franklin was a necromancer?"

"I think I read something about that somewhere," I said.

"Fascinating stuff," Godfrey said, excited.

We entered a natural cavern lit from high above by electric lights that had been hung from a precariously mounted iron grid. The room itself was full of activity. The trappings of an office were scattered throughout, including some ancient-looking file cabinets that lined the walls and

several dozen wooden tables stained with ink from ages gone by. A half dozen of Godfrey's fellow archivists were busy at several of the desks—writing, filing, and even a few working with computers.

Godfrey pointed to one of the desks with two empty chairs. I walked over to it while he stared at a section containing several of the old filing cabinets.

"Give me a few minutes to pull some records on Cleopatra's Needle. I think I'll start with Egypt, Monuments, Central Park, and, on a long shot, Sewing."

Godfrey disappeared into the darkness of a nearby row of cabinets, leaving me to watch the rest of the Gauntlet in action. All the scurrying around reminded me of that old kids' game Mouse Trap. Every movement of Godfrey's co-workers seemed like part of a well-oiled machine. When one got up from a workstation, another took his or her place. One woman's sole purpose seemed to be working the room and handing books to various employees in a pattern that looked random but definitely had a rhyme and reason all its own.

Several minutes later Godfrey returned with a stack of books and file folders that were piled up to just below his eyes. He let them loose on top of our table and they scattered across it.

"Well, this should be a start," he said, sitting down next to me. He scooped up several folders and quickly started flipping through file after file, scanning them like lightning. He had a researcher's prowess that I was pretty sure I could never equal.

After watching Godfrey in action for a bit, I said, "Well?"

"Well," he said, shaking his head like he was pulling out of a trance. "Like you said Dave Davidson mentioned to you, there *are* three of these needles. The second is in London and the third in Paris, but all three of them originally hail from the city of Heliopolis in Egypt."

He paused as his brain accessed another mental file.

"I'm unfamiliar with that city," he continued. Godfrey pulled out his personal notebook and scribbled down *Heliopolis, Egypt.* "I'll have to check it out later."

He started to zone out again, but I tapped the folder he was holding.

"Is there anything about the markings on the obelisk?" I asked.

"Do you know how to read hieroglyphs, Simon?" Godfrey asked, snapping out of it. I looked to see if he was being a smart-ass, but he was dead serious.

I shook my head no.

"Sorry," I said. "I took Spanish. They didn't offer Ancient Egyptian at my high school. Can you imagine?"

Godfrey didn't even crack a smile.

"The school systems these days," he said with a shake of his head.

I hoped they had a section on Humor down here. Perhaps I could go find a few books for him.

Godfrey turned back to the file he had opened and scanned the page. "It looks like the monoliths were cut from Aswan quarries circa 1450 B.C. under the orders of Thutmose the Third, *but* the inscriptions are far more recent. They weren't added until two hundred years later."

"By who?" I asked, feeling a little excited now that we were getting somewhere. "Please tell me it was some kind of vampire lord or something, because that would *so* jive with what I'm chasing."

Godfrey checked the page and shook his head. "Not unless there's something seriously paranormal about Ramses the Second that we don't know about. It's only in truly bad fantasy books that popular historical figures ever turn out to be supernatural or dabbling in the dark arts."

He scanned the page with his finger. "Sadly," he continued, "the monolith needles were erected in celebration of Ramses's military victories, not to celebrate a dark covenant or anything like that. You know, I'm starting to think this Cleopatra's Needle might not be as evil as you think it is. After all, I doubt Egypt would have gifted it to America if it was a lightning rod for collecting evil. Don't you think?"

I couldn't argue with him.

"You talk sense," I said. He saw the look on my face and gave my shoulder a collegial pat. It felt awkward and forced, as if Godfrey didn't often have much contact with other people.

"I *can* work on the hieroglyphs," Godfrey said with a spark in his voice, "but that's going to take a while. It's also going to take some time to go through all the cross references too, but on the surface I don't see anything terribly supernatural about this needle of yours. Sorry."

I stood up and gave him a reciprocal pat on the back. When I was done, Godfrey pulled at his lapels to smooth out his coat where my hand had touched him.

"Well, thanks for trying," I said.

Without another word, Godfrey shoved his face back into the pile of reading on the table and was once again off in his private mental world. I slowly backed away so as not to disturb him and headed back to the stairs, alone.

I had to figure out how to best utilize what remained of my day. I checked my watch as I climbed back up to the Department's office level. I could go to the Javits Center, but by the time I got there most of the day on the show floor would be over. Perhaps I could serve the Department better by staying at the office and working on my backlog of paperwork. Having a break from Connor would be nice, too. I'm sure we'd have a jolly old time later staking out Central Park for the jogger's ghost at the crack of "Oh God" o'clock, but for now, some mindless office work seemed the perfect remedy.

Once I was back at my desk, I started sorting through my mountain of paperwork, looking for anything to fill out in conjunction with the vampire case. There had to be something I could do to help move things along while the office bureaucrats flowed with their molasseslike efficiency. Ever since the Inspectre had secretly put me in charge of the investigation, I had felt like a bossy ass, but at least I had some time alone for now to get some paperwork out of the way.

Not that I was able to get anything started. After looking through the first few inches of paper, I realized I was fresh out of Form SSO—Shufflers, Shamblers, & Others, where the vampire qualified under Other. Filling it out would speed up the Enchancellors, and without it I was screwed. Connor, seasoned pro of pencils and papers, probably had it, though. I snuck over to his desk to snag a few. Connor's desk was locked this time. I thought back to when I had been looking for the Spidey PEZ Dispenser but found his folder of clippings about me instead. Maybe he thought I might accidentally find it—like I had—and decided to lock it away just in case.

Without being able to check the drawers for the form, I hoped he had some of them in the shuffle of paperwork on top of it. Psychometry was a great tool when it came to playing lost and found.

I sat down at his desk and placed my hands flat across the top of it and paused before throwing my power into it. The electric connection was instantaneous and I set my mind to finding the forms I needed.

The world in my mind's eye switched to some time yesterday, the only indicator being the slightly smaller piles of paperwork on both of our desks. It was disorienting being Connor, because I was staring across the desk at yesterday Simon filling out the incident report on the party boat massacre. At that moment, that version of me wasn't paying attention to Connor at all.

Connor, however, was focused on a single sheet of paper, which I assumed was the form I was looking for, but something was wrong. I tried to change my focus to the paper itself . . . only to find it blank. I could feel Connor's eyes moving. He was definitely reading something on the page, but I couldn't see it, even though I was staring straight at it.

I threw all of my concentration into it, pressed my power into reading the paper. Something that felt like a sinus headache started to throb, but I pushed even harder in my attempt to read the letter. The world went black.

When I woke up, I found myself lying on the floor, tipped over in Connor's chair. Luckily, since I had fallen over behind both our desks, I was blocked from the view of anyone who would have been passing down the aisle. The back of my head hurt like crazy, and when I felt it, there was a painful lump just above the base of my skull from where I had hit the floor.

I stood up, shaking worse than I usually did after a psychometric episode. I stumbled over to my desk and fished around in my drawer for a roll of Life Savers. Erring on the side of caution, I grabbed two of them. This wasn't normal. Usually I felt a little drained from using my power, but it shouldn't have been this bad.

Someone or something had blocked me from reading Connor's letter.

16

I headed home nursing the goose egg on the back of my head. I was all prepared for a good sulky walk and then a few hours of sleep before meeting up with Connor at Central Park again, but sadly, what I wanted didn't seem to matter much to the universe at large. When I parted the curtains of the movie theater, there was Mina, sitting in one of the coffee shop's comfy chairs, waiting for me. Her back was pressed into one corner of the chair, and her legs were thrown in irreverence over the opposite arm of it, showing off her evil little curves. She was still dressed as if she had come from watching *The Matrix* one too many times.

"What are you doing here?" I said. I quickly closed the curtain behind me, not really sure what I was trying to hide. The offices were well obscured behind the door at the very back of the theater, so all I really ended up hiding was the movie theater itself. I quickly looked around the coffee shop. At this time of night there weren't too many people I knew from the D.E.A. in there. More important, I was glad to see that Jane wasn't there. Her running into Mina right now was the last thing I wanted.

Mina swung her legs off the arm of the chair and crossed them at the ankle as she sank farther back into the cushions, giving a catlike stretch that accentuated every curve of her body. I tried not to notice, but failed miserably.

"You must really like vampires, huh?" she said when she settled down.

I wasn't following. "I'm sorry . . . ?"

Mina looked at me like I was thick in the head. "I've been sitting here for hours," she said. "You must have sat in there and watched *Nosferatu* a million times today."

Right, *Nosferatu*. It all came clear. For a moment I'd forgotten that Mina didn't know what I really did for a living, so she assumed I had been sitting in the movie theater all day.

Still, what was *she* doing here at all?

I sat down across from her and leaned in close, whispering. "Have you been following me, Mina?"

She laughed, a little bit of that old-school crazy lighting up in her eyes. "God, that sounds so stalkery . . ."

"And yet here we are."

"I didn't follow you the *whole* day," she said, as if that somehow excused following me at all. Her face turned to a mask that was a combination of disgust and disdain.

"Okay, look, yes, I followed you," she continued, "but I didn't want to pay to get into the Javits Center, not with all those comic nerds there. They kept approaching me outside of the place, getting their skeevies all over me, asking if I had come as Trinity or some chick from BloodRayne, whatever the hell that is. Creeps. Anyway, I just had to wait you out. I lost you for a few hours after that, but caught up with you again. When you came into this coffee shop, I followed you in, but man, you and your vampires."

"I'm sorry," I fired back. "Are *you* giving *me* shit over vampires?" I laughed. "Yeah, *I'm* the one who loves vampires, *Mina*. Me. Yep. Pot, have you met Kettle?"

I stood up, fuming. "Look," I said, staring down into her eyes with the darkest, most serious look I could muster. "You can't follow me like this, Mina. So knock it off."

I tried to walk away, but she grabbed my sleeve. She tugged it much harder than I thought her capable of, and I fell off balance into the same chair she sat in. Mina wrapped her arms around me to hold me in place, cradling me on her lap. Before I could wriggle free, her voice was in my ear.

"I *can* follow you, and I *will*," she said with commanding sharpness. "You forget. I don't have a 'day job' to go to, and who'd hire an ex-con, anyway? An ex-con, by the way, who ended up in jail in the first place because *someone*—and I'm not naming names here, *Simon*—didn't have my back. I've got all the time in the world to follow you around, thanks to that. Until you agree to help me, I've got nowhere else to go. So stop hanging out at comic conventions and watching movies all day, and say you'll do what I'm asking you to. I need to get my hands on *The Scream*."

Despite her obvious delight in torturing me, there was also that note of desperation in her voice again.

"Don't you think *need* is a little strong, Mina?" I said, trying to twist out of her hold on me. To anyone watching it might have looked like we were a frisky new couple fooling around. That would turn a few heads around here, since everybody knew I was with Jane. I wanted to break free, but Mina was even stronger than I remembered. "You don't need that painting; you *want* it."

"That's really none of your concern," Mina said, finally pushing me away. I slid onto the coffee table and across several open magazines before falling to the floor, but not before slamming my hip bone on one of the corners of the table.

Pain shot down my leg in tiny needles.

"The only thing you should be concerned with," Mina continued, "is what I'll do to your precious little Janey if you don't go along with my plan. Help me out and we part ways, no harm done. I'm out of your life forever." She stood up, not even bothering to give me a hand from where I was on the floor. The look on her face was one of disbelief as she shook her head at me. "God, how can you stand it? Doesn't living an upright life just drive you nuts? Going shopping instead of taking what you want, having a happy little girlfriend, going to the *movies* all day? You used to do bold, beautiful, brash things. You used to be somebody worth knowing. If I lived your life now, I'd die of boredom."

For a second I wanted to just get it out of my system and tell Mina everything—about my psychometric powers, the Department of Extraordinary Affairs, the Fraternal Order, even about the fact that Jane and I weren't such the happy little couple—but I held my tongue.

I knew Mina too well. If I even hinted at any part of my new life or showed any signs of weakness, she would only twist it to her advantage.

Could I believe her? Would she keep her word and leave me alone if I just did this one last job for her? Mina had always had a strange honor-among-thieves thing she stuck to. Her words might be crazy, her legality was questionable, but in matters with her associates, she kept her word. Just get rid of Mina by simply helping her out with this one job. Get in, get out, say good riddance, and have her get the hell out of my life for good, as she promised. I could compromise myself this one last time if it would protect the people I cared for. I could already feel myself justifying it. It wasn't like I was doing the actual stealing. More of an assist, really . . .

I picked myself up off the floor of the coffee shop. "You may find my life boring," I said. I brushed a bunch of muffin crumbs from the table off my pants. "But I like it just fine, thank you very much. Just tell me when we're doing this."

"Tomorrow night," Mina said. "I've got previous obligations tonight in preparation—'casing the joint,' as they say in all the cop shows. Bring whatever you need for picking locks, Mr. Golden Touch. I need you to get me in and then watch my back while I actually switch out the painting. I'll be busy not setting off the sensors on it, and the last thing I need is to have to handle some guard at the same time. So be ready for a fight. I hope that fits into your busy schedule. If it doesn't, tough."

I just stared at Mina, wanting to yell at her, but the Lovecraft Café was not the place for it. I stepped away from her.

"You're a real piece of work, Mina. I'm surprised some lucky guy hasn't snatched you up and married you yet. Really, I mean, with a soft side like yours . . ."

"Bite me," she said, and spun around, heading for the door. "Better brush up on your lock-picking skills, Boy Scout."

17

The encounter with Mina left me all riled up, and I gave up on the idea of sleep before meeting up with Connor at the park. It was around eight, and I thought I had enough time to try to patch things up with Jane. With a fresh idea in my head, I called her and told her to meet me around ten at Eccentric Circles.

When Jane found me at the back of the Department's favorite watering hole in one of the dark and secluded booths, she stopped in her tracks and smiled. The bar was the usual hangout for our unusual crowd, but I had chosen the back dining area for a quiet meal alone with her. I had set the booth up for dinner for two, complete with a red-and-white-checkered table cloth I had picked up along the way, candles, and an array of Italian dishes.

As she walked up the booth, she stopped when she saw everything. "Isn't it a little late for a big dinner? And Italian? Does Eccentric Circles even *do* Italian?"

I nodded my head.

"For the right price they do," I said, standing up. "I

would have made it for you myself at home, but my schedule's been pretty crazy."

"You arranged all this?" Jane's grin widened.

I nodded. "I've been feeling pretty Lady and the Tramp lately." Flashes of my Lovecraft Café encounter with Mina filled my head. "Let's just say I've gotten a little perspective on how healthy you are for me, and I wanted to make up for the way I've been acting."

I took her hand in mine and raised it to my lips. I was glad to see she didn't pull away when I kissed it and her smile remained. I helped her slide into the booth.

Jane picked up the glass of wine on her side and raised it. "Well, you're certainly off to a good start."

I raised mine as well, clinked it with hers, and the two of us drank.

"So *Director* Wesker told me about the book that attacked you," Jane said.

I wasn't thrilled to hear that he had told her about my embarrassing little incident, but I was glad she had thrown "Director" in in place of "Thaddeus" as a peace offering.

"Yeah, well," I said, "at least it was only one book this time. Plus, double bonus, I remembered to wear my gloves."

She laughed.

"Well, that *is* something, isn't it?"

I liked seeing her smile.

"So," I said. "Any new developments with the technomancy? Have you figured out how, exactly, you saved me from those rats?"

I shivered at the thought of the Oubliette and whoever had sabotaged it against me.

"Actually, I'm trying to cut back on using it," she said, "for now."

"Why?"

She shrugged. "I don't know. I just feel a little funny suddenly having all this power at my disposal. Doesn't feel right."

"If you say 'with great power comes great responsibility,' I might gag."

"Well," she said. "It *is* true, but that's not my main reason. I just don't feel as happy, I guess, when I use it. Of course, Wesker keeps encouraging me to experiment with it."

"Of course he does," I said.

Jane cocked her head at me, the blond tip of her ponytail momentarily swinging into view.

"What I mean," I continued, "is that he's all about the accumulation of resources, and I'm sure he considers the development of your power as one of the new shinies in his dark little toy box."

Jane shifted her face into a half smile, half frown.

"You make me feel so owned."

Now it was my turn to shrug. I didn't want to say anything too damaging. I wanted her to mull over the possibility that maybe she shouldn't get so chummy with her potentially evil boss, especially when the two of them spent so much time alone together at Tome, Sweet Tome. I pushed away fantastical images of Jane and Wesker bumping uglies in the Stacks.

Of course, it would only take touching something of Jane's that had been with her all day to find out the truth, if I really wanted to know. But I resisted. I hadn't learned to control the very type of incident that had led to every ugly breakup of my adult life only to turn around and use it now simply because it was the easy way. Instead, I dove into my food.

"Oh, I almost forgot," Jane said, her eyes lighting up. She turned to her shoulder bag on the seat beside her. "I brought this for you." Jane produced a book and put it on the table, sliding it across to me. *The Rough Guide to Supernatural New York City*. "This is the book you came for, isn't it?"

"Jane," I whispered, pulling the book off the table and out of sight in a flash. "I thought the Stacks were a no-lending area?"

"They are," she said, giving me a devilish grin, "but who says I can't use my occasional evil tendencies to benefit my man every once in a while?"

It was a tiny bit wicked, but who was I to lecture her on flouting Departmental rules? Besides, I was the one who was about to by involved in an art heist. "Thank you," I said. "I'm hoping I can figure out just what the hell the significance of Cleopatra's Needle is, if any, before I meet up with Connor in Central Park at three a.m. I appreciate it, but no more evil on my behalf, okay?"

"Sure thing, cutie," she said, her grin still in place. I felt her foot start to trace its way up my calf under the table. "Sure I can't coax you into a little more evil?"

Oh, I could definitely have gone for some of the horizontal evil Jane was hinting at. Then I remembered that Mina was staying at my apartment, and even though she was out making preparations for our heist tomorrow night, she could come back at any time. "Can we make it your place?" I said. Jane's eyes narrowed.

I slid the book into my own bag.

"I've got to meet Connor in a few hours," I said, skirting the issue of my houseguest, "and Chelsea's a little closer to Central Park. It'll give me more time to cuddle . . . ?"

"Cuddle?" she said. "Honey, when I'm done with you, you'll be lucky if you can even move."

I'd worry later about the delicious damage Jane might do to me and how I was going to be able to walk to meet Connor afterward. This was certainly a much better distraction than irrational jealousy, psychotic ex-cons, and vampires.

18

When I met Connor at the base of Cleopatra's Needle, it was three a.m. and I was too exhausted to even speak. Aside from the mind-blowing sex, my body had already been pushed to its limit today—physically from the chase Connor and I had engaged in with the ghost, and emotionally from trying to deal with both Mina and Jane.

Just being in the silent darkness of the park after hours was clearly freaking Connor out. This was on top of whatever had spooked him in that letter I had seen in my psychometric vision—or rather *hadn't* been able to see. There was no way in hell I could ask him about it directly, though, so for now I was happy to meet Connor's silence with my own. My brain was thinked out.

I took a seat on the steps of the white pedestal supporting Cleopatra's Needle. I stared up at one of the four bronze crabs standing guard at each corner. Connor paced back and forth. Curiosity eventually got the better of me and I spoke up.

"I don't get it," I said. "You think the jogger or maybe the vampires might return to the scene of the crime?"

Connor shook his head. "Not the vamps. Just the jogger hopefully," he said, and went silent again.

I became bored and stood on the top edge of the white base, reaching up to grasp my gloved hands onto one of the metallic crab claws. I hung my full weight from it, letting my feet dangle, feeling a bit like a prize from one of those arcade claw vending-machine games. The mental image caused me to laugh out loud.

Connor twirled around, full of nerves.

"Jesus, kid," he said. "How can you laugh at a time like this?"

"It probably helps that I'm dangling from this here crab," I said, but Connor wouldn't even smile at that. "My arms are numb, but it's a nice, cooling sensation."

"Just keep sharp," he said, and resumed his pacing. "That's gotta be nine hundred pounds' worth of bronze crabs yer dangling from."

"I'm not sure how important this is," I said, dropping down, "but it would help if I knew what I was staying sharp *for*. Or rather, what we plan to do should anything show up here tonight."

"Huh?" Connor said, looking up from his pacing. "Oh, right. Sorry, kid."

Connor's bag sat on one of the benches and he went to it. He pulled two shapes from it, but I could barely make them out in the pervading darkness.

"Are those . . . hair dryers?"

"Close, kid," he said, "but no cigar."

Connor stepped closer. In each hand he held identical hair-dryer-shaped devices. Both were bright yellow with red stripes down the sides.

"Bubble blasters?" I asked, and Connor nodded. "I don't get it."

"What's not to get?" he said. "They blast bubbles."

"Yeah, I gathered that."

He handed me one. "Go on, give it a try."

As if things couldn't get more surreal, I pulled the trigger. Bubbles filled the air—but they weren't ordinary bubbles. The smell of patchouli rose from the gun. I popped one of the bubbles and it splashed onto my face. "Great," I said. "I smell like one of the squatters in the East Village now."

"Look, kid. These vampires, or whatever it is we're hunting, might not return to the scene of the crime, *but* the jogger might. A free-floating ghost almost invariably repeats the patterns it formed in life, like jogging this path. It's just a matter of time."

I held up my bubble blaster, waving it at Connor. "I thought mentors were supposed to be older and wiser. You've got the older part down."

Connor stared at me. "Just get away from the crab and get on the other side of the path, will you? When we see the guy coming, we get the blasters going and create a wall of this stuff."

My memories of the foul-smelling scent were always intertwined with the night we defeated the Sectarians at the Museum of Modern Art. Hundreds of ghosts, including my then-ghost-crush Irene, had been trapped by barrels filled with the stuff. I shook it off, heading down to the path at the bottom of the steps that led up to the Needle. I crossed to the far side of the path and waited for Connor to join me.

"We don't have anything more high-tech?" I asked hopefully. I didn't want to bet my life on something from the summer clearance bin at Toys 'R' Us.

"After you just did all that paperwork to requisition a new phone from Supply?" Connor asked. "We'd do double that to get any gear for an op like this, and then add a two-week wait for signatures, plus possible back-order time. It was just easier using these."

I flexed my finger against the trigger of the gun. It felt plastic and flimsy, like it was just waiting to snap off at a crucial moment.

"And if this doesn't work?" I asked.

"It'll work," Connor said, offended.

I looked at the white streak in Connor's otherwise sandy brown mop of hair. "I don't want to become part of your Hair Club for Men," I said, using my favorite name for the White Stripes.

"It'll *work*," Connor said, and huffed. "And if it doesn't, we'll at least have had a fun time in Central Park blowing bubbles together."

"You really need to work on your deadside manner," I said.

"You really need to shut up and get ready," Connor said, looking down the path. "It's Don Ho time."

"Eh?" I said, cocking my head.

Connor looked at me, exasperated. " 'Tiny Bubbles'? Get with the program, kid. Jesus, you're making me feel old."

"That would be your white hair talking," I said, "and midthirties *is* old."

I shifted my focus down the path. I could barely see anything through the mist covering the pathway . . . until I realized the mist was actually the see-through body of the dead jogger coming toward us. He looked exactly as we had seen him the other day in his "Sherlock Ohms" T-shirt. He appeared to be oblivious to our presence.

"Start your engines," Connor said, pulling the trigger on his blaster. I did the same. The tiny whirr of the fans felt anticlimactic considering what we were doing here, but the bubbles started flowing freely back and forth across the pathway. If only there were a mirror ball present, we'd have had a full-on disco.

Onward ran the jogger, still not noticing us, until he hit the first of the bubbles. He stopped abruptly, like he'd been shot. One of the bubbles hit his arm and popped, and he looked down as he hissed in pain. A sticky-looking patch formed on his translucent arm. Connor frantically waved his blaster up and down around the ghost in an attempt to contain him.

"Get around the back, kid," he said. "We've got to encircle him before he makes a break for . . ."

Connor's words were cut short as the spirit shot backward. Connor and I jockeyed for position to get around him, but that was when the jogger finally seemed to take notice of us. The ghost's eyes widened in cartoonish horror, and his face distorted beyond the way a normal human's could.

"N-n-no!" the spirit stammered. He turned and shot up the stairs toward the needle.

"Crap," Connor said. "Looks like were gonna have to Scoob and Shag it, kid."

"Scoob and Shag . . . ?"

"Improvise," he said, and dashed off up the stone steps after it. I fell in behind him, my legs already aching. The spirit limped in a circle around the base of the needle, trying to shake free of a few of the bubbles that had popped on his leg. When he saw us coming, he circled around to the far side of the needle.

"Don't hurt me," the jogger shouted.

"We're not here to hurt you," Connor said, trying to calm him. The spirit gave Connor a look of doubt.

While the two of them continued their exchange, I crept around to the jogger's side of the needle. Connor kept talking while I snuck up on him.

"We just need to know a few things," Connor said. He checked my position by stealing a glance at me, but the spirit noticed and twisted around. His face was a contorted mask of inhuman rage. His sudden ferocity scared the crap out of me. I pulled the blaster's trigger, and the bubbles started blowing. The jogger stumbled back in terror to avoid them.

"Nooo," he screamed again, and cowered toward the needle, backing through the railing that surrounded it. Although the jogger was immaterial, he fell back like he had tripped on something, and phased into the base of the monolith, disappearing altogether. The park fell silent around us. Connor hurried over.

"That could have gone better," he said, looking around with caution on his face.

"Better *how*?"

"We could have *not* failed completely," he said with optimism.

"That's not terribly mentor-y," I said, turning to head back down the stairs. "I'm going to . . ."

I was interrupted by something akin to the screech of Godzilla coming from behind Connor. I looked at Cleopatra's Needle. It took me a moment to identify the sound, but then it struck me—the sound of wrenching metal, coming from the pedestal at the base of the monolith. Not one, but all *four* of the bronze crabs were pulling free from their moorings, the sound becoming overpowering and painful to listen to. Connor covered his ears.

I shoved the blaster into my coat pocket, threw back the other side of my coat, and pulled out my retractable bat. I thumbed the switch and the bat jumped to full size.

Connor was still facing me, clutching his ears, stunned by the sound.

Not sure of what the hell they were or what to call them, I screamed over the sound of the crabs tearing free. "Umm . . . mecha-crabs behind you . . ."

Connor narrowed his eyes at me as he tried to figure out what I was saying, but seeing the bat in my hand was enough to get him to turn and face our foes.

The crabs hit the ground with an immensely solid clang.

"What was it you said?" I asked. "Nine hundred pounds of bronze? That makes each of the crabs roughly two hundred pounds!"

I looked at the thinness of my hollow bat and collapsed it back down, resheathing it.

"I say we err on the side of actually living and run," I said. "Not that I'm ordering you."

"No, that's an order I can take," Connor said, and ran for the stairs. "C'mon!"

The tiny legs of the bronze crabs clacked across the cobblestones while their claws snapped like sharp, tiny vises. That was all I needed to get running.

Connor was already down the steps and turning south along the path. I skipped the steps entirely and jumped straight to the ground in two bounds, catching up to him.

Even with my eyes somewhat adjusted to the light, it was tough following Connor through the darkness. The path led under a footbridge, the sound of rapid crab claws echoing against the tunnel walls. On this side of the bridge the path began to wind in and out of trees and my pace slowed a little as I fought to keep from losing an eye to low-hanging branches.

"Don't slow down, kid," Connor yelled, and then I heard him begin a low litany of *"Oh shit, oh shit, oh shit, oh shit . . ."*

I wanted to go faster, but all I could think of was a jagged branch skewering my eyeball or that, like in some movie cliché, I'd trip on an unearthed root that would be my undoing. I shielded my eyes, picked my feet up high, and ran faster. Off to either side of the path, I noticed thousands of tiny lights flickering off in the trees like I was running past a Fourth of July display.

"What the hell are those?" I shouted.

Connor slowed a little as he looked, but he didn't slow much.

"Beats me, kid. Probably one of the million reasons I hate fucking being in the park at night."

For a short while they brightened, and I swore I could see a city among them, one much different from Manhattan. It looked part Blade Runner, mixed with a dash of Tolkien, both gorgeous and terrifying to see out here in the middle of the night. I was determined not to fall and returned my eyes to the path. The lights faded away and the darkness of the woods returned. The sight of the speck that was Connor receding up ahead urged me to sprint even harder.

I caught up with him as he came to a stop, wrapped his arms around a tree, and shimmied up it.

I had no idea why Connor had opted to climb a tree at this point in our escape. Surely the crabs could wait around the base until he tried to come down. I congratulated myself for keeping moving and staying on the ground.

Until I saw nothing but lake spread out before me.

19

"Dive in, kid," Connor shouted from up in the tree.

I dove.

As the ice-cold water nearly sent my body into shock, I propelled myself underwater and out across the lake. When I surfaced, I twisted myself around and looked back to shore. The crabs had left Connor alone up in the tree, having preferred to continue after me as the grounded target. All four charged into the water, clicking their claws as they came. I was thrilled, however, to see that, despite chasing me into the lake, the one thing the vicious little crabs couldn't do was float. They used their back legs to try to propel themselves as a regular crab would, but the weight of their bronze bodies dragged them to the bottom of the lake. As long I kept myself floating at the surface, I should be fine. I watched as each of them sank into the mud of the lake bed below, their claws frantically clicking toward the surface.

I swam back to shore. When I crawled back onto dry land, Connor was just coming down from his tree. I slowly peeled off my coat. It weighed a ton.

"Son of a bitch," I said, trying to wring it out as best I could. "What the hell just happened?"

I looked at Connor, but his concentration was mostly focused on the lake behind me.

"Kolb," he said, "just possessed those things. And here he comes again . . ."

I stood there soaking wet, shivering, and turned myself around. Beneath the water, a faint white light started to form, growing like a searchlight rising to the surface. The water bubbled like it was a giant stew pot of WTF, and out of it rose glowing bubbles full of swirling mist, some as large as basketballs. With an alarming pop, the mist broke free and swirled together until I recognized a distinct shape forming. It was the jogger, gasping for air and clawing his way toward the shore. He still acted like he was human and that breathing was an issue for him.

The jogger pulled himself up onto shore and collapsed. His dark wreath of hair was wet, hanging down on one side at least half a foot from a bad comb-over. Everything else on him was wet, too—running shorts, track shoes, and his "Sherlock Ohms" T-shirt. He lay there, sputtering and catching his breath.

"Why is he wet?" I whispered to Connor. "He's dead. Doesn't that mean he's immaterial?"

Connor shook his head.

"I don't think he understands that he's dead," he said. "Mr. Kolb here thinks he's alive so his spirit is reacting somewhat accordingly. He expected to get wet being in a lake, therefore he's wet. Didn't they teach you anything as a F.O.G.gie yet?"

"I *am* too alive," the jogger said, forcing himself up onto his knees, "and it's *Doctor* Kolb to you. I didn't go to MIT just for the parties, I'll have you know."

He snickered at what he must have thought was some great private joke, then stood up. With care, he scooped the hanging section of his comb-over back onto the top of his head and arranged it. It was a futile attempt at best, looking nothing more than someone with a wet cat sitting up there, but he looked happy with it.

"Sorry, about that, *Dr.* Kolb," I said. Politeness was the cornerstone of the D.E.A.'s training manual *Deadside Manner* . . . or what I had read of it, anyway.

His initial fear from when we had first seen him tonight seemed to be gone, replaced with fascination. He turned away from us and looked down into the water.

"Astounding," he said. "Did you catch all that? The way my body broke down on a molecular level, and reconstituted itself by manifesting within those four statues?"

"That doesn't seem odd to you?" I said.

"Odd, certainly," Dr. Kolb said, his face a mask of excitement, "but think about the scientific implications of this. This is on par with King Midas or the myth of the philosopher's stone . . ."

Before I knew what was happening, Connor had reclaimed his bubble gun from the base of the tree and fired it at the jogger, blasting him with the spirit binding. The ghost's face went slack.

"What the hell?" I asked.

"Sorry," Connor said, not really looking like he was. "He was rambling. I need him a little more sedate than that—I'm certainly not going to argue with him whether he's dead or not."

Connor had a point. Back when we had found the ghost of Irene Blatt in the coffee shop, she had been pretty adamant that she was still alive, too.

"You were attacked yesterday," Connor said to him. "You died."

The jogger, although much more sedate now, still shook his head. "I don't see how that's possible. I mean, you *are* talking to me."

Connor pulled out his cell phone. He flipped it open and called up one of the pictures he had taken at the scene of the crime yesterday.

"Not to be harsh or anything," Connor said, "but do you

recognize that guy lying there half covered in a sheet?"

The jogger squinted at the tiny screen. His eyes widened, and he nodded. His wet hair fell from its perch and hung off the side of his head again like damp seaweed.

"Hate to break it to you like this," Connor continued, "but the good doctor? He's *out* . . . for good. Someone or some*thing* did this to you. Can you think of anyone who would want you dead?"

Dr. Kolb laughed at that. "Want *me* dead? You're kidding, right? I'm a scientist. My specialty is developing polycarbonate thermoplastic resins for communications and buildings. Who's going to want me dead? Someone from a rival nerd consortium?"

Connor looked agitated, but pointed at the camera phone. "Well, scientifically speaking, something made you dead, Doctor. Personally, I'd like to know who. I would think you'd like to know as well."

Dr. Kolb looked at the picture on Connor's phone again. He screwed up his face, struggling to remember. If he could recall who had done this to him, or why, I was fairly certain it would be a huge step toward figuring out our case, not to mention helping Dr. Kolb pass on to the next life.

"Anything you can give us," Connor continued, his voice less harsh this time. "Anything at all, no matter how insignificant."

"I can almost see it in my mind," the dead jogger said, still struggling.

While Dr. Kolb gave it a good think, I watched the water for any signs of the crabs, even though the spirit that had been mechanizing them now stood before us. I shuddered at the thought of them crawling back up to shore.

"It was like . . . like a dog," he said with conviction.

"A dog?" I repeated, then looked to Connor, raising an eyebrow. "Werewolf?"

"Doubtful," he said. "We're not even close to having a full moon right now."

"I said *like* a dog," Dr. Kolb said, clearly irritated that he was dealing with two people he felt were his mental inferiors. "Not an *actual* dog."

I tried to keep him focused. "Why don't you describe it to us, then?"

The dead jogger's attitude morphed as he recalled the creature, his face full of fear.

"Like I said, kinda like a dog, only hairless . . . with sunken red eyes . . ."

Connor perked up at this. Dr. Kolb started to stutter, his fright overtaking him as if he were reliving the experience.

"I couldn't look away. I wanted to, God knows, but I was paralyzed with fear . . ."

"This creature," Connor said, "was its back kinda spiny?"

Dr. Kolb nodded. His arms were held out in front of him, trying to push something invisible away.

I moved closer to Connor.

"You know what it is?" I whispered.

He nodded and hit the speed dial on his phone. HAUNTS-GENERAL popped up on the display.

"Could it have been a vampire?" I asked. "Can't vampires take canine form, do that whole shape-shifting thingie?"

Connor rolled his eyes. "Don't believe everything you see on the SCI FI Channel, okay? Believe me, kid, it ain't vampires."

20

I was freezing by the time Haunts-General showed up twenty minutes later. They started going about the business of releasing Dr. Kolb's spirit. Whatever that entailed, I really didn't know. My last encounter with them had been over Irene's spirit, and the paperwork for dealing with a spirit like hers *sans* body had been enough of an excuse for them to leave her case in Other Division hands. Haunts-General had simply walked away from it. Tonight, thankfully, we already had the body and now the spirit of the late Dr. Kolb. Hopefully they'd be able to send the poor guy off to wherever it was that spirits were supposed to go after death, and Dr. Kolb would be one less apparition running through the park.

As Haunts-General took over the scene, I described what had happened while Connor walked off for a bit. When I was done, I searched around for him, only to find him alone heading toward the nearest exit of the park.

"So, if it's not vampires, then what is it?" I asked when I was by his side. Connor really didn't look like he wanted to talk, and when he finally spoke he sounded pissed.

"Dammit, kid. You shouldn't have reported it as vampires. You said it was vampires in the vision."

"I know," I said.

Connor stopped and turned to me. "Now the Enchancellors are probably going to come down on you for blowing the call. I'm sorry—come down on *us*. You were so quick to call it. Is that what they teach you F.O.G.gies? To make rash judgments? You know, for a secret society, you sure seem pretty keen on showboating."

I gave up. Connor started walking again, and I followed him.

"So are you going to tell me what type of creature we're dealing with or not?"

Connor sighed. "Well, from what our dear dead doctor had to tell us—red, hypnotic eyes, a doglike creature with pronounced spinal ridge—I'm guessing we're looking for a chupacabra."

I knew the name from the D.E.A.'s three-hour seminar entitled "Fee Fie Foes: A Refreshing Look at Cryptozoology from A to Z." There had been handouts, but I was sure mine were lost somewhere in the paperwork scattered across my desk. What I did remember of the chupacabra was one key factor. It, too, was a bloodsucker.

"They're from New Mexico," I said. We were at the edge of the park now. Connor walked though the gate, moved to the edge of Fifth Avenue, and hailed a cab. "Why would there be one of those in New York City?"

A cab pulled over and Connor got in. He made no effort to move over, leaving me to stand, wet and freezing, on the curb.

"Maybe you'd better read up on them, then," he said, sullen. "And while you're at it, why don't you fill out the paperwork for reporting the missing crab statues? Maybe next time you'll *think* before causing a stir in the Department."

He slammed the door shut and the cab sped off as the horror of more paperwork filled my head.

I stood there, soaking wet, wondering if I'd ever again be able to go a whole day with dry pants. The odds weren't looking good.

By the time I got back to my apartment, I was shivering involuntarily, thanks to being soaked through. I barely had control of my hands as I went to unlock my door, but I finally managed to get it open on the third try.

Thankfully, Mina was already passed out in my guest bedroom, so I wouldn't have to deal with her. I considered that my luckiest break in the whole of my night—well, morning. I hadn't really thought about what I would have told her had she seen me coming in like this anyway. She never would have bought a made-up story about the old version of me getting mugged, but since she held the straight-and-narrow version of me in such low esteem, maybe she would have bought it. It was no matter—she was busy sleeping, something my body desperately wished it was doing.

I counted myself lucky that I wasn't scheduled to be on the floor at the Javits Center until noon the next day, but I still wanted to get up early to take care of a few things over at the Lovecraft, like seeing if my phone had come in yet or if Godfrey had anything on Cleopatra's Needle. I peeled myself out of my cold second skin of clothing and took the most scalding shower I could stand in an effort to raise my core temperature back to normal. I hoped it was enough to kill whatever ick I had been exposed to just from jumping into the lake.

The next morning I was up and out the door without having to interact with Mina, though I remembered to slip my lock picks in my coat pocket. The less I interacted with her, the quicker she would be gone when she got what she wanted out of me. When I hit East Eleventh, the front of the Lovecraft Café buzzed with activity, which was no surprise. At this time of day there was always a heavy mix of agents among the locals, which made what I was about to do slightly easier.

I hurried back through the theater, which, for once, wasn't running a horror movie, paradoxically giving it an eerie feeling. The general bull pen area of the offices was mostly empty, to my relief. I looked up at the dry-erase board high on the wall. It currently read "It has been 2 days since our last vampire incursion."

My feet felt heavy as I climbed the ladder. When I reached the top I wiped away the 2, recalculated the number, and wrote in 738. I slid back down the ladder before anyone could notice and headed for my desk, but there was the sound of someone clearing his throat nearby and I turned to look.

Godfrey Candella had just come in through the movie theater into the offices, a notebook in one hand and a coffee cup in the other. His suit, as always, was impeccable, his tie knot perfect.

"Good morning," I said. "Anything about Cleopatra's Needle yet? Translate the hieroglyphics?"

Godfrey shook his head, then cocked it to the side, looking up at the dry-erase board.

Damn. I had hoped to distract him from what I had just done.

"Sorry, not yet. Too soon," he said. "I wasn't aware that there were any changes in the alert." His voice was more curious than accusatory. Had there been any accusation in it, I might have just turned and walked away as fast as I could, but instead I stepped closer.

"Yeah," I said with a whisper and a sheepish grin. "My bad. There's probably going to be a lot of paperwork involved in retracting that, but I just thought I'd get it off the board first."

"A lot of paperwork?" Godfrey said, his eyes bulging. "Please. That's the least of it. I already have the Gauntlet updating all the archives in preparation for documenting the antivampire operation. I even had overtime approved by the Enchancellors, and that *never* happens."

"I'm sorry," I said, and I truly was. I didn't want to create more work for anyone. I sat down heavily on the edge of a nearby desk and rubbed my eyes. "I just thought it would impress the Order if I had something big like that under my wing, you know? And when I saw all those dead people on the boat, I was almost chomping at the bit to call 'vampires' on it all."

Godfrey seemed to process that for a minute before speaking up. "So, if it's not vampires, what is it, then? Do you have any other guesses?"

"Connor said it's probably a chupacabra. I hoped to get a little research in before I have to head up to the convention center. I need to grab some reference materials on them."

"You don't need books," Godfrey said. "Chupacabra, eh?" Behind his glasses, his eyes rolled up and to the right as his brain accessed some little referential nook or cranny. He smiled. "What would you like to know?"

I pulled out my still-wet notebook. I read through the few notes I had made.

"So they're bloodsuckers, yes? Piercing fangs and red eyes?"

Godfrey nodded. "They can hypnotize with those eyes as well."

I flipped through my notes to where I had written down the description that the booze cruise employee Maggie had given me of the strange creature she had encountered on Pier 84.

"Could this thing be mistaken for a dog?"

Godfrey thought a moment, then nodded. "I could see that," he said. "Yes. Some have been noted to have these spiny ridges or thick fur all over them. I've only seen a few *National Enquirer*–level photos of them. A dead one was supposedly found in Nicaragua. But from some of what I've seen, they could probably pass for, or at least be mistaken for, a dog."

"Good," I said, making a few new notes.

"Does that help?" he asked.

I nodded. "Yeah. It confirms a lot of what Connor was thinking."

Godfrey smiled, pleased. It made my own shame over calling "vampires" on the case by mistake easier to bear.

After Godfrey left, I was a lot more knowledgeable than I had been several minutes earlier, but still wondering why a chupacabra was now in New York City.

I pulled out the photo blowups of the Dr. Kolb crime scene. I had been sure that Cleopatra's Needle figured in to this. Maybe I had watched *Nosferatu* one too many times, but I had already imagined a lone vampiric figure skulking around the base of the monolith, finding secret meaning in the ancient hieroglyphs chiseled there. I found it hard to believe there was nothing arcane about it, except now I imagined this doglike creature piddling on the base of it before moving along. If there was any significance to the needle, it was beyond me. I gave the pictures another look, this time checking out everything the camera had captured, ignoring the monument.

In the photos, there were trees, lots of them. Then there were shots of the crime scene itself. It wasn't terribly gruesome as far as crime scenes went, except for the bloody bite marks on the victim's neck. Other than that, there was very little blood left, which was what foolishly led me to think vampires in the first place. Several photos showed the police officers who were blocking off the crime scene, many of whom I recognized. And then I saw one more face that I recognized as well, off in the distance and just barely visible through the trees. I leapt from my desk, folded the picture, and stuffed it into my jacket pocket as I headed for the streets. I needed to get over to the Javits Center right away.

I needed to know why Illinois gypsies had also been in that area of Central Park that day.

21

I stopped by our booth long enough to throw the picture in front of Connor. He was still trying to figure out what was so important in it when I took off at a run through the crowds and toward the stall where the Brothers Heron were set up. I heard him cry out behind me, "Kid, wait," but I didn't turn back. I was too pissed off.

When I spied the quaint old gypsy wagon, all three of the brothers were busy rearranging their wares on the tables in front of it. The older, balding one, Marten, looked up and smiled at me at first, but it faded in an instant when he saw that I was running toward the three of them. I was cruising now and people were getting out of my way. Before Marten could warn his brothers, I leapt up over their table, tackling the weakest-looking one, Lanford. He had been the one I'd spied in the photos. There had been no mistaking his gawky features in the background of Connor's pictures.

"What the hell did you release out there?" I shouted. I scrabbled onto my knees and sat on his chest, pinning him down. I pulled off one of my gloves. "You tell me, or so help me God, I'll rip it out of your mind."

I could feel the electricity swirling in me. The more emotional I got, the harder it was to control my power, but right now I didn't care. I had only dragged information out of one other person before—Faisal Bane, the leader of the now-defunct Sectarians—and it had left me a gibbering idiot afterward. I was willing to take that chance here if I had to.

If I'd had a chance, that was. Two hands grabbed the sides of my shoulders and lifted me like I weighed nothing. Julius had me completely under his control, like I was a prize in one of those claw vending-machine games. He set me on my feet. Then, before I could move, he wrapped one of his meat hooks around each of my arms to restrain me.

"I don't think you want to be attacking my brother," he said.

Marten reached up and patted Julius on the shoulder.

Lanford slowly got back on his feet, but he was visibly shaken. Despite the odds turning totally in his favor, he was still afraid.

"Do you know what the penalty is for bringing crypto-zoological contraband into the tristate area?" I shouted at him.

Lanford shook his head. I didn't know what the penalty was either, specifically, but at least I knew it was illegal.

"Did you bring a chupaca—" I started to say, but Marten stepped around behind me and shoved his hand over my mouth.

"*That* will be quite enough of that on the show floor," he whispered, leaning in. "We don't need you screaming that out." His face softened and he gave me his best huckster smile. "We're not bad people, Simon, but it's true we sometimes do bad things. Or bad things happen to us. It's the curse of being born Romnichal, sadly. Still, we can't have you drawing attention to us."

I wanted to shout into his hand or at least bite it, but I decided to conserve my energy for now. I could feel my power coursing wild through my body, and I needed to calm myself down. My fingers were starting to glow with power.

Marten grabbed my left arm by the sleeve of my coat, careful not to touch my hand as he pulled my other glove off.

"Very interesting," he said. Lanford stepped closer.

Marten flipped my hand over, palm up, and looked over at his skinny brother.

"Lanny? Will you do the honors?"

Reluctantly, Lanny leaned over my hand. I closed it into a fist, but Julius put the squeeze on my arms and Marten pried my hand back open. Lanford ran one of his bony fingers across my palm, hovering over the various lines in my hand.

When he was done, he turned to Marten and nodded. His voice was solemn. "He's marked."

Marked? I thought. What the hell are they talking about? The only thing I saw on the palm of my hand was a sliver of graphite under the skin from when I had accidentally jabbed a pencil tip into it when I was twelve.

"Do you think so?" Marten asked with a hiss of sarcasm toward his brother. "What? Did you think his hand was glowing just for fun?"

"Hey," I heard Connor yelling from far off in the crowd. "Get your goddamn hands off my partner."

Julius's meaty grip on my arms tightened painfully.

Marten looked into my eyes as if he was studying me. I tried to look away, but it was no use.

"Such a pity," he said, disappointed. "Would that there was more time and we were meeting under more auspicious circumstances . . . Still, we can't have you hounding us, can we?"

Marten raised his free hand up to my face, the pinkie and index finger extended and practically touching my eyeballs. I struggled to pull my head away, but Julius's chest pressed against the back of my head, making it impossible to move. Marten then muttered something barely resembling a language, and all of a sudden I felt like I wanted to throw up.

Julius let go of me, and I was surprised to find that I couldn't stand. I fell to the floor, gagging. I turned my head to the left and saw Connor arriving just on the other side of their tables.

The Brothers Heron stepped over my body, heading toward their wagon.

"Time to pull the old Baba Yaga, boys," Marten said. Lanford and Julius looked at each other, total "is he serious" looks on their faces. They decided that their brother was indeed serious and made short work of stuffing themselves through the doorway of the gypsy wagon, Julius barely fitting. Marten backed up the steps. "We're really not bad guys, honest."

He pulled the door shut as he backed in, and smoke started pouring off the tiny wooden wagon, forming voluminous black clouds. It reminded me of those black snake fireworks I'd had as a kid. Cloud after cloud of black smoke rolled off it and rose toward the convention center ceiling high overhead. When it cleared, the entire gypsy wagon had vanished.

A few of the people who had stopped to watch applauded the spectacle, most likely convinced they were seeing some kind of staged Comic Con event.

Connor helped me up. I choked on the last of the smoke, but thankfully the sickening sensation in my stomach was gone.

"You okay, kid?"

I nodded, winded and unable to speak.

"Those guys had something to do with the chupacabra?" he asked.

I nodded again.

"I kinda figured that after you left me back at the booth playing 'Where's Lanford?' with the crime scene photo."

Finally my throat cleared enough that I could speak.

"Those douche bags are what gives gypsies an evil name, you know that?" I said. "Evil."

"One of them actually looked like he was evil-eyeing you," Connor said, looking me over. He put his hands on my face and pried my eyes open to examine them. "You sure you're okay?"

"I'm fine," I said, then stopped myself. "Hold on." The stomach pain had passed and the smoke inhalation too, but I somehow felt . . . off. I walked over to the table of goods the brothers had left behind as a result of their hasty exit.

I scooped up one of the totems at random with my bare hands. I pushed my power into it and . . . nothing. I threw it down and grabbed a deck of Tarot cards. Nothing. I scooped up several items at once, trying to roll my power into them.

All nothing.

"Kid?"

"My power," I said. "It's gone." Then, as an afterthought, "I hate Illinois gypsies."

22

While I stared at my hands, Connor checked through the space previously occupied by the gypsy wagon just to make sure we weren't having the wool pulled over our eyes by some sort of illusion.

When we determined that the wagon truly wasn't there anymore, I said, "Well, that's pretty damn impressive."

The crowd that had cheered when the wagon disappeared had dispersed, since it looked like the magic show was over and the wagon wouldn't be reappearing anytime soon.

Connor paced in the now-empty booth. He looked hopeful, like maybe the wagon might suddenly reappear.

"I thought gypsies only did folk magic," I said. "Trinkety stuff . . . lucky rabbits feet, love potions, wart removal, that kind of thing."

Connor stopped pacing and looked up at me. He held his arms out and waved them in the empty space.

"Usually, yeah," Connor said. "I guess some folk magic is a little bigger than others."

"A *little* bigger?" I said. "We're talking David Copperfield vanishing the Statue of Liberty proportions here. I think we should go fill the Inspectre in."

Connor agreed and the two of us returned through a sea of geeks and nerds to our booth to give the Inspectre our rundown of what had just happened. Including the fact that I had lost my power.

"Don't worry, kid," Connor said once we had finished telling him. "We'll figure something out."

"Oh, really?" I said, agitated. "That's pretty positive sounding coming from someone who hasn't just *lost their abilities*. You'll figure something out? Tell me, Connor, just how much folk magic have you reversed in your day?"

Connor held up his hand, his fingers tracing a circular goose egg.

"Exactly," I said. I turned to the Inspectre. "Sir, I'm sorry. I have to get out of here."

"Nonsense, my boy," Inspectre Quimbley said, giving me an encouraging slap on the shoulder. "There's plenty you can do around here to help with recruitment that doesn't require a lick of power."

I walked out from behind our table and went over to the next booth. It was just your average Comic Con booth, set up with a wide array of collectible comic memorabilia. I ran my hands up and down through the cardboard coffins of comics.

"Nothing," I said, moving to the next table and the next one after that. "Nothing, nothing, nothing, nothing, *nothing*."

I must have looked insane.

Connor and the Inspectre stared in silence until I calmed down.

"Feel better, kid?" Connor said.

"Not really," I said. "I feel kind of naked without my power, you know? It's been a part of me for so long, I can't remember life before it."

The Inspectre gave a loud *ha-room*, stroked his mustache, and walked around the table to the outer side of the booth.

"Perhaps I'll give you two a moment to collect your-selves while I check out this disappearing wagon for my-self," he said.

As he headed off in the direction we had just come from, Connor and I lapsed into awkward silence.

Several passersby sidled up to the booth, took a few pamphlets, and moved on. I was still shaking from the dawn-ing realization of what losing my powers really meant. In many ways, they had defined my very existence up until this point.

"Listen, kid," Connor said after a while. His voice was soft when he spoke. "Up until you joined the D.E.A., you considered your powers mostly a curse, right? Always messing up any chance with the ladies. So look on the bright side—now you don't have to worry about your power getting in the way of your life anymore."

I didn't think I could feel worse than I already did, but apparently I was wrong.

"Yeah," I said, "I can ruin my life all on my own just fine. Thanks."

Connor cocked his head.

"Troubles in paradise, kid?"

I stepped back into our booth and sulked toward the rear of it.

"I don't know," I said, thankful for the change of sub-ject even if it was also a dark one. "I don't know if I can take her being in Greater and Lesser Arcana. I just don't like Jane working so closely with Wesker. Every time I see them, she's laughing and having a good time, but whenever I'm around her lately, it's like she's reserving all her linger-ing bits of darkness just for me. You don't think that she and Wesker . . . ?"

I couldn't even finish my sentence without my brain feeling like it might explode. My heart jackhammered in my chest.

"Wait, wait, wait," Connor said. He came over to me.

"Jane and *Wesker*? What? You think she's doing the dark deed with the Dark Dud?"

He started laughing and shook his head.

"What?" I said. "I'm dead serious. What's so hard to believe about that? He's powerful, commanding; they share an affinity for dark things . . ."

"But he's *Thaddeus Wesker*," Connor said, unable to control himself. I felt the uncontrollable urge to smash him in the face. When he saw the serious look in my eyes, he composed himself. "Look, kid. I know that actually maintaining a relationship is new to you. It's probably why you're having all these out-of-whack jealousy issues. It's like you're in high school."

Connor was right, though I hated to admit it. I felt my rageful urges calming down.

"I've never had to deal with any of this before," I said. "I'm in uncharted water here."

"You and Jane make a cute, if annoying, couple," he said. "Don't blow it over something as ridiculous as your imagined jealousy, okay?"

"Should I really be taking this advice from someone as single as you?"

Connor's face darkened.

"Hey," he said. "My being single is a choice. I made that decision when I entered the Department, so that no one close to me would ever come to harm. Let's not get off topic here. We're talking about you."

I stared down into my hands—my powerless hands.

"Believe me," Connor said. "There are worse problems than not having paranormal powers."

"Things okay with you?" I said. Like the lights going out in a house, Connor's eyes changed right before me, and he looked away.

"It's nothing, kid," he said, but I could still see he carried some kind of extra burden. That letter he had received had something to do with his brother. I would have bet money on it. Why had it been blocked from me in my psychometric vision, though? I had to find out.

"You know, you *can* talk to me," I said. "About anything."

Connor gave me a sidelong look of suspicion. "Is that an order?"

My stomach clenched at his words.

"Knock it off," I said simply.

The Inspectre pushed his way back through the crowd, elves and Klingons flying to his left and right. He approached the booth, breathless.

"Anything?" Connor asked.

"As you said, the blasted wagon of theirs is nowhere to be found," the Inspectre said.

"So there's nothing we can do," I said, frustrated. The only people who might have any sort of answers about the chupacabras or my power loss had literally vanished into thin air. It was all I could do not to scream. "I have to get out of here."

The Inspectre, still winded, gave me a stern look.

"Sir, please," I begged. I held my ungloved hands up to him. "We're called the Department of *Extraordinary* Affairs. Right now I'm barely qualified for ordinary affairs, if that. I just need to get away for some time to think."

My pleas seemed to soften the Inspectre, and he nodded.

"Of course," he said finally. "Why don't you take the afternoon off from the show floor and collect yourself."

"Yeah, kid," Connor said. I turned to him.

"Can I use your phone?" I said.

Connor hesitated. I never asked to borrow it from him, but that had been because I generally didn't want to trigger off anything personal of his unless it was under the right circumstances. Without my powers, it really didn't matter what I touched, but Connor didn't move to hand it over.

"Mine melted in the Oubliette, remember?" I reminded him.

Connor nodded, and reluctantly pulled out his phone.

He started to hand it to me, then pulled it away. "Maybe I should dial whatever number for you, just for safety's sake."

I reached over and snatched the phone from him. It felt oddly liberating not to have to worry at all about keeping my power in check while holding it. Liberating, yes, but also a little bit empty.

"Give me that," I said, stepping away before he could grab it back. "I just need to get in touch with Jane."

I'd have to contend with Mina and the heist details later, but now that I was powerless, the desire to see Jane was suddenly overwhelming. Sure, I had poor impulse control, but I wasn't scheduled to take "Controlling Your Poor Impulse Control" until next spring anyway, so I couldn't feel guilty about it.

23

I called Jane and begged her to meet me once again at Eccentric Circles in half an hour. I didn't feel like heading into the Black Stacks over at Tome, Sweet Tome in my current condition. Jane agreed to meet me downtown. I hurried off the floor of the Javits Center and headed down to the bar.

Eccentric Circles was jumping considering it was midafternoon, but I wasn't in the mood to talk to anyone. Thanks to the gypsies, I could walk around gloveless. Normally a bar was a potential minefield for my psychometric powers. It felt weird to be bare-handed.

Since Jane had farther to travel coming down from Tome, Sweet Tome on the Upper West Side, I grabbed a beer and settled into the same booth Jane and I had dined in at the back of the bar the other night. By the time she showed up, I was down to the dregs of it. She had her trademark pile of arcane books sticking out of her shoulder bag. She didn't look happy.

"All this research is going to kill me," she said, "or, at the very least, crush me."

"I hope you didn't bring any books that have a vendetta against me," I said, holding up my hands in a defensive posture.

"It's not the books you should be worried about," she said, with a little attitude to it.

I was a little blindsided after our time spent patching things up last night.

Jane's eyes went to my bare hands as she slid the bag off her shoulder and onto the seat. She raised an eyebrow.

"You're not wearing your gloves," she said.

"Yeah, about that . . ."

I told her everything that had happened since seeing her last—about Central Park, chasing dead Dr. Kolb, and about the confrontation with the gypsies on the convention floor at New York Comic Con.

"So they just evil-eyed you?"

I shrugged. "Something like that. All I know is that I haven't been able to read a single thing psychometrically since."

Jane took my hands across the table.

"Wow," she said.

We sat there in silence for a minute, the bar and the rest of life continuing on around us.

"You okay?" she asked.

"Actually, yeah." I smiled. "For so long, my power dictated who I was, or limited what I could do. I came to the Department of Extraordinary Affairs because, let's face it, where the hell else was I going to fit in with what I could do. Now I feel kinda free. I thought about it while waiting for you . . . Maybe I should leave the Department. I thought I'd run it by you before I came to any real decisions, though."

Jane looked wounded, but then she shook her head.

"I don't think you want to quit, Simon. I really don't."

"Why shouldn't I?" I asked. "It's not like I fit in with our little Island of Misfit Toys anymore. Besides, I wouldn't have to deal with seeing you working for Wesker anymore . . ."

Jane sighed but squeezed my hands.

"Despite whatever issues you seem to be having with me, Simon, you're good people. This job is in you, even if you're never able to read another item in your life."

"How do you know I'm all that good?" I sure didn't feel like all that good a person. I was a jealous boyfriend and a deceiver. I thought about Mina and the fact that I was about to help her steal something. Was that what a good person let himself get wrapped up in?

"How do I know you're good?" Jane asked with a look of *duh* upon her face. "Because I'm constantly fighting my dark tendencies, especially these days. But you? You made a choice to walk away from all the bad in your life, and look at you now."

I squirmed in my seat. I was desperate to tell her that I wasn't a saint, that right now I was plotting a nefarious heist with Mina. Sure, I had the best of intentions in doing it, but still . . .

"If anyone's made a change here, it's you," I said to Jane. "Coming over to the D.E.A. like you did, giving up everything that Faisal Bane and his organization had to offer."

Jane raised a hand and waved it away.

"But working for the Sectarians was a delicious brush with dark power," Jane said, "and that changes a girl, mostly for the worse."

"But you're turning out okay," I said.

"That's why I said *mostly*, dum-dum," she snapped with dark anger, then caught herself. I sat back like I had been pushed. "See? See what I mean? It's a hard habit to break."

"Hanging with Thaddeus Wesker probably doesn't help," I muttered to myself.

"Whoa," Jane said, pulling her hands away. "Can we stick to one mental crisis at a time?"

"Sorry," I said, but it was too late.

Jane scooted herself out of the booth and pulled her bag of books toward the edge of the bench seat.

"I've got to get back to the office," she said, her face

looking like she had tasted something unpleasant. "I want you to give something some serious thought, Simon. Maybe it'd be best if we took a break until you get your act together and get over this thing about me and Wesker."

"What?" My stomach balled up in an instant.

"I don't like what's been happening between us," she said. "I don't need you going all jealous on me around Director Wesker every time you see me when I'm just doing my *job*. It's like you only call me when you want to apologize and get all needy like this. I know you're going through a lot right now and I know you've never really had the opportunity to be in a relationship like this before, which is why I'm not telling you to get lost. But honestly, there's only so much a girl can take before the dark thoughts start taking over."

This day was rolling downhill from suck to double suck.

"Are you . . . breaking up with me?"

Jane shook her head.

"We'll see about that," she said. "I just think you need to focus on where your head is at for now."

Other than up my ass? I thought. It sure sounded like she was breaking up with me, but before I could speak, Jane headed back up to the front of the bar and out the door. I walked toward the front, too, but not out the door. The call of one more beer was too strong, and frankly I was in the mood to self-medicate.

God only knew what Mina would have in store for me later tonight, heistwise. Plus, now I didn't have my powers to help me out. But until then, there was a lot of stuff I wanted to forget, and liquid courage seemed the best way to do it.

24

On my way back to the Lovecraft offices, I touched everything I saw with my gloveless hands, but it was no use. Whatever the Brothers Heron had cast on me seemed to be sticking.

I settled in at my desk. I felt pretty useless, and it meant the best I could do was dig into the mountain of paperwork in my in-box. Just as I was contemplating driving a pen into my eye to save me from filling out the multiple forms, case briefs, requisitions, and follow-up reports in triplicate, I was given a momentary reprieve when Supply called to tell me that my replacement cell phone had finally come in. After a quick trip down to them, I felt victorious but only a little better with my shiny new cell phone in hand. There was no way I could go back to tackling my mountain of paperwork madness. Being powerless was making me too antsy to concentrate. I needed to get away from my desk and get some actual legwork done on one of my cases, and luckily I knew just where to chase one of my hunches. I thought of how Batman detective-y I'd have to be without my powers, and this idea actually got me excited.

I found Godfrey Candella in the coffee shop scrawling away in one of the Gauntlet's trademark Moleskine notebooks.

"Hey, God."

He finished the sentence he was writing and then looked up from his notebook.

"Simon. Hey."

"Do you think we could head down to the Gauntlet and, I don't know, maybe just hang out and talk in private?"

Godfrey looked wary. "Is this about a case?"

"Not really," I said, shaking my head. "More of a social call."

He looked surprised but excited, and without another word he closed his notebook and we headed off to the offices and down the carved stone steps that led to the Gauntlet. There were fewer people down there than in the bull pen, and he led me to a private office where he had a large wooden desk covered with books, along with several comfy chairs. He went into one of the lower drawers of the desk and pulled out a bottle of scotch and two glasses, pouring an ample amount into both of them.

Godfrey was practically bouncing in his seat. "Sorry," he said. "No one ever asks us Gauntlet folks to do much of anything social. This bottle of scotch has had a few extra years to age because of it."

"Really?" I said. Godfrey smiled and gave a modest nod. I reached over and loosened his tie for him. "For God's sake, man, relax a little. Consider yourself off the clock for a few minutes."

"Oh, okay," he said, as if he hadn't thought of relaxing until I prompted him. Getting his story out of him was going to take more prodding than I thought. I decided to help my odds of getting anything out of him and raised my glass. He raised his, and, despite my buzz from earlier, I took a long pull of scotch from mine until I drained it, to make sure he followed suit and loosened his lips.

Not being a scotch man, the burn of it filled my throat,

and I waited for it to pass as Godfrey poured us a second round. Already I felt it hitting me stronger than I'd thought it would, and I decided to slowly sip the next one. Unfortunately, drinking in the late afternoon only helped me to feel worse about losing my powers, and I found myself staring blankly into my glass instead of pumping Godfrey for info.

"Simon . . . ?" Godfrey said. I don't know how long I had been staring, but I lifted my head. "You okay?"

I actually thought about it for a second. Was I okay? A wave of anger overtook me and I slammed my glass down onto the corner of his desk. "Frankly, no, I'm not. Fucking gypsies . . ."

Godfrey sat upright at my language and pushed his glasses back up on his face. "I'm sorry, what?"

"I don't want to bore you with the details," I said. "I just . . ."

"No, really, please do tell," he said. "If I'm about anything, I'm about the details."

"I just . . . crossed paths with the wrong Romnichal, and now I'm jinxed or cursed or whatever you want to call it. I'm powerless. I haven't been able to get a psychometric reading off anything all day."

Godfrey looked at me with sympathy.

"I'm *normal* now," I said, with bitter distain in my voice. "I always wondered what type of life I would have lived had I never had my power."

I didn't want to get into my past with him, but questions about my whole life started flooding my head. Would I ever have gotten mixed up with Mina and her gang when I had worked the antiques stores? Would I ever have worked at an antiques store? But the scotch was bringing out my darker heart about it all. "The truth is, I miss having them so far. It set me apart from the rest of the world. Not to mention I feel a little scared to be without them. I feel like I'm missing a limb."

I looked up at Godfrey. He looked hurt.

"What's your problem?" I asked.

"You act like being normal is a curse," Godfrey said, a little upset. "Some of us like being 'normal,' you know. Most of the planet deals with it."

I hadn't come down here to argue. I had come here to try to wean a little information out of my archival little friend.

"I'm sorry," I said, hoping to swing the conversation back around. "I wouldn't label you as normal, Godfrey. I mean, think about it. You have a real knack for being at the right place at the right time."

"How do you mean?"

Godfrey took a long sip of scotch, wiping his mouth with the sleeve of his jacket. Daring to soil his coat must have meant Godfrey was flying pretty high already.

"Well," I said, "the night we took the Sectarians down at the Met, for example. By the time we came rushing out of the building, you were already there taking down details. You were even there before the cops came. And at the boathouse the other night."

Godfrey nodded, excited to once again be talking shop. "Well, I can't be everywhere all at once," he said, "but I'm pretty lucky when it comes to things like that."

Luck? I wondered. Or something more? I nodded and let a moment of silence pass between the two of us. I didn't want to seem too eager leading him on, but I needed to know more about his past if my hunch was correct.

"Have you always had this sort of luck?" I asked, hoping I sounded nonchalant about it.

Godfrey Candella took the bait, his eyes lighting up. He seemed more than eager to talk about his life.

"Before I was recruited into the Department," he said, pushing his horn-rims back into place, "I had lived what an Other Division agent like you might call a quiet and mundane life. Five years ago, I experienced what I thought was a stretch of bad luck. The law firm I had been a clerical assistant at for four years fired me very suddenly, and for no apparent reason that I could figure."

"That must have been tough."

Godfrey nodded. "For someone as meticulous about details as I am? Yes, it was. I was devastated, but that only lasted for a couple days."

"What changed your mind?" I asked.

Godfrey gave a bittersweet smile. "Two days after I was let go, the building exploded."

"What?"

"It's true," Godfrey continued. "They were redecorating the office suite next to my old office and an errant nail gun punctured a gas line. It must have sparked, and *WHOOM!* Destroyed the whole place."

I gave an appropriate moment of silence out of respect for the dead. "Yeah, I'd definitely call that lucky."

"Being the only survivor really shook me up for several months," he said. Godfrey pulled off his glasses. He looked on the verge of crying. "Survivor's guilt over my dumb luck."

"It's okay," I said. I reached over and patted him on the shoulder.

Godfrey needed a moment to compose himself, taking the opportunity to pour us another round.

"So, then what did you do?"

"Nothing," he said. "After my near brush with death, I found myself unable to procure another job, which I found astounding, but no one wanted to hire the sole survivor of such a tragedy. Everyone thought I was bad luck. Heck, even I thought I was. I went three months just trying to figure out what I should do with myself. I had no idea. That's when the letter showed up."

"Letter?"

"An invitation to become a clerical official to a government office—one that I didn't realize was secret until I found it hidden away behind the Lovecraft Café, that is. I don't know how they got hold of me or why they even chose me, but I was running out of money. The timing was perfect."

Too perfect, I thought, but remained silent. I doubted the D.E.A. would have done anything so nefarious as blow up a building full of civilians to get a new recruit, but there was something weird about all this. No one was this lucky. Maybe Godfrey possessed a power even *he* didn't know about.

The D.E.A. didn't send out blanket snail mail to people hoping to find recruits. They preferred more cryptic means of drawing members to our organization. For instance, I had found them in the classified ads, and the Inspectre was busy screening the people who gravitated toward us at Comic Con. Someone had specifically sent that letter from the D.E.A. to Godfrey. But who, and why? I had my suspicions, but testing them would have to wait until I sobered up just a little. I checked my watch. It was almost time for my daily training with the Inspectre, and hopefully that would yield some answers, too.

25

Even though the immediate threat of vampires seemed like it was gone, Inspectre Quimbley insisted I had to be prepared for the day I met one, so he was once again dressed in his long black Dracula cape, with a padded chest piece bearing a heart target. I found myself fighting both the Inspectre and an entire six-piece dining room set. If I was supposed to "stake" him like the vampire he was pretending to be, I needed to overpower the enchanted furniture and smash it to have something pointy. Compared to things like the rampaging bookcases uptown at Tome, Sweet Tome, an embroidered chair seemed much less menacing . . . or so I thought.

What the dining set lacked in size and crushing power, it made up for in speed and viciousness. The six chairs galloped around the open area of the training room like miniature racehorses. My shins already sported several bruises, and the longer I had to contend with them, the harder I found it to walk around. I hadn't even managed to grab one of them and break off a stake. My vampire had nothing to fear yet.

To my surprise, I found that showing up a little buzzed for my training actually kept me loosened up. My reflexes were generally slower, but the buzz kept me from overthinking every possible move. I reacted more out of instinct, which saved me from what I could only imagine would have been three times the bruises I was already sporting.

Four of the chairs surrounded me, poised to hurl themselves at my body. I waited until the first of them sprang at me, and I dove onto the table, which was also making its way toward me. I landed on my shoulder, thankful the table could support me. The four chairs collided with one another and became a hopeless mess of legs. I rolled over the edge of the table, landing on the two other chairs, which seemed to collapse under me, smashing apart and leaving me stunned on the floor. Unfortunately, that gave the table enough time to throw itself down on top of me, crushing me under its weight.

The Inspectre whistled, and, with some reluctance, the table lifted itself off me.

"That, my boy, is why we F.O.G.gies are taught to think six steps ahead."

The table meandered off toward the remaining tangle of chairs and started to help pull them apart like a mother dog sorting out her pups. The Inspectre walked over to me and offered his hand. I took it and let him help me back up as I dusted splinters of wood off my clothes.

"Sorry, sir," I said. I felt my face turn red.

"Nonsense," the Inspectre said, encouraging me with a clap on the back. "You're getting there. I'm sure one of those shattered chair pieces could have been driven through my heart if you'd grabbed one. You were already thinking three or four steps ahead, which, for an initiate, is tremendous progress."

"Thank you," I said, humbled. I hadn't felt like I was improving, but I suppose I had fared well enough, given my current mental state.

" 'Course I suspect your lack of focus might have something to do with your trip down to the Gauntlet," the Inspectre said, and I felt my face go flush again.

Busted.

"I owed Godfrey Candella some details for the archives," I said, giving him a semitruth. "Just thought it
would be a little more sociable to knock back a few."

"I see," he said, running one hand over his walruslike
mustache.

"Speaking of Godfrey, sir, I was wondering . . . What's
his story? He called himself 'normal' today. He seems to
be under the impression that he doesn't have any power of
any kind."

"And why shouldn't he be?" the Inspectre said, more
defensive that I would have imagined. "None of the Gauntlet staff have any extraordinary abilities to speak of, other
than a deep love of history."

"Oh," I said, somewhat disappointed. "I just thought . . ."
I stopped myself. I was being ridiculous.

"You just thought what?" the Inspectre said. His voice
softened. "My boy, more than any other division that in-
teracts with the Department, you should know that the
Fraternal Order supports independent thought over mere
compliance with Departmental policies. The Order predates it by several hundred years. It may have provided the
foundation of the governmental branch, but it serves more
than just whatever the political flavor of the times is. It's
why we exist outside the mainstream. So, by all means,
speak up. If you've got a theory, I'd like to hear it."

I paused for a moment to gather my thoughts before
speaking. Talking to the Inspectre always made me feel
like I was twelve.

"Well, Godfrey and I got to talking, and he told me a
little bit about his past—how he had been let go only days
before the company he worked for was destroyed, that he
was the lone survivor of the incident, how he first received
an offer to join the Department . . ."

The Inspectre nodded. "And you wondered how the Department came to recruit him."

It was my turn to nod. "I mean, I lucked into finding out about the Department in the back of the newspaper, and even then it was hidden in a cryptic ad. You must have seen *something* special in Godfrey to have extended an invitation directly to him."

I felt a little nervous putting the Inspectre on the spot like this, but I couldn't help it. I had to go with my hunch.

When I stopped, the Inspectre smiled.

"I knew I was right to choose you for the Fraternal Order," he said, beaming.

The Inspectre turned to the table and chairs and whistled. The four surviving chairs had just finished untangling themselves from one another and trotted over to the table. The Inspectre gestured for me to sit. He looked serious, even in his Dracula cape.

"What I'm about to tell you is strictly the business of the Fraternal Order of Goodness. That means no telling Connor, or Jane, and *especially* not Godfrey Candella. If he finds out that shortly after his escape from certain death, at least ten pairs of eyes started watching him almost every waking moment of his life, he would have certainly considered his existence to be less than mundane. Do you understand?"

I nodded yes. I was eager to find out anything I could, whether it confirmed my suspicion or not.

"Good," the Inspectre said. He leaned in, even though there was no one else in the expansive room, and lowered his voice. "Godfrey Candella is unknowingly one of the prime archival tools of the Department of Extraordinary Affairs because he seems to possess some innate ability."

"I *knew* it," I said, pounding the table. One of the table legs kicked me. "Sorry."

"Godfrey caused a spike in the radar of the Gauntlet when its professional newsreaders picked up the story about the freak building explosion. The idea that there had been only one survivor lucky enough to have escaped that tragic fate sent up red flags. It was enough for us to dispense a small Shadower team to investigate Godfrey Candella further.

"The initial reports on Godfrey showed an abnormal amount of coincidental and luck-based activity surrounding the man. However it works, he certainly has a knack for being in the right place at the right time, or avoiding the wrong place at the right time, as the case may be. It's not that he has a nose for trouble so much; it's that he seems to be fairly lucky. A walking deus ex machina, if you will. We think that's why he's often first on the scene when something happens, which is an invaluable tool for an archivist. However, the kicker is that it appears that he has absolutely *no idea* that it is happening around him. None at all."

"So why not tell him? Let him hone it the way I'm learning to hone my own ability."

The Inspectre shook his head. "You don't understand. You've always been aware of your powers, even when you couldn't control them. Many of the other people in the Department simply aren't wired that way. Everything that's happened to Godfrey Candella was because of innate ability, which means that if he ever becomes aware of it, it might disappear altogether. We can't risk that, and there's no foreseeable harm in him not knowing."

No wonder Godfrey always seemed to be there in a timely fashion. That explained his appearance at the docks the other day. He was the perfect historian, always on the scene to record events as they happened. But the way the Department kept him in the dark about this power irked me to no end.

"So he doesn't suspect anything?"

"Nothing," he said. "The files on him aren't even on record down in the Gauntlet for fear he might come across a mention of himself. His unusual case even caught the eye of the Enchancellors. It was decided from the top down, Simon, that in order to keep his potential within the Department viable, Godfrey Candella must never be made aware of what he truly is."

I sat there in quiet after the Inspectre finished. I didn't know exactly what to say. Godfrey was definitely a boon to the Department. Having information in our line of work was crucial, and having someone who could be on the scene to record it was a definite advantage. Didn't he have the right to know, though? With a power like that, it sucked that Godfrey Candella remained in the dark.

It also sucked that I was going to use him without his knowledge, but I had to do something to keep more people from dying at the hands of the chupacabra.

I swore myself to secrecy with the Inspectre and headed off to my rendezvous with Mina, for what I hoped to be my last crime ever.

26

A late-night crowd filled the coffeehouse and Mina was once again waiting in one of the comfy lounge chairs when I emerged through the curtains of the theater, her legs kicked up over the arm of the chair. Her head lolled back in boredom. A black duffel bag with a shoulder strap sat next to the chair. She noticed me walking toward her and rolled her eyes.

"Moved on to the Grim Reaper, I see," she said.

"I'm sorry?"

"Bergman's *The Seventh Seal*?" she said, standing up. "Once again, you've been in there for hours. I even tried to find you, but the theater was too dark and filled with way too many people cloaked in black."

I forgot they had switched over to a Bergman film in the theater today, but with Mina semistalking me, at least my cover still hadn't been blown.

"You're starting to creep me out, Mina."

"Whatev," she said. Then she clapped her hands together and rubbed them vigorously. "You ready to get up to some crime?"

I shushed her. "Not here. Could you be a little more reckless? Jesus."

"Sure thing, Candy," she said, scooping up her bag. She started for the door, then turned around. "You have whatever you need on you?"

I felt my sleeve to make sure my lock picks were secure and discreetly felt at my waist for the retractable bat hanging just inside my coat. I liked to travel light but prepared. I scanned the room, trying to not appear too guilty. Several of my fellow D.E.A. members were in the coffeehouse, and although none of them was paying any special attention to me, I felt like I had a huge sign over my head: OFF TO COMMIT A CRIME.

I turned back to Mina. I was angry at her for getting me wrapped up in something like this again, for coming back into my life and pulling the comfy rug I had made for myself out from under me. But if I was being honest, I was more upset with myself for ever having associated with someone like her in the first place.

I stormed past her, knocking into her with my shoulder on my way out.

"Hey," she yelped. A couple of the regulars turned their heads, but I kept on going. Sure, I might have allowed myself to get stuck helping her, but I didn't have to be pleasant about it.

It was after one when we made our way up to the Museum of Modern Art, but I didn't speak to Mina. At least the cab ride gave me a chance to cool down a bit. Going into a break-in hotheaded only left room for error, and I was determined not to screw up my one criminal transgression since going straight. Everything about this had to be as discreet as possible, not only because it was wildly insane to go after *The Scream* itself, but because there was also my future with the Fraternal Order of Goodness to think of. I was pretty sure that helping to steal a painting worth millions didn't fall under the broad banner of "goodness." I justified my involvement by telling myself that I was serving a greater good by getting Mina away from everyone I cared about as quickly as I could. Just this one job and she was out of here. And if I could later trick her and turn her over to the authorities in the process . . . well, so be it.

Mina had the cab stop about half a block from the museum entrance, and she got out. She pulled a small plastic shopping bag out of the large duffel and threw it at me. Inside was a fairly realistic, high-quality blond men's wig and a pair of aviator sunglasses. She stood and crossed to me, pinching my cheeks.

"Who says I don't take care of my little sunshine?" she said, then pulled out a blond wig of her own. She put on the glasses. I was surprised how well the disguise worked. She helped me with my wig and slid my glasses on. "There. Now Mr. Straight and Narrow can be safe from those pesky cameras."

Mina's bravado and odd playfulness were probably all brought on by nerves. It only helped to intensify her already manic disposition. She swiveled around, scooped up her bag, and ran off toward the main entrance of MoMA.

I adjusted my wig in the reflection of one of the panes of glass in the building next to me. I looked ridiculous. I looked like every teen villain in every teen movie from the eighties *ever*.

My new phone went off in my pocket. I pulled it out. Jane. I walked away from Mina to answer it.

"Hello?"

"Simon. I see they were able to give you the same number." I hadn't heard from her since she'd walked out on me at Eccentric Circles earlier, and just the sound of her voice pained me.

"Yeah," I said. Now was *sooo* not the time. I stared down the block, watching Mina pace in front of the outer doors to MoMA like a panther. I noticed movement even farther down the block, across from where she stood. Three men on the opposite side of the street were walking toward the museum along Fifty-third Street, stumbling in and out of little pools of light and shadow, but there was something oddly familiar in their movement.

Something from my training in the "Shufflers & Shamblers" seminar last spring kicked in. Zombies.

The bodies moved down the sidewalk with disjointed jerks—classic signs of undead motor skills. What else had the seminar told me to look for? The clothes. None of them was wearing what I would call funereal dress— jeans, a hoodie, a heavy black cable-knit sweater, one in a Misfits T-shirt—which meant these three had been freshly killed for the very purpose of being put to work for a necromancer.

I turned around to see if any passersby were coming from the other end of the block, only to see three more figures shambling toward us from that direction. We were being boxed in from both avenues.

"Simon?" Jane said over the phone. When I had spotted the zombies, I had forgotten I was even on it, so I almost dropped it when she spoke up. "You there?"

"Yeah," I said, distracted. A passing taxi honked as it narrowly missed running into one of the zombies crossing the street toward us.

"Are you outside?" Jane asked.

I couldn't deny it, not with all the sounds of the city around me. "Yeah."

"You and Connor on a stakeout or something?" Jane asked. "You're not watching me through my window from the opposite rooftop again, are you?"

Running a surveillance job on Jane when she'd been a Sectarian had been one of my more pleasurable (if highly intrusive) ops.

"No, all alone," I lied. "I just . . . couldn't sleep so I decided to go for a walk."

"Oh," Jane said. "Look, I'm sorry about earlier. I know

I've been a little absorbed in everything that's changing in my life."

"Simon," Mina shouted from the entrance to MoMA. I threw my hand over the mouthpiece, but was too late. "Hurry up."

Was she doing this intentionally? I shot her a look that I wished would cause her to burst into flames. Would that I had been blessed with pyrokinesis instead of psychometry. At least then I could end all my troubles in one glorious blaze.

"Was that *Mina*?" Jane said, suspicion and anger rising in her voice. "That's what you call being alone?"

"I am," I said when I took my hand away again. "Mostly."

"Mostly?"

"Can we get into this later?" I said. The shuffling figures were getting closer by the second. I had to get off the phone fast, even if it meant forcing Jane off it. I went with the behavior that had been getting me in trouble in the first place—jealousy. "What's the matter, Jane? Feeling guilty about all your time with Director Wesker? Redirecting it at me, perhaps? Why so suspicious?"

"I wouldn't be suspicious if you weren't lying to me, jackass." I was thrown for a minute. The Jane I knew had never called me a jackass before, but there were those evil tendencies of hers rising up again. It was either that or the simple fact that right now I *was* being a jackass to get her off the line.

I hurried toward MoMA, keeping an eye on the zombies closing in on us.

"Look, I'm sorry," I said, trying a new tack and going for as close to honesty as I could. "There's just some old business I need to clear up right now. I can't really talk about it. Think of it as classified, like all that stuff I can't tell you about the Fraternal Order of Goodness."

Jane scoffed over the phone line.

"Don't think that you can hide any of this with the Or-

der's secrecy, Simon. If whatever's going on with you tonight is such a secret, why is Mina there?"

I didn't really have a good answer. I gave up. "We'll
discuss this later. I promise." Then I hung up on her.

The walking dead were making good time and closing
in on us faster than I would have liked, despite their physi-
cal limitations. I put my phone away and dashed the last
little bit down the sidewalk to Mina, sliding my lock picks
free from inside my sleeve to save time.

Mina gave me an innocent smile. She hadn't noticed the
zombies yet, and why would she have? She lived in a world
that didn't think they existed.

"Don't give me that look," I said, irked. "Are you trying
to ruin my relationship? Does the word 'covert' mean anything to you, Mina?"

Mina laughed. "Oh, don't get your panties twisted, Simon. I need your full concentration on getting that painting and not pining away on your cell phone. Now, according
to my casing of the place, we've got about twenty minutes
to get into the lobby before the guards come back through
here . . ." Mina glanced past my shoulder and finally noticed one of the packs shambling toward us. She squinted.
"Are those guys okay?"

"Just drunk," I lied. I was still pissed, but now there was
a greater problem: incoming zombies. I couldn't let Mina
catch on to that part of my life. "Let's just get inside before
they cause a scene."

This late at night, there was little crosstown traffic by
the museum, and even the cars that passed seemed to be
paying very little mind to what was going on. To them, the
zombies *were* a pack of guys who'd been out too late drinking and were stumbling home.

I dropped to my knees in front of the outer door and
examined the lock. It looked simple enough, if I had the
time to do it right, but the approaching zombies really put
the pressure on. Lock-picking wasn't easy when I was shaking with nerves and a horde of zombies was approaching.

"I don't think those guys are drunk," Mina said, her toughness disappearing for a second, "but whatever they are, they seem to be coming for us."

They're coming for me, I thought to myself, but I couldn't very likely tell Mina that without exposing what I did these days for a living. The Sectarians had used zombies as muscle—and for administrative work. Could they have something to do with this? Either way, I had to get us inside the museum. I slotted one of the tension wrenches and two picks into the lock.

"Can you work a little faster?" Mina said, still managing to fill her voice with condescension despite the nervousness in it.

"I'm sorry my breaking and entering isn't to your liking," I said. "Now, shut up and let me do this."

I didn't dare chance a look to my left or right while I concentrated on the lock. The sound of shuffling and dragging feet was enough to tell me that I needed to tumble it, and fast. I took a deep breath and pushed the pick in against the last pin, gently letting it slip up to the shear line. I felt the pin give and twisted the tension wrench. The lock turned and the glass door clicked open. Behind me the air was suddenly putrid, and I felt familiar cold wafts of it against my neck. The zombies were upon us.

Mina pushed through the open door and I rolled into the vestibule. I turned over and reached for the door. Mina threw her weight against it and slammed it shut just as the zombies stumbled against it, decaying bits of their hands and faces streaking the glass.

When I was sure Mina had her weight pressed firmly against the door, I pushed myself away from it to examine the secondary door that led to MoMA's actual lobby.

Getting into the vestibule had been relatively easy, thank God. The exterior glass door's lock had been pretty standard, probably hadn't been changed in years, but the interior lock was another story. It was electronic.

"Hurry up and get us in there," Mina shouted.

The sound of the undead against the glass was making my nerves twitch as they pounded at it with their decaying hands, making a squishing sort of sound with each thump.

"Uh, I think we're kinda stuck here, Mina," I said, standing back up. I continued examining the electronic box built into the glass door. "Lock picks don't work on this kind of lock." I slid the rest of my lock pick set out of my sleeve and unfolded the case. "I thought you said you cased this joint? You can't *pick* an electronic lock. Maybe you should have thought this through better, picked a better ex-con to help you out."

"No," Mina said from behind me. "I picked the right one. But don't you think you really ought to try using that little psychic thing of yours on that lock right about now?"

My skin went cold and I froze where I stood. How the hell did Mina know about my power? How could she? All my years of working alongside her on crimes, I had done my best to hide my wild talent. As far as she and the other miscreants from my past knew, I simply had an eye for finding extremely lucrative scores.

I turned around to question her, only to find myself face-to-face with the barrel of a gun.

"I think it's in both our interests if you get that door open," she said, shoving the gun even closer to my face, "and fast."

I had always wondered what could be worse than being trapped by a brain-thirsty pack of zombies. Now I knew.

27

"How do *you* know about my power?" I said, trying to ignore the gun.

Like most other D.E.A. agents, I was more nervous about being on the receiving end of a gun than encountering anything supernatural. Sure, we dealt with terrors and other things that were beyond the normal, but when faced with the blunt brutality of a gun, its very finite and real nature freaked me out in a way I wasn't used to.

Behind Mina, the zombies continued to pound on the glass of the door, smudges of blood and grime streaking the apparently shatterproof glass. Only her continued weight against it kept them from pushing their way in. Mina rolled her eyes, but didn't lower the gun.

"Oh, *please*," she said. "You think you could keep something like that secret? Now use your damn power and open the door."

The zombies struggling behind her gave the whole scene a surreal aquarium effect.

"Just touch the lock," she continued. "Read the entry code off the last person who used it."

Whoa, I thought. That was far more articulate a summary of how my powers worked than I would have expected out of her. Something didn't quite seem right about that, but there was no time to think about it with her shoving a gun in my face and giving me orders.

"Yeah, about that . . ." I said. "Thing is, I don't really have those powers at my disposal right now."

"Yeah, right," Mina said, and cocked the gun. "Just hurry up. Do you want to be stuck here when the guards come back through?"

"I'm serious," I shouted. "There were these gypsies . . ."

Mina wasn't buying any of it, despite the fact that I was telling the truth.

"If you had been stalking me properly," I continued, "you'd know that. They cursed me. My powers don't work."

"Sucks for you," she said, her finger ready on the trigger. The door behind her pushed in just enough for one of the zombies to wiggle its hand in through the opening. To my relief, she uncocked the gun, slid it into her waist, and pushed back on the door with all her might. I ran up to her side to help, and the door slammed shut underneath our combined weight, but not before several rotting fingers snapped off of the hand and fell to the floor. The smell coming from them was putrid, but the severed fingers continued to move, rolling back and forth on the floor of the foyer.

"You shoot me," I said, "and then you're just stuck in this little glass box with a bunch of zombies pouring in on top of you."

"Then it's really in our best interest that you get that second lock open, isn't it?" she said, some of the venom gone from her voice. Mina was scared. One of the fingers rolled onto her shoe and, with a nervous jump, she flicked it away.

"You've got the door by yourself?" I asked. Mina nodded. I turned and looked into the actual lobby, on the other side of the glass doors, with its large, gray tiles on the floor, its open atrium, and the tiny squares of color all over the wall. It looked like freedom and I wanted it bad.

I changed my focus to the lock that kept me from all that. There was a screen at the top of it and it prompted me for a five digit pass code. I wrapped both my hands around it. I braced myself, hopeful for something to happen . . . anything.

"Well?" Mina shouted over the low moaning coming through the glass.

I kept my hands firm on the lock, but it was no use. "Nothing."

I turned to face her. Maybe there was a way to get my psychometry back. Stress had always been a trigger back when I couldn't control it, so maybe . . .

"I have an idea," I said. "Pistol-whip me."

Mina turned from looking out the door. "I'm sorry, *what*?"

"Just do it."

"Simon, are you crazy? I'm not going to pistol-whip you."

"A second ago you were willing to shoot me," I spat out.

She shook her head and sighed. "I wouldn't have really shot you."

"Looked like it to me," I said, moving closer to the door she held shut. I reached for its handle. "Now, pistol-whip me or I'm going to pull this door open and let the undead have their merry way with us."

Mina started to argue, but gave up when she saw how dead serious I was. "This is the Simon I remember," she said with a smile. "Reckless and steeped in crazy. You realize it's a fine line in pistol-whipping between rendering you unconscious and killing you, right?"

I hadn't really thought of that. Pistol-whipping just seemed like one of those great movie clichés to try.

"I suppose irreversible brain damage might not be worth the risk. Fine. Just hit me like you mean it."

"No problem there," Mina said, and pulled back her arm. She let fly with a right hook, catching me upside the head. I stumbled back, stunned and a bit shocked at how jarring the blow was.

"Again," I mumbled.

"Again, no problem," Mina said. There was a perverse anger on her face now, and my ire was rising as well. She drew back, this time missing my face and punching me in the shoulder while still keeping the door secure.

The blow spun me around and I was once again facing the lock. I reached for it.

"Agai—" I started, but I felt a sudden sharp pain in my ass as Mina drove her foot into it. I fell forward into the glass from the kick's impact, clutching onto the lock itself to keep my face from smashing into it. Mina was in pure vengeance mode, and all my years of repressed anger toward her flooded my mind. Female or not, I wanted nothing more than to get up off the floor of the foyer and take a swing back at her, but all these emotions overwhelmed me like I had been hoping they would. I felt the tiniest electric spark of my powers returning, building until it washed over me. I could only hope that by the time I came out of this fresh vision, Mina wouldn't have beaten me to death by accident.

As I expected, the life of an electronic locking system wasn't an exciting one, but it certainly got a lot of action. Multiple flashes filled my head—fingers, chubby, wrinkly, young, old, keyed their pass codes into the system. Each of their IDs was different, but the numbers were flying by so fast I couldn't make out any single code. I slowed the psychometric vision as best as I could, like I was watching it on replay. A harsh-faced woman with an armful of books paused by the electronic lock and keyed her code: 24601.

When I pulled from the vision, I found myself passed out on the floor of the little lobby, and the first thing I noticed was how sore my ass was. The second thing I noticed was a tickling sensation by my nose, accompanied by a wretched smell. I tilted my head, only to see one of the severed zombie fingers wiggling far too close to my mouth for my liking. I shot up to a sitting position, the pain in my ass screaming now, and I found myself shaking with low blood sugar. I hadn't expected the return of my powers, but there was half of a lint-covered roll of Life Savers in my coat pocket, and I crunched them down as I went to stand up again.

Three arms were poking in through the door now as Mina struggled to keep the rest of them from coming in as well.

"Jesus, my ass," I said.

"Sorry," Mina said. "Got a little carried away there with the kicking. Didn't realize you were out for the count."

"Enough of this shit," I said, batting the one zombie arm away. "Time to go."

I ran to the lock and pressed in 24601. Tomorrow, the security people might wonder why their favorite scholar's code was being used this late at night, but I was more concerned with the guards patrolling the museum right now. If we didn't get the hell out of the vestibule before their return, our choices would be fighting them or fighting the zombies. Probably both.

The light went green with a pleasant beep, and the magnetic lock clicked. I pushed the door open all the way. Mina was still concentrating on holding the outer door shut against the zombies and wasn't aware of what I had done at all.

"Mina! Let's go."

She craned her head around and her eyes lit up. When she saw me inside the museum, she slammed the glass door on the zombie arms once more, eliciting a bone-cracking crunch, then ran toward where I stood just inside the main lobby. As she ran past, she grabbed me by the arm and started dragging me with her.

"No," I shouted, pulling free. I had wanted to shut the inside door against the zombies, who were already stumbling over one another as they streamed into the foyer. I ran back toward the door, but there was no way I was going to get to it before they entered the museum. I looked back over my shoulder. Mina stood there watching me, dumbfounded.

"Go," I said, raising my bat and turning back toward the oncoming zombies. "Do what you came here for. They won't bother you. They're after me."

Mina hesitated for a couple more seconds, then ran up a set of white stairs leading to the next level. Now that she was out of the way, things would be much easier. Zombies in small numbers were easy to outrun, and if I led them off into the museum away from her, I should have no trouble playing keep-away. And there was always the bat to fall back on. If I got lucky, I'd be able to pick them off one by one. I had never dealt with zombies all by myself, but I really couldn't call in the D.E.A. to help me with this one. I *was* in the middle of a crime, after all.

I started backing off in the opposite direction from the one Mina had gone, jumping onto one of the dark wooden blocks of a bench . . . only to watch the entire pack of zombies start shuffling off toward the white stairs instead.

"What the hell . . . ? Hey! Dicks! Over here!"

I leapt off the bench and crept to the edge of their pack, my bat choked and ready for action. Not a one of the monsters swiped at me. I poked my bat at one of them. It pushed the bat away, but ignored me and my juicy, juicy brains.

They continued toward the stairs. Definitely going after Mina.

"Crap on toast!" I said, and ran ahead of the pack. I took the stairs two at a time. The next floor had even less light than the main floor, but was lit in dim little pools here and there. I spun around, looking for signs pointing to the traveling exhibition that held *The Scream*. I couldn't read anything in the dark, but I did see a pool of light move across the wall off to my left and I ran toward it as quietly as I could. I didn't want to run up too boldly thinking it was Mina, only to startle a guard.

I stopped at the arch near where the light had come from and peeked in. Mina stood there in front of *The Scream*, the lone figure in it looking horrified that it was being stolen for the umpteenth time. Jane finished unfolding a painting-shaped soft case from the bag she had brought with her. She then pulled out pieces of an adjustable frame and started assembling them.

"You want to speed this up?" I whispered.

Mina jumped.

"What are you doing up here?" she said. "I thought you were going to take care of your friends."

I shook my head.

"Apparently, they're not *my* friends; they're *yours*."

"What?" She stopped what she was doing and turned to me.

"Seems like I'm not the only one around here with major secrets. You been pissing off the wrong people, Mina?"

She wouldn't respond, and turned back to her now-assembled frame, which was roughly the size of *The Scream*. "Shit."

"You didn't just figure out I had psychometry all on your own, did you?" I said. Mina remained silent. "Because normal people don't have zombies coming after them, do they, Mina? You want to explain just what it is that you're into here?"

"Nope," she said, and continued working. She started attaching tiny blocks of weight to the interior of the frame she had just assembled.

Low moans came from one of the other rooms. The zombies were no longer downstairs. Contrary to popular culture, zombies weren't stair-challenged.

"Fine," I said. "It's not going to matter once they shamble their way over here."

"Quiet. I've got to counterweight this for the switch out," Mina said. "I'm going with forty-five pounds, more or less."

"Are you even listening to me?" I hissed. "They're coming."

Mina looked at me, her eyes calm and her voice evening out.

"So deal with it," she said. "Listen, this next part has got to be pretty precise, and if they ruin it for me, we're both going to get caught."

I turned away from her and stormed off toward the zombies. I was going to have to be creative if I was going to stall or beat down an entire pack by myself without disturbing any of the art or setting off alarms. I prayed that some of my new training with the Fraternal Order of Goodness would be of use.

The zombies had all but ignored me before, but I was pretty sure that if I stood between them and their target, they'd try to rip me apart. Still, I couldn't just wait for it. I'd have to dodge them and play to the fact that I was faster, despite being outnumbered. Stalling them until I could thin their numbers was my best chance for survival.

I backed myself just to the left of the arch leading into the room that Mina and I occupied. I could make a stand against the first few before they tried to converge on Mina. I counted heads. Six of them, one sans fingers. All of them had made it up the stairs. Damn.

Given the width of the opening into the room, only two could force their way in at the same time, and I came down hard and fast on both of their heads with the bat.

In my short time doing all this, I'd never quite gotten used to braining something so identifiably human, but the dull crunch of the skull caving in did the trick on one of them, and it collapsed. The other was more resilient and stumbled into the room with two more right behind him. I backed away, tracking the damaged one, and swung down at it again. It dropped to the ground and stopped moving. I backed up and stepped to the side of the arch.

The zombie closest to me made a beeline for Mina,

which was what I had hoped for. I grabbed it by its rotting arm and used its own momentum to swing it off into the open space of the room. I did the same to the others as they entered. As long as I could keep moving and using my brain as more than snack food for them, I might get through this.

I shifted myself back between them and Mina. She was taking forever to swap the weighted adjustable frame with *The Scream* on the wall. Any bumps or pushes from my fight, and she'd set the alarm off.

I pushed one of the zombies away from me with the tip of my bat. A closer one lunged for Mina, and I swung around and down with a strike to the back of its head as I sidestepped. There was a crunch and it dropped. I paused for a moment. My arms were shaking. I realized that despite my adrenaline rush, I was still truly terrified.

"Almost done," Mina said. She had the frames swapped out and was busy stuffing *The Scream* into the padded bag. Cold, rotting breath filled my nostrils. I turned and one of the undead was inches from my face, its lips peeled back as it moved in for a bite.

"Ready," she said, and I felt a tug at my arm as she whisked me away. I felt slimy teeth brush against my skin as she pulled me along behind her. I shuddered and felt at my neck to see if the skin was broken anywhere. I couldn't feel anything, but it did cause me to go weak in the knees, forcing me to lean on Mina. By the time we hit the top of the stairs, I started to feel a little stronger and made it down without breaking my neck. When we reached the main lobby, I looked back up them to see the three remaining zombies just coming into sight.

Mina stopped. I thought she was winded since she was breathing heavily, but there was a lustful sparkle in her eyes. I remembered that type of high from back when I was a thief. I felt the sensation a little now and realized that I had missed it. Mina gave me a wicked smile.

"Thanks for keeping me safe," she said. Then she kissed

me. Her mouth was warm and inviting, but it wasn't what I wanted from her. Not now, not ever. I pushed away from her.

"Mina, I . . ."

I stopped myself. I was at a loss for what to say.

Mina turned away from me and slid the painting bag over her left shoulder. The moans of the remaining zombies came from the top of the stairs.

"Oh, and Simon?" she said, turning back.

"Yeah?" I was still somewhat dazed.

She raised her right hand. Her gun was in it, this time held by the barrel like a set of brass knuckles. "For the record, *this* is how you pistol-whip someone."

She swung, hitting me squarely above the shoulder blade, right in the neck meat. If it hurt, I wasn't sure. I was already unconscious and falling.

28

When I came to, I was thrilled to see that I didn't have a sudden craving for human brains. I did, however, find myself in the back of a cab parked outside my apartment in SoHo with the driver giving me a gentle shake into consciousness. The side of my head throbbed to a bossa nova beat and I felt dizzy when I tried to reach for my wallet, but the driver waved me away. Apparently, the ride had already been paid for. I guess it was the least Mina could do after giving me a potentially life-threatening concussion and making away with a multimillion-dollar painting. How she had managed to drag me out into the street while carrying the painting *and* fleeing the zombies, I had no idea. But at least we hadn't been caught, and now I hoped I'd never see her again.

On my way up to my apartment, I almost passed out several times as my head swam. After I let myself in, I shuffled across my darkened living room, surprised to find my psychometric powers triggering off everything I touched. Apparently, they were back for good . . . or at least until I ran into the gypsies again. I felt oddly comforted by their return, less alone.

I lowered myself onto my couch, letting it swallow all my pains and kinks from the night. I sat there for a long while, enjoying the quiet. It was nice for a change not to get jumped or find someone lurking in the shadows. My head still ached, but I could live with it.

I made my way to the kitchen and fished some aspirin down from one of the cabinets. Then I noticed my answering machine blinking.

Seventeen new messages.

My stomach tightened. Given my less-than-savory dating history, over ten messages usually meant that I was being dumped. With some hesitance, I hit play and was relieved to discover that only three were from Jane, which meant the likelihood of us still being a couple was high. Those messages were fine, more concerned and checking up to make sure I hadn't gone off the deep end after hanging up with her. It was messages four through seventeen, though, that had me freaked. All of them were Connor asking me to call him back, and he did not sound happy. Still a bit groggy from my evening, I pulled out my cell phone. Sure enough, there were even more messages from the both of them. The last one simply said to meet Connor at the office; he'd be working late.

Although it was past two now, I ditched my disguise and cleaned myself up in the bathroom before heading over to the Lovecraft Café. A few night owls were sitting in the coffee shop and movie theater, but I paid them only cursory attention as I headed out back to the office. It felt like a long, slow march to the gallows. We hadn't talked since the gypsies had cursed me earlier in the day, but I had left the show floor all freaked-out.

Connor was at his desk, working his way through a stack of case folders.

"Hey."

"Ah," he said, looking up from the file he was writing in. "I was wondering when you were gonna check in with me, kid."

"Sorry, busy night," I said, averting my eyes to my own desk. I sat down. "Got a friend in from out of town. We were at dinner."

"I see," he said, then fell silent. He went back to work on the file. "So you didn't catch the news yet."

"What news?"

"Thought you might be interested in this story they're running," he said, "you being all into the art scene. Somebody, or should I say somebodies, broke into the Museum of Modern Art tonight."

He looked up from his desk and met my eyes. I didn't dare look away.

"Really?" I said, forcing as much surprise into my voice as I could muster. "Anything interesting stolen?"

He stopped writing, sat back in his chair, and folded his hands over his chest.

"The news isn't saying what, exactly," he said, "but here's the interesting thing. They've got David Davidson handling all the press coverage of it."

"Over a burglary?" I said. I was afraid I knew where this was going.

As far as I knew, Davidson only handled politicking things for the mayor that fell into supernatural jurisdiction.

"Well," Connor continued matter-of-factly, "the news is already showing footage from the security tapes at the museum. Looks like a small gang of people broke in, at least that's how Davidson is spinning it. Thing about the footage, though, is how herky jerky most of the gang members look . . . and with Davidson out there running a denial campaign to the local networks, I'm thinking we've got a little shuffler and shambler action going on there."

"Zombie robbers?" I said, once again trying to sound more surprised than guilty.

"That's the way it looks to me," he said. "From the footage, it appears that only two living people were the ring leaders on this, a blond couple."

"How clear are the security tapes?" I asked. "Can you make out their faces?"

"Barely," he said, and I felt a small wave of relief cool my nerves a bit. "It's a guy and a girl. From what I can tell, the girl's kind of hot. I'd hit that."

I'd hit that too, I thought, rubbing my pained jaw. I'd hit that with a bat if I ever saw her again.

Connor looked at my hands. "I see you're wearing your gloves again."

"Yeah," I said, realizing I had put them back on after triggering off everything in my apartment. "Crazy thing . . . those Illinois gypsies must not be as powerful as we previously thought. Their curse just kinda wore off while I was out . . . with my friend . . . during our appetizers."

Connor stared me down, but I refused to flinch.

"Anyway," he said, drawing his words out slowly, almost painfully so. "Hope you enjoyed . . . dinner with your friend."

He was making it so obvious that he had pieced it together himself that the hair on the back of my neck stood up.

"Fine," I hissed across to him. "Her name's Mina. She's from my past, alright? What do you want me to say? You want a full confession?"

Connor shook his head with disappointment.

"You think that wig would fool me, that I wouldn't recognize my own partner?" he asked. "I just wanna know why, kid."

I paused. Mina was my business, and I was damned if I was going to bring everyone into it when it was my mess to clean up. "I . . . can't tell you," I said finally.

"There's a world of difference between *can't* and *won't*, kid."

There was such superiority in his voice, I snapped.

"Why don't you tell me about your letter, then?" I asked.

Connor looked like he'd been slapped in the face.

"We've *all* got our dirty little secrets," I continued. "So don't get holier than thou on me, alright?"

"So you know about the letter, then, eh?" he said, standing up. He grabbed his coat from behind him. "Yeah, why don't we both mind our own business?"

"You're keeping things from me," I said, feeling defensive about having been caught. Now I was lashing out.

Connor put on his coat, fished out his keys, and made sure to lock his desk.

"There's a world of difference between keeping something private and breaking the law while *lying to your partner about it*," he shouted. "You don't want to trust me enough to help you? Fine, kid. But don't expect me to keep this from the Enchancellors forever, especially since you seem to think you're running the show around here now, giving the orders."

"I am giving the orders," I shouted back. Connor fell silent. "The Inspectre put me in charge of this whole vampire chupacabra mess under the jurisdiction of the Fraternal Order of Goodness. I didn't tell you because . . . well, because I didn't want to pull rank, and also because I knew you'd fly off the handle, just like you are now."

Connor's eyes widened and he opened his mouth to speak, but couldn't. Instead he just turned around and stormed off, heading for the doors.

I felt like the worst partner in the world. I couldn't even bring myself to stand up to follow him. What good would it have done anyway?

Fucking things up with everyone around me was becoming my new pastime.

29

I went home and slept, but woke up the next morning good and depressed. I unlocked the door that led to my Fortress of Solitude, the White Room. I flicked on the light. Every piece of furniture and even the walls were all the same shade of white, and, more importantly, nothing in the room would set off my psychometry. I was hoping to clear my head by sitting in the neutral room, but it was no good. Its blinding whiteness and blank features only served to depress me further, and so I decided to skip out on going to the Javits Center later. If I didn't see Connor, I wouldn't have to deal with him, right? Instead, I would work on this chupacabra case all on my own. Well, mostly on my own, anyway. First I had to bait Godfrey.

"Donut?" I said, holding out the box I had just bought from the front counter of the Lovecraft Café. Godfrey Candella looked up from the wingback chair he was sitting in, pausing his pen on the page of his open Moleskine notebook.

"Oh," he said, quite surprised by my offer. "Thank you."

"Try the powdered ones," I said. "They're lemon filled, I think."

"I don't do powdered donuts," he said, quite serious. He took one of the plain ones out of the box. "The powder gets all over my suit."

Given the fastidious nature with which Godfrey dressed himself, it wasn't surprising. I sat down across from him and helped myself to one of the powdered ones.

"Suit yourself," I said. "I don't care if I get all powdery. Brushes right off the leather."

I bit into the donut. Jelly. I hated getting jelly when I was expecting lemon. I swallowed the bite, but put the donut back in the box. I grabbed the other powdered one. This time when I bit in I was rewarded with the taste of delicious lemony goodness.

When I looked up, Godfrey was staring at me.

"Is there something that you needed, Simon?"

"Me?" I said, nonchalant. "Not really. Just . . . enjoying my donut here."

"Oh," Godfrey said, finding his place in his notebook. "Okay. You don't mind if I get back to my notes, then?"

"Not at all," I said. Godfrey's concentration fell back to his work while I finished my first donut in silence.

"Another donut?" I asked when I was done.

Godfrey held up his first one; only three bites were gone from it.

"Still working on this one," he said. "Thanks."

"Sorry," I said, then started poking around the remaining ones in the box.

Godfrey seemed put off by my being there.

"Honestly, Simon, if there's something that you need . . ."

"Well," I said, "now that you mention it, I was kind of looking for a little help with something."

"Ah," he said, and closed his notebook. "I see. Now we're getting somewhere."

"Thing is, I really can't tell you what it's about," I said, feeling bad about being so cryptic.

"Is this something to do for the Fraternal Order?" he said.

"Yes," I lied, but it was only a half lie. I had discussed Godfrey and his history with the Inspectre and the both of us were F.O.G.gies, so didn't that count a little?

"But I really can't tell you," I continued.

Godfrey gave a sad but knowing smile. "You'd be surprised how often I hear that. For someone as archival as myself, a lot of people prefer me in the dark around here. I've never quite understood why."

After talking to the Inspectre, I understood. No one ever wanted to run the risk of letting Godfrey in on his innate luck power.

I stood up.

"Can you come with me?" I asked, gesturing toward the street.

Godfrey looked astounded. "You mean . . . out into the field?"

"Why do you look so shocked?" I asked. "I've seen you out on operations plenty of times."

He shook his head. "No one really asks me to go there. I just happen to be in the neighborhood and catch some of the commotion. But no one's ever asked me officially to come on an operation."

"And you still haven't been asked officially," I said with pointed wariness in my voice. I sat back down and leaned in conspiratorially. "I need you to keep this under wraps for now."

He smiled like a little kid, then wiped it from his face before nodding his head with vigor.

"Sure," he said. "Absolutely. Do you think I should change?" He looked down warily at his suit.

"Do you own anything other than suits?" I asked.

He considered it for a moment. "Truthfully, no," he answered.

"Then don't sweat it." I stood up. Godfrey stood as well, ready to follow, his eyes already showing his excitement. "Should just be a walk in the park."

* * *

"When you said it would just be a walk in the park," God-frey said, taking off his suit coat and throwing it over one shoulder, "I thought you meant it figuratively, not, you know, an *actual* walk in the park."

During the day, Central Park was far less spooky. I led Godfrey toward the crime scene. We stood at the base of Cleopatra's Needle, staring up the side of it. The crabs, I noticed, were still missing.

The Gauntlet archivist stood there, stone still, as if his eyes were recording every last detail of the monument, writing it to the hard drive that was his brain.

"God?" I asked. "You okay?"

"Sorry," he offered when he pulled out of his trance. "I don't usually get to see many of the things in our archives up close. Fascinating."

I wanted to give the poor guy a hug. Godfrey looked kind of lonely. Given that it was daylight in a park full of people, I opted for clapping him on the shoulder in reas-surance. That seemed to do the trick for now.

"You need to get out more," I said.

The park was unseasonably warm and the two of us were sweating bullets. Godfrey even loosened his tie, a feat I wouldn't have imagined possible for him.

"So now what?" he said after we had stood at the crime scene for a couple minutes.

"I hoped having a second set of eyes might help me fig-ure out something more about what happened to that jog-ger here," I lied.

Honestly, when I'd talked Godfrey into joining me, I didn't know what was supposed to happen. The Inspectre had told me about his powers, but I had no idea how they worked. I had simply brought Godfrey here because I thought I might be able to use him as some kind of clue lightning rod that would lead me in the right direction.

I was grasping at straws just to keep this case moving.

The shame of having called a false alarm on vampiric activity stung, and in my desperation I needed a break in the case. I'd hoped that, however Godfrey's power worked, whatever innate ability he had would have kicked in by now.

"Let me clean my glasses, then," Godfrey said, untucking his shirttail, nearly causing me to die of shock. Candella was a fastidious dresser, but he was so focused on actually being out in the field that he didn't care what was happening to his outward appearance. He wiped his glasses clean before sliding them back onto his nose just as one of his lenses popped out and rolled off across the stones.

"Oh, bother," he said, and knelt down to find it. I joined him in his search.

People walked by, giving us strange looks as they went, no doubt wondering why two grown men were crawling around together in Central Park. After several minutes, Godfrey found his lense and we stood back up. Earlier I had printed out a map to mark the two incidents I had dealt with so far—the attack at the pier and the one on Dr. Kolb—and I pulled it out now to examine it.

"I'm sorry," Godfrey said as he fished around in his pockets for something. "I don't notice anything. I'm afraid I'm not much use out here."

"That's okay," I said.

I looked up from my map, and Godfrey was heading back up past the monument and toward the East Side exit onto Fifth Avenue.

"Hey, God," I called after him. "Where the hell are you going?"

Godfrey turned, and his face was slack. When he spoke, it was like he was in a fugue state. "I need to repair my glasses. Have to find a repair kit."

He turned back around and started walking off again.

"God!" I called out after him, but it was no use. Godfrey Candella was on a mission, and with every passing second, I started thinking that maybe he was on to something. I folded up my map and followed him, but still kept far enough away so as to not disturb whatever mojo he had going on.

At Fifth Avenue he crossed against the light, almost getting himself run over in the process. Tires screeched and horns blared, but Godfrey didn't react to any of it. He entered a Duane Reade that was on the corner. Minutes later he reappeared at the door with an eyeglass repair kit, which he quickly opened, using the tiny tools to pop his lense back into place before fishing out a miniature screw to hold it in his frames.

When he was done, he noticed that his shoe was untied. Godfrey leaned against a lamppost to steady himself while he lifted his foot to retie it, but even so he stumbled and had to reach out for the post. His fingers grabbed for it, but only ended up tearing away one of the flyers affixed to the post itself. He read it and started heading up Fifth Avenue. This was the strange sort of stuff I had been hoping for out of him. I followed.

When he stopped in front of the Guggenheim Museum, I finally ran up to him.

"Oh, hello, Simon," he said, coming out of his trance. "Have you come for the show?"

"Huh?" I said. "What show are you talking about?"

Godfrey held up the flyer, and I snatched it from him. It advertised a modern art installation currently going on, but other than that, it looked normal enough.

"This is why you came here?" I said. Godfrey nodded.

There had to be more to this. He *had* stopped here, of all places. I pulled out the map and consulted it again. I found the tourist icon for the Guggenheim, then the one for the boat at the pier. Running in a straight line between them was the very spot where we had found the body of Dr. Kolb. The chupacabra hadn't been after Dr. Kolb. The good doctor had merely gotten himself in the way of its direct beeline for the museum. I put the map away.

"Follow me," I said, and started walking around to the side of the building. If the chupacabra had come to this spot, I doubt it had gone in through the main entrance of the museum. I doubted they could open doors, anyway. There had to be another opening. I crept along the wall and tried every door I found, only to find each and every one locked. At the end of the building, however, was a gated area and the gate was slightly open. The door inside of it sat oddly ajar as well. I ran over to it.

"We're not going in there, are we?" he said, his eyes widening like a fifth-grader spying an ice cream truck.

"Not we," I corrected. "Just me. This is where you get off."

"Are you sure?" he asked.

I nodded.

Godfrey looked nervous, scared, and a little relieved that his field trip was about to end this way. I had no other choice but to send him back to the offices. I wouldn't put him at further risk. Using him like a lightning rod for what I was looking for would probably get me in trouble anyway.

I reached for the door just inside the broken gate but pulled away from it.

Up close, the door wasn't just open, but its lock had been busted by force. I looked for whatever security system was attached to it, only to find that someone had already looped the exposed circuits in an expert manner so there would be no danger of setting off any of the alarms. Professional work, something I was pretty sure a chupacabra couldn't do.

I turned back to Godfrey.

"Listen," I said. "You can't breathe a word of this to Connor or the Inspectre, okay? They'd just get pissed off or worried. But if I'm not back in the office by six or so, let them know where I went. Got it?"

Godfrey nodded and backed away from the gate. He gave an all-too-enthusiastic thumbs-up at me. Not wanting to hurt his feelings, I returned it before entering and closing the door behind me.

With my power back, I could certainly handle a little re-
con with just my bat by my side, couldn't I? After all, it
was just a museum in the daytime.

The interior of the Guggenheim corkscrewed downward
underground the same way the museum proper did up-
ward. A set of dimly lit stairs ran down into the depths of
the abandoned part of the building and I followed them,
contemplating the finer differences between bravery in the
face of potential danger and stupidity. I blamed my time
with the Fraternal Order of Goodness for blurring the line
so much.

30

As I crept downward inside the museum, I tried my best to keep as quiet as I could. Muffled sounds came from farther down the corridor. I quietly pulled my retractable bat out and cupped my hand over the end of it as I slowly extended it, hoping to hide my own sounds from whoever might be listening. The wall of the downward-spiraling corridor opened up to an archway off to my left. I could barely make it out in the little amount of light in this subterranean area, but the noise definitely seemed to come from that direction. I hugged myself to the curved wall and moved closer to the archway.

As I approached, the sounds I heard became more familiar. It was the sound of someone digging through packing materials, without a doubt. Given the state my living room was often in, with all its own half-packed antiques and art finds, I could hardly mistake it. I chanced a peek around the corner of one side of the arch.

The room before me was so dark and long that it disappeared into the shadows. Wooden packing crates marked with symbols both arcane and simply illegible cluttered the entire area, reminding me of the government warehouse at the end of *Raiders of the Lost Ark*. At first glance I didn't notice anyone, so I quickly slipped around the edge of the arch and sank into the shadows of the piled crates. As I crept forward, my mind began to play tricks on me in the darkness.

Be vewy, vewy quiet, I thought. I'm hunting chupacabras.

Row after row of crates formed a labyrinth as I proceeded toward the sounds. Within several minutes my sense of direction was shot to hell. I had zero idea of which path actually led back to my escape route after the first few turns, but I supposed I'd improvise if a hasty retreat were called for. Knowing my luck, it would probably be hastier than not.

I peeked around one corner and spied movement up ahead, and for once the sound didn't seem muffled anymore. Light, however, was not at its best here, and all I could make out was shadowy movement against the backdrop of three half-opened crates that looked like they had been searched through in haste. I pressed myself against the opposite row of crates as hard as I could and moved forward, keeping the bat hidden on the far side of my body to prevent it from catching any light on its metallic surface by accident.

As I got closer, a lone figure came into view, but before I finished closing in on it, I was able to identify it by the curvaceous shape of its dark silhouette.

"Mina," I hissed.

Mina Saria bolted upright from the crate she was leaning halfway into, fistfuls of crumpled packing paper in her hands. She brandished them at me like weapons. Then she squinted, realized it was me, and threw the two handfuls back into the crate, looking relieved.

"Jesus, Simon," she whispered. "For a second there I was almost scared."

I pulled my bat out from behind me. "I'm still holding a bat, you know."

"As if you're gonna brain me," she said, then turned back to the crate and began rummaging around again. "Didn't I just save you from the walking dead last night?"

My jaw ached with a phantom pistol-whipping just from seeing her again.

I closed the distance between the two of us, grabbed her by the arm, and pulled her back up to standing position. I pushed the end of the bat up under her chin.

"I owe you one," I said, trying to sound as threatening as I could.

Mina looked me straight in the eye. I wasn't comfortable with the idea of smacking her around, and she knew it.

"Give me a break, Simon. It's not in your nature to beat down a lady."

"Maybe in your case I'll make an exception," I said, then tried to flash her as intimidating a look as I could, but it was no use. I lowered the bat. "Fine, although there's some argument to be made as to whether you qualify as a lady. My jaw thinks otherwise."

Mina considered this. "You wound me," she said, "but in all fairness, I *did* pull you out of there. I could have left you to those . . . those things. Now, if you'll just stand guard, maybe I can find what I came here for."

She dove back into the crate, almost falling into it as she leaned over to check deeper down inside it.

"Mina, what are you doing here?" I asked. "You were supposed to leave town."

She ignored me.

I sighed and gave a nervous look around. Dark and dangerous nooks and crannies were everywhere. If the chupacabra was here, I'd have to get Mina out fast, if only to beat her senseless later myself.

"Mina, trust me, you don't want to be messing with whatever's going on here. There are things going on that you don't understand, that *I* barely understand. Just get out."

All I could imagine was an evil, red-eyed attack from one of the creatures I had seen sketches of, the same one

Dr. Kolb's spirit had described to us and that I'd seen for a brief moment when I was the DJ.

It suddenly came to me what didn't fit in this scenario. In my mind, Mina and my casework had always been in two separate compartments that had nothing to do with each other. Why, then, in the middle of my work-related investigation, was she here?

"I just want my painting," Mina said, and for once, I actually heard nervousness in her voice.

"Wait . . . what's going on, Mina?" I asked, concerned. "I helped you steal *The Scream*. What happened to it after you stole it? What have you gotten yourself into?"

"Nothing," she said with sharpness, but she kept on digging. A few seconds later she stopped. "Shit. It's not here."

Mina checked a series of numbers marked on the three boxes she had looked through.

"What have you gotten yourself into?" I repeated.

Mina looked more worried than ever and started pacing.

"Nothing," she said, repeating herself again, more frenetic this time.

"Bullshit," I said with anger in my voice, but then I softened. She was spooked, no doubt. "Those zombies were after *you* last night at the museum. If you tell me what you've gotten yourself into, maybe I can help."

Mina looked hesitant.

"Trust me," I said, almost blushing with pride over the fact that I was in my element. "I'm sort of an expert on these things. It's my day job."

"I know," she said.

That took me aback.

"What? How? How do you know?"

Mina crossed her arms over her chest as she paced, looking lost in her own world of thought.

"Last night," she said, "with the zombies . . . you were right. They weren't after you. They were after me, but I couldn't take the time to explain why. I couldn't. So I knocked you out."

"Why would zombies be coming after *you*, Mina?"

"That's not important," she said, and before I could beg to differ, she continued. "Look, I made some deals in exchange for my freedom. My employer asked me to do something that . . . I just couldn't."

"You were supposed to kill me," I said, "weren't you?"

Mina nodded. "Before the heist, I called him and told him that, tried to reason and bargain with him, but to no avail. I had to get out of town, but you know me . . . I still hoped that I could snag *The Scream* before that. I didn't think he'd send fucking zombies after me."

"Then why knock me out?" I asked. "I thought for sure I'd wake up craving brains once the zombies got to me."

"Sorry," Mina said. "I panicked. I didn't have time to explain any of it and the zombies were coming, so I went with my usual answer to things—violence. When I saw you lying there it would have been so easy to just take the painting and run, but even then I couldn't do it. Even after you had turned your back on everything our gang used to have. I hated you for that, but I couldn't just leave you there to die. So it was either carry you or the painting. I put the damn thing down to get you out of there, but by the time I went back for it, the remaining zombies were there. I had to flee."

It was strange seeing the softer side of Mina. Strange, and a little creepy.

"Mina," I started, "I don't know what to say . . ."

She put her hand up.

"Don't say anything," she said. "You're just making this next part harder."

"Making what harder?" I asked, but it was too late. I saw the crowbar she'd used to open the packing crate in her hands. She raised it and swung for the base of my neck before I could even raise my bat. Once again, I had let my guard down around her, and part of me almost felt like I deserved what was coming.

"A lady's got to do what a lady's got to do," she said as the impact sent instant stars across my vision.

Fuck chivalry, I thought on my way to the ground. The next time I saw Mina it was going to strictly be on a "bat first, ask questions later" basis. That was, if there was a next time.

31

There's nothing quite as disorienting as waking up to someone poking you repeatedly in the same sore spot on your neck, but that was what I had to contend with when I came to. I looked up from where I was on the floor to see Mina leaning over me.

"Honestly," I said through a mouth that felt cottony, "you can stop that anytime you like."

I went to move my arms to help myself sit up, but my hands were trussed up behind my back—with what, I had no idea.

"Up and at 'em, sunshine," she said, back to her perky malicious self. "Places to go, people to see . . ."

Using both of her arms, she swung behind me and lifted until my legs were under me once again. I put the bulk of my weight on them and my knees buckled at first, but Mina held me up until I found the strength to stand on my own.

"Why the hell are you doing this, Mina? Have you finally flipped the last crazy switch in your brain?"

She scooped up my bat from where it lay on the floor

and stepped behind me, giving me a shove with it. "Just walk, unless you want me to gag you as well."

I limped forward at a slow but steady pace, my knee aching. I must have hit it when I fell, and it twinged with every step.

"No, seriously, Mina, why are you doing this?"

"This is just economics now," Mina said, "pure and simple. I tracked the painting here, hoping to find it, but you saw . . . Those crates are empty. If I give him you, though, maybe he'll give me what I want in exchange. Maybe he'll give me *The Scream* back once he uses it for whatever messed-up psycho ritual or blood sacrifice he has planned."

"Him *who*?" I asked. "Wait . . . blood sacrifice? Are we talking cultists here?"

Mina nodded.

"Great," I said, loving how much deeper I was sinking into trouble. "Why do you want that goddamn painting so badly?"

Mina grabbed me by the face, moving me to within an inch of hers. "Because I stole it. Possession. Don't you remember what it was like when you used to take things that weren't yours and *made* them yours? I never intended to hand it over to them."

I had no idea how Mina had gotten mixed up with cultists in the first place, but before I could ask we reached an intersection in the maze, and Mina pulled out a Maglite to check the ground. A trail of little multicolored dots ran down one of the aisles and she dragged me off in that direction.

"Are those Skittles?" I asked.

Mina nodded. "Easier to follow than bread crumbs. Tastier, too."

I didn't want to admit it to her, but it was actually a good idea.

"So you're handing me over to cultists just so you can get your stupid painting back?"

Mina lifted her hand and stuck her finger in my face.

"Don't call it that," she said. "*The Scream* is the most perfect thing in the world. The exquisite torture in that lone figure's face, the loneliness, the madness. You're a collector, for God's sake. You understand."

I liked the painting well enough, but leave it to Mina's twisted mind to turn it into the pinnacle of her own private obsession.

Mina continued to guide us out of the crates, the lights growing brighter and brighter as we approached the entranceway to another room.

"So I take it you know everything about me, about the Department?" I asked, after several moments of silence.

Mina nodded.

"How? Who are you working for?"

Mina remained silent, dragging me along.

I let my legs go out from under me and landed hard on my ass. I sat Indian-style to make it harder for her to move my dead weight.

Mina stared down at me and sighed. "Get up, Simon."

"No."

Mina poked my chest with the end of my bat. "I don't have the patience for this, Simon," she said. "*Get up.*"

I shook my head. "You want me to walk, then you tell me what you know."

"I could just cave your skull in," she said matter-of-factly, shaking my bat in the air.

I didn't put it past her, but I kept my face a blank slate, if only to deny her the pleasure of a reaction.

"I'm much harder to carry as dead weight, wherever you're taking me," I said, hoping my false bravado wasn't as transparent as it felt. Even if I complied and kept going, there was no way in hell I'd be able to get up of my own accord now.

After a quick visual Mexican standoff, it was Mina who finally gave in. With a final nervous look down the aisle, she squatted down behind me and started picking me back up.

"Fine," she said. "I know everything about you."

"Even . . . ?"

Mina held up her hands and wiggled them at me. "*Zap.* Yes, even that. I always wondered how you were so astute about things when we were ripping people off. I didn't just happen across your apartment by mistake. I was given a lot of information on you: your address, the Department you work for . . ."

"By who?"

Mina dropped her eyes from mine, unable to look at me. "Let's just say you meet a lot of interesting people in jail . . ."

"How long were you in jail?"

"If you're going to follow everything I say with a question, I'll get straight to using the bat on you," she said.

"Sorry."

"Two years into my jail sentence, I was transferred to this hard-core coed facility, and you wouldn't believe what I ended up hearing through the rumor mill. Seems one of the most badass inmates of them all had a real mad-on for one Simon Canderous. He was delighted to make my acquaintance when we met. You might recall him . . . a European gentleman recovering from a stab wound through his shoulder?"

"Faisal Bane," I said, and my stomach dropped out from under me. Suddenly I wanted to throw up.

Even though I had run the leader of the tristate area's largest cult through with one of the historical swords at the Metropolitan Museum of Art less than six months ago, I should have realized that no matter what type of jail time he might serve, he wasn't done with me.

"You say his name with about as much contempt as he said yours," she said, amused.

"I suspect that's the only thing we have in common," I said.

"Even in jail, you could tell people respected him, if

only out of fear. A tiger, even when caged, is still a tiger. And besides, I like powerful men. They can do things for a girl . . ."

I thought I saw where this was going.

"Like get her out of jail earlier than she's scheduled to be released?" I asked.

Mina smiled. "Something like that. I don't know what you did to piss him off, Simon, but Faisal is someone you want to have in your corner, someone who can do things for you."

"And my life is the price you paid for your freedom, right?"

Mina didn't answer, but she had me standing once again and shoved me off in the direction of her colored candy trail.

"And you're doing all this for what? So you can get your hands on *The Scream* again? This is a sick obsession. If Faisal and his people have it, they're not going to just hand it over, you know. They have to want it for some special reason."

"I'll burn that bridge when I come to it," Mina said, her face determined and with purpose now. "Besides, Faisal isn't the worst of your concerns right now."

"Oh, great."

"Don't sound so disappointed," a familiar voice boomed out. The last time I had heard it was that night at the Met. A figure stepped out from behind one stack of crates, the minotaur of this particular crate-formed labyrinth—Cyrus Mandalay.

"Hello, Simon."

There was no mistaking the imposing figure of Cyrus— a huge white man with dreads, sharklike teeth, and ritualistic tattoos weaving across his face. He had escaped the cops, and here he was now. He was even wearing the same pirate costume he'd worn to the gala at the museum. It hung in dirty tatters now and he looked like he had been living like the mad king of the hobos ever since his narrow escape. I thought normal Cyrus was scary, but this new, unhinged version terrified me even more.

"We really have to stop meeting in museums like this, Cy," I said, trying to keep my cool. "People will start to talk."

"Glad to see you're in such good spirits," he said, smiling with his row of razor-sharp teeth. They were yellow now. "I, unfortunately, am not. You cost me my business."

"Tome, Sweet Tome? We're having a field day just trying to wrangle some of the more aggressive books, but we'll manage. Great acquisition for the Department."

"That's not what I'm talking about," Cyrus said, his eyes blazing with hate. "That bookstore was just a cover for my real business. You know that."

"Oh, Ghostsniffing?" I said. "Yeah, I'm really broken up inside over the fact that we put an end to your little soul-destroying narcotics operation."

Cyrus started walking toward us, but Mina held up the bat, pointing it at him.

"That's close enough for now, Cyrus," she said. "I can let him go, or you can give me what I came for."

Cyrus stopped where he was, peering at us. It was like he was noticing her for the first time.

"Mina, was it?" he asked. "You think your life means anything to me after you refused to kill your little boy toy Simon? Wasn't that what you exchanged for your freedom? Now I'm afraid you may have to be put on permanent display at our little exhibit here . . ."

"I brought him to you," she said in desperation.

"Actually, I found her—" I started.

Mina kicked at me, catching me in the shin and sending a shiver of pain up my leg.

"I'm willing to trade you Canderous for the painting," she said. "I'm kind of attached to *The Scream*, and I honestly think the painting would be far happier in my hands than yours. Especially after you sent a group of hit zombies after me . . ."

"Hired help." Cyrus sighed. "They were just supposed to take the painting from you. If I had my way about it, I would have sent more zombies after you with instructions to eat brains first, ask questions later, but someone in jail thought rather highly of you."

"I'll be sure to send Faisal a nice care package," Mina said. "The painting, please."

"Don't be sure he'll be all that forgiving this time. Besides, that painting is integral to what we're going for down here."

"I'm sorry," I said, interrupting, "but are we going to bash my head in now or would you rather wait till later? Because if I get a vote, I can tell you which camp I'm siding with."

Mina raised the bat over my head and held it there like a blunt guillotine waiting to drop. "Just give me the painting."

Cyrus gave an arcane gesture, and the sound of shuffling rose from several points behind me. I craned my head back to take a look, but it was no use. I had a pretty good idea what was coming, though.

"Umm . . . Mina?"

"Quiet, Simon," she said, pissed off. "I'm negotiating."

"You might want to negotiate nicer, then," I said. Mina looked at me. Since my hands were still bound behind me, I gestured over my shoulder with my eyes. Mina's eyes widened. She swore under her breath, lowered my bat, and let go of me.

I could understand her frustration. I was just as surrounded by dozens of zombies as she was. Apparently, somebody had been studying up on his necromancy.

32

Having a tight ring of brain-hungry zombies surrounding Mina and me was unnerving, and it was only after they relieved Mina of my bat and forced us to follow Cyrus into the next room that I took a moment to really look around.

In this new section of the unused underground part of the museum, there were only a few crates, mostly open and unpacked. This room was nearly identical to the one previous to it, except that I could actually make out what was going on in here. The lighting was still running at low generator levels, but it looked like an assortment of art exhibits mid-setup.

"Good to see you've found ways to entertain yourself other than destroying souls," I said. "What is all this?"

Cyrus smiled and shook his head at me, then pointed straight up above us. Directly overhead hung a banner, done up in a mix of black and bloodred fonts:

Para-lyzed!

Where Art and the Paranormal Ar't

When I looked around the room again, I saw signs of an art installation that I hadn't noticed before, all of them in various states of preparation. The most prominent was a section of wall where *The Scream* hung. Next to it were the beginnings of a life-sized diorama re-creating the long stretch of dismal road from the painting.

"Well, this looks sufficiently fucked-up," I said. "*This* is what you've been spending your time on, like some kind of demented subterranean Phantom of the Opera?"

Mina elbowed me in the gut. "I'd kind of like to live a little bit longer, so could you at least *try* not to antagonize him? Dammit! Trading you for *The Scream* was the last ace up my sleeve."

"Sorry," I whispered. "I don't listen to people who repeatedly threaten to bash my brains in."

At the mention of brains, the group of zombies let out a soft moan. I shuddered.

Cyrus *tsk-tsk*ed me. "You see?" he asked. "That's exactly the problem with you people. You're limited by your solipsistic point of view. If you would only open up your mind and see the greater picture, the high art in all this . . ."

Cyrus circled around a large glass display case that stood near him, and I noticed a stirring at the bottom of it. Two distinct figures rose, stretching themselves on their four legs and arching their spiny backs. Their red eyes glared at Cyrus, then one of them charged forward. It hit the glass and bounced off, letting out a whine before it stood and shook its head, regaining its composure.

"The chupacabras," I said.

Cyrus raised an eyebrow. "I see they're actually teaching you something in that department of yours."

Cyrus squatted down next to it and stared at the chupacabras from eye level. The two animals pulled themselves to the far end of the case. "Yes, they're for this special little exhibit I'm putting together. A kind of deconstructed Will Wegman piece with a twist that I think will really wow our patrons. You won't believe how hard these creatures were to come by. I had initially paid for only one, but two days later, a second one showed up out of nowhere, scratching around. I think these things mate for life, like they're the swans of the paranormal world. The poor thing was a little bloody, but I could hardly turn it away from its mate, now, could I?"

Parts of the puzzle started to fall into place. The mangier of the two must have broken free from the gypsies near the docks, which had explained the shattered crate in their storage area behind the gypsy wagon. It must have been disoriented when it found itself by the docks on the west side, first killing everyone on the booze cruise, then taking the life of Dr. Kolb as it made a beeline for its mate's scent all the way across town.

"So I *did* see you at the Javits Center," I said. "I thought I was going crazy with there being so many damned pirates. You bought one off of the Brothers Heron."

"Pirates are so de rigueur at those types of conventions," he said, tapping on the glass of the display case. "I barely had to disguise myself. Apparently those imbeciles didn't realize that these fine creatures mate for life. When one of them was taken away, the other simply followed. That hardly sounds evil, does it? Tell me that's not the act of a loving creature."

"Evil or not, it's still illegal to sell them in the tristate area," I said. "And they're evil through and through. They've got some kind of demony thing going on with all that blood sucking. I think that technically counts as evil . . . and illegal."

Cyrus stood up, mock horror on his face. "Oh heavens, no . . . not *illegal*!"

"Listen," Mina said, speaking up. "I think the two of you have a lot to get off your chests here, so why don't you just let me go? I've thought it over, and you know what? You're right. I've been paid fairly and honestly already. You can keep the painting. I'll leave town; you won't have me to worry about."

That was Mina, always looking out for herself. I would have kicked her if I didn't think it might rile up the zombies.

Cyrus laughed out loud at her for several minutes, almost unable to control himself.

"Mina, Mina, Mina," he said, when he could catch his breath. "So gothic, and so aptly named for what I have in mind for you. I think I have the perfect exhibit that could use a little bat bait." Cyrus gestured again. "Bring her."

A section of the zombies broke away, taking Mina with them. I managed to reach out to grab her arm, but caught one of the zombie arms instead, snapping it off with a squishy mess as the loose flesh clung under my fingernails. Grossed out beyond gross, I tossed it away and fought back the urge to vomit.

Cyrus crossed over to another glass case approximately the size of a telephone booth—on second look, more like a large glass coffin. The interior of it was filled with a cloud of gray mist. A small, sealed-off fan unit was affixed to the top of the case, keeping the mist in a constant swirl. Every so often I thought I saw the formation of a hand and the hint of a face in it, but I wasn't certain.

"Time to saturate," Cyrus said. He pulled out a set of keys, unlocked a tiny control box that stood about waist high, and flicked the switch inside it. What could only be blood rained down from a spout at the top of the coffin into the mist, turning it from white to pink to a dark crimson. The mist sank to the bottom of the case, and Cyrus turned off the pump. "That should put him out of commission for a few moments."

Mina struggled to pull away. "Him?" Mina said. "Him *who*?"

"Your new roommate," he said with a smile. He flipped another switch in the box and I heard the sound of decompression. When it stopped, the front of the box swung open and I noticed there was a high lip around the bottom of it that kept the near-liquid form at the bottom from spilling out. The zombies forced Mina toward the box. She fought back, but it was no use. There were too many of them on her, pushing her. When she had stepped all the way in, Cyrus swung the glass door shut and powered up the compressor to reseal the box.

"What are you doing to her?" I shouted. "She'll suffocate."

"No worries," Cyrus said. "The compressor is merely to seal the box from any form of leakage. Air is circulated in through an exchange mechanism. It's the overhead fan that keeps our vampiric guest from fully forming, although I suspect he'll be good and blood drunk for some time to come."

Already a red mist was beginning to swirl around Mina's feet. She pounded on the glass in soundproof horror as she realized what she was locked in with.

"Oh, my God. Will she live?" I asked.

Cyrus considered this for a moment. "You know, I'm not quite sure. That's what I love about this type of performance art. It's an experiment of sorts; just the type of thing I suspect will get a fabulous write-up in *Cultist Quarterly* when the show opens. True, the vampire can't fully form, but I wonder if it will find a way to feed nonetheless." He turned to contemplate the box with Mina in it. "That's what good art does, Simon. It inspires thought."

"I don't mean to argue with you, Cyrus, what with being surrounded by your undead minions, but I'll just say beauty is in the eye of the beholder and leave it at that."

"Oh, yes," Cyrus said, turning to me once he was done with his morbid meditation. His eyes lit up. "I almost forgot . . . Thanks to your little magic hands, you're a bit of an expert on art, aren't you? Don't worry. I have something better lined up for you, too. Something special."

"For me?" I said, trying to hide my nervousness. "Gee, you shouldn't have."

"Oh, believe me," Cyrus said, walking off to another end of the great hall. "It was my pleasure. I've got something lined up for everyone who brought down my Ghost-sniffing operation. The good thing about being in hiding as long as I have is that downtime is good for the creative soul. I've had plenty of time to think up fitting ways to make everyone's life miserable, especially yours."

Cyrus breathed out a small chant and his zombies started moving me across the floor toward an ever greater assortment of cases. If my hands had been free, there was a chance I might have escaped, but I couldn't with them bound behind my back as they were. I missed my bat already.

"Had Mina followed through with her end of the bargain, you would have been dead by now," he said, stopping by another case, this one covered with a red curtain, "but when that seemed unlikely, I started thinking. The artist's mind is always turning, and you know what? I'm glad she didn't kill you. Death would have been too easy on you, I realized. Then I was struck with inspiration. I wondered how and when I was going to be able to get ahold of you. I knew I shouldn't have worried. I should have known that you possess the meddling gene and it was only a matter of time before *you* found *me*."

"Hey," I shouted defensively. "I didn't just stumble across your little project here. I worked this case very hard to get as trapped as I am right now, thank you very much."

"Take what little pleasure you can in that, I suppose."

Small comfort that it was, I did take a perverse joy in having gotten this far. Of course, right now it would have been much better to have Connor or the Inspectre or, heck, even Godfrey at my side. The closest thing that I had to a friend in all this was Mina, but she was currently occupied. I chanced a look back at her. She was still freaking out in the glass coffin, but given the deep shade of red that the mist was, she looked safe enough for now. Relatively speaking.

I turned back to Cyrus, only to find him standing less than a foot away, holding a coil of rope in one hand and a foul-smelling rag in the other.

"I'm afraid that this next part is going to be a little tricky," he said, placing the rag over my mouth and nose.

As my eyes slid shut, my last thought was how much quicker chloroform seemed to act in real life than in the movies.

33

Compared to the last few times I had regained consciousness, waking up this time felt relatively pleasant, although what I guessed to be chloroform had given me a headache. I'd have to get myself checked out by a doctor if I got through all this. The assortment of traumas today couldn't be good for my body.

As I struggled to rouse myself, I found it hard to breathe. I thought it might be due to the drugs, but when I opened my eyes, I found I was inside a sealed clear box myself, this one more confining. My hands stuck out of the front of it through two small, circular cutouts and were tied together on the outside. When I looked down at my arms, I realized that I wasn't even in my own clothes anymore. Around my waist was a fake wooden table with a crystal ball on it, but above that I was wearing a shiny gold shirt and a brown vest, and in my reflection in the glass I could see I was wearing a turban with a large red jewel in it.

"What the . . . ?" I started, but my mouth was thick with spit. I swallowed. "What the hell am I doing in this getup?"

"Don't you recognize it?" Cyrus said.

The cloud over my mind lifted a little.

"Am I . . . one of those gypsy fortune-telling machines? Like in *Big*?"

"Zoltar!" Cyrus said, putting his finger on the point of his nose. "Ding! Yes. Think of it, a living, breathing Zoltar machine, reading the psychic fortunes of others. It borders on genius."

"Forget it," I said. "I'm not going to participate."

Cyrus tapped on the see-through box.

"I don't really see where you get a choice," he said, and then looked down at my hands.

Yes, they were tied, but they also were no longer covered. My gloves were gone.

"I've added a feature or two so our patrons get their money's worth," Cyrus said, gesturing to a button on the front of the machine. "Nothing too dangerous, mind you. Wouldn't want to accidentally kill one of our star attractions."

He pressed the button and a mild but slightly more than annoying electric shock ran up my leg from a metal cuff I hadn't realized had been there until now. My teeth clamped shut, gnashing against one another in pain. My body shook with the mild dose of electricity until Cyrus released the buzzer.

"I trust that will win your cooperation," Cyrus said, and backed away from the machine.

He studied me. I felt like an animal at the zoo.

"Perhaps we'll need to add a little facial hair to get the look right. A goatee or a Fu Manchu."

"Good to see you're paying attention to the details," I said. Muscles throughout my body twitched.

"You should see the Edward Gorey section I have planned. We've done the whole alphabet, a different death for all our foes."

"I'd love a look around," I said, then rattled my hands

where they were tied, "so if you just want to undo these . . . I promise I'll keep the swami outfit on."

Cyrus came up to the case and started rapping on it.

"We can't have our little Zoltar escaping on us," he said, "not before we have a chance to see our most favorite piece of art brought to life in re-creation."

Mad pirate Cyrus danced his way across the floor and up to the wall where *The Scream* hung. I could hear the sound of Mina pounding on her glass box, no doubt enraged that Cyrus was showing it off. Next to it was a contraption that was waist high and clearly meant to hold a person in it. There was more to the diorama now that had been set up while I was unconscious. There was a torture device set up in the center, a torso-high container riddled with slits, all of which had blades on the outside just waiting to be inserted.

Cyrus stood before the painting, his hand hovering over the lone figure, almost like he wanted to caress it.

"The look on this face, the pure horror, the agony . . . The real artistry here, of course, will be to re-create it as a three-dimensional vision."

Cyrus rapped his knuckles on the top of the Pain-o-Matic machine.

"I'm sure we'll find just the right amount of blades to get the look right on his face," Cyrus said.

"He? He who?"

"Why, the biggest betrayer of them all, of course," Cyrus said. "Thaddeus Wesker. All that time with the Sectarian Defense League and all the while deep cover for the Department of Extraordinary Affairs. He's got a good time coming to him, believe me."

I had no love for the guy, and if there was anyone in the Department who *might* deserve a bit of torture, it was Wesker, but honestly, even I didn't think he guy deserved to be shish-kebabbed.

It looked like Cyrus had really given some sick, twisted

thought to how he would seek his revenge on everyone he
blamed over at the D.E.A. If this weren't the project of a
deranged mind, I would have been even more impressed.
I kicked myself a little for having slept through the seminar "Madmen & Their Master Plans: Downfalls or Das-
tardly?"

Cyrus turned back to *The Scream*, staring deep into the
face of its figure. If he started licking the painting or trying
to tongue-kiss it, I was going to throw up in my little swami
booth.

I sensed movement out on the rest of the exhibit floor.
The chupacabra pair had turned their attention to the
stacked crates over by the entrance to the room from which
Mina had dragged me in. I glanced there and found further
signs of movement, thankful it wasn't the zombies who,
with their master focusing on his art fixation, had gone
slack from lack of command.

A single figure crept into the room. *Jane.*

She was dressed in jeans and a singular T-shirt that
read *"Brrrains . . . "* across the front of it, and carried a
dark tote bag over one shoulder. In the same moment I was
both thrilled and terrified to see her. The odds of her being
torn apart were looking pretty high, all things considered.
I started rocking back and forth in my booth to get her attention.

There was so much spectacle in the room that she didn't
see me at first. Instead, she saw Mina panicking in the glass
coffin and stealthed her way across the floor toward it.

When Jane reached it, she slid along the side farthest
from Cyrus as she examined the glass coffin. Mina saw
her and started screaming directly at her, but thanks to the
vampire-resistant strength of the glass, and being encased
myself, I couldn't make out a word she was saying.

Cyrus, however, heard Mina and turned. Even though
Jane was blocked from his sight by the swirling blood and
Mina's body, it was clear something was up by the particu-
lar way Mina was freaking out in the box. In response,

Cyrus incanted something and the zombies started shuffling toward the glass coffin.

I bent down as far as I could to the holes from which my hands stuck out and pressed my lips against my wrists.

"Jane!" I shouted as loud as I could. "Incoming!"

Jane peeked out from behind the coffin and looked around the room, assessing where my voice had come from. She spied me, her eyes lighting up. Then she noticed the zombies and gave up trying to hide and stepped into plain sight. Cyrus couldn't miss her now, and sure enough he waved his hand and the zombies corrected their course, heading straight for Jane instead of the coffin.

Jane continued to look around. The only thing close to her was the power box for Mina's holding cell. Jane slapped her hand on it before pointing toward me, emitting that piercing electronic noise I had heard first in the Oubliette. Power danced up the length of the box. It arced across the room and up the front of my display case.

Cyrus watched the whole thing with grim fascination but ran for cover, taking only long enough to incant some commands to his zombie minions.

The raw power flowed up my case and shot into the cords around my wrists. I felt electricity touch me and made sure my tongue was out of the way so I wouldn't bite it off.

The power shocked me and the cords around my wrist burst into flames, which would have been fine had I been wearing my gloves. The smell of burning flesh, of *my* flesh, filled the booth, and pain I could do nothing about overtook both my hands. All I could do was wait for the cord to burn enough so that I could snap it, but the pain was intense. Seconds felt like minutes. I viciously tried to pull my hands into the booth in a desperate attempt to free them. The flaming cord snapped the glass between the two holes and my hands were inside the booth, along with the flames. The cheap vest I had been dressed in caught on fire in seconds. I gave another tug at the cord before I felt it snap.

Apart from the reinforced glass front, I noticed that the rest of the case was nothing more than the gutted remains of an actual Zoltar unit. Now that my hands were free and I could get some leverage, it was easy enough to smash through the more flimsy back of it. My jacket lay on the floor nearby, and I scooped it up, throwing it on over my charred outfit.

I looked around for Jane, spotting her near where she had come in, retreating from the swarm of zombies. Mina, on the other hand, was still trapped in her clear glass coffin. As pissed as I was at her, I just couldn't leave her there like that.

I ran across the room and lunged for the case, throwing my weight against it.

"Brace yourself," I shouted, hoping she got the picture even if she couldn't hear me. Apparently she did, and she raised her arms to press out on both sides of the coffin. I ran at it again, rocking it to its tipping point, and it went over from my momentum. I landed hard on the glass, and a fraction of a second later it shattered beneath me and I came down hard on top of Mina. There was a sickening wet swirl of mist around the two of us, and although I had just had the wind knocked out of me, I resisted the urge to take a deep breath. I wanted no part of this creature somehow entering me. I grabbed Mina and rolled the two of us out of it, hoping the vamp would choose flight over fight in this situation. I looked back to see the red cloud pause as if to register us, then dart off toward the roomful of crates.

Mina was out for the count, as far as I could tell. I rolled to a standing position. Cyrus had run for cover, but where was he now? I couldn't see him, but since he was the necromancer controlling these zombies and they were still coming, it meant he was still alive somewhere nearby.

Jane had pulled back to the edge of the crate room and began scaling the towers of boxes. It was a smart move—zombies weren't strong in the climbing department.

I caught up with her and joined her at the top of the

crates, my burnt wrists screaming with pain. I pressed them against my body.

"Sorry," she said. "It was one of the few bits of helpful arcana I know."

"It's okay. I'm fine," I lied. "At least I'm not in that box anymore."

"But, sadly, you're still in that gold swami shirt and it's burnt. It smells like hair on fire."

"What are you doing here?" I said. "How did you find this place?"

"I came here to get you, and I almost had to beat it out of Godfrey," she said with wickedness appearing at the edge of her eyes, "but that man caves real easy. See how having evil tendencies helps sometimes?"

There wasn't really time to argue about the finer points of good and evil right at the moment. We needed to get out of there.

"We're so screwed," Jane said.

"Yeah, well, at least we've got vampires now, so Connor will be happy," I said. "Somehow I take some comfort in that."

"Simon," Jane said, pointing back into the exhibit room.

I turned around. Mina was gone from where I had left her. My eyes shot over to the main wall.

So was *The Scream*.

34

We needed to find a way out of this subterranean madhouse, and if we were lucky, we'd find Mina as well, so Jane and I could recover the painting.

We had to get moving. I looked down into a sea of flailing arms and undead eyes. The zombies couldn't climb, but there were enough of them that they threatened to topple over the already precarious stack of crates.

"You know," Jane said as she tried to keep her balance, "they seemed a lot less scary when they were working in the typing pool at the Sectarian Defense League."

The crate underneath me shifted and I jumped to hers as mine fell away and disappeared into a group of zombies.

"Time to go," I said. Jane nodded and reached for my hand, hitting my wrist by mistake. I yelped.

Jane jumped back, almost toppling over, then started digging through her shoulder bag. "Hold on a second."

"Is that . . . ?"

Jane nodded. "The Greater and Lesser Arcana Welcome Kit, yeah. A little more fashionable than the one you guys have, and easier to wear in the field, too."

Jane pulled out two dirty-looking finger-shaped rolls of bandages and placed one against each of my wrists.

"Mummy Fingers?" I said. I haven't seen them since . . ."

"You found me lying in the alley outside your apartment," Jane dashed out. "Yeah, yeah, yeah. Just hold still."

Magic caressed the area as the bandages uncoiled themselves and proceeded to wrap around each of my wrists. The sensation felt creepy as hell, like a snake slithering against my skin, but when it was done, I could feel the healing, or at least painkillers, kicking in.

"Better?" she asked.

I nodded. "Okay. Let's try our great escape again," I said, and this time I grabbed for her hand first. "Let's go."

I jumped for the next set of crates just as the ones we were standing on toppled over. Leaping from crate to crate, we made our way to the far end of the darkened room. Halfway across the vast expanse, Jane overtook me and started going off in a direction different from the one I thought we should be headed in.

"Uh, Janey?" I said, almost losing my balance as I changed my course. "You sure this is the right way out?"

"Just follow me," she snapped, a little bit of her darkness resurfacing. "We don't have time for that male macho bullshit over directions."

Considering how lost I had been by the time I had found Mina earlier, I shut up and followed. As the end of the room got closer, Jane dove over the edge down to ground level with her blond ponytail streaming out behind her. I followed, landing on my feet, thankfully not needing to use my hands to steady myself.

Jane, however, hadn't landed on her feet. She was lying on the floor, intertwined in a pile of limbs with Mina. *The Scream* stood swaying nearby, precariously balanced on one of the crate corners that threatened to tear through the canvas. Art won out over chivalry and I dashed over to the painting to save it. I guess it showed where my priorities were.

When I turned back to the two of them, Mina was already throwing Jane off of her and getting to her feet. In Mina's hand was my bat, but before she even realized what was going on, Jane snatched it away from her.

"No problem," Mina said, turning her attention to Jane. "I can handle Miss Needs to Dye Her Roots without it."

Jane gave her a pained smile. "Natural blonde here. That red of yours looks straight out of the box."

The low moan of the approaching zombies came from behind me, sounding much closer than I had expected. I turned my attention away from the two women, but not before I saw Jane flip herself up into a standing position from prone on her back.

"Here's the thing, bitch," Jane said, again using harsher language than she normally did. "If you're going to mess with someone like Simon, you want to keep in mind who his friends are . . . and in this case, who his girlfriend is."

It was of some comfort that Jane still thought of us as a couple, despite the past few days.

"Ladies . . ." I started, but I could no longer spread my attention between the oncoming zombies and them. I didn't know which I found scarier—Jane's attitude or the approaching brain munchers. "Jane! Bat! Now!"

She tossed it to me and I caught it, spinning it until I had the handle firmly in one of my hands.

Holding the bat like it was a rapier, I poked several of the approaching zombies back into the others, causing a delay in their advance as they stumbled around. It slowed them, I hoped, to the point where I could deal with only one or two at a time, but I wasn't sure how long I could make that last, with more and more piling up behind them. I caved in the head of the closest one with a noisy squelch and chanced a look over at Mina and Jane.

Mina threw herself toward Jane, but I could see desperation and fear in her wild eyes. Jane, on the other hand, looked pissed off and determined, a look I hoped I never found myself on the receiving end of in our relationship. The two of them fought. Mina had fighting technique on her side, but fear was making her sloppy and Jane was blocking everything Mina threw at her with ease. Even with constant blocking, though, Jane had been pushed back up against the wall, almost smashing her head into a junction box and leaving her with nowhere to go. I had to help her.

Room-temperature fingers raked against my neck and another set dug into my gold shirt, pulling at it until it tore. I spun back around. Three of the zombies had closed in on me, and the one with its fingers on my neck moved in for a bite, its putrid breath hitting me full in the face.

I grabbed the bat tight with both hands and brought it up in a circular swing, hoping to knock away the arms clawing at me. It worked, almost too well. Both of the zombie's arms snapped free and went flying off into the darkness, landing with a wet thud.

"Do . . . not . . . WANT!" I grunted as I started swinging like wild to fight off the squickening sensation of having literally disarmed them. Something slimy dripped down my face but I ignored it in my berserker rage.

Winding up like one of the Yankees, I drove back the closest three with one swipe.

Jane screamed from behind me. I turned back around. Mina had slammed her into the wall, and though hurt from the impact, her eyes were dark with anger.

Mina stopped beating Jane long enough to look over at me. "You like watching a little girl on girl? Or maybe you just like watching me kick your girl's ass . . ."

Despite the look on Jane's face, it was clear she *was* getting her ass kicked now, but what could I do? The zombie hits just kept on coming and I wasn't getting any closer to helping her.

Not that I needed to. Right then, Jane reached her hand out along the wall, coming in contact with the metal junction box she had almost clocked herself on. She opened her mouth to speak, but instead of words, out sprang that sound of a thousand modems dialing for connection, louder than

I had heard it before. Mina's hair started to rise as if charged with static. Then I felt mine do the same. One of the darkened fluorescent tubes blinked to life overhead, glowing brighter than it should have until it shattered as if from a massive overload. Electricity shot from the open sockets and rained down and through both the zombies and Mina, but not channeling through me.

The remaining zombies, as electrified as they were, didn't have the capacity to react to pain, but instead kept coming until something in their wiring cooked to the point that they fell to the floor, smoldering. The smell of burnt hair and charred meat mixed with that of rotting flesh and I gagged.

Mina was screaming bloody murder behind me. Unlike the zombies, she felt everything that was happening to her, and I realized that at this point Jane was actually electrocuting her.

"Jane," I called out. "Stop."

Jane's eyes stayed focused on Mina, but she made no motion to detach herself from the junction box. Sparks were pouring from the ceiling in a cascade around Mina's still-twitching form.

"Jane," I shouted, reaching for her, but stopped short. I hadn't been trained in how technomancy worked. I wasn't sure if I'd electrocute myself in the process or not. Still, I couldn't let Jane kill someone, not while I had a chance to do something about it. I ran between her and Mina, fully passing into the stream of electricity arcing to her.

Although the power only arced into me for a few seconds as I cut across its path, it was like getting kicked hardcore in the breadbasket, except given the intensity of it all, my whole body felt like it *was* the breadbasket getting kicked.

Jane faltered when she saw me take the hit and her one hand dropped from the junction box as she screamed.

The electricity in the air dissipated and the two women both slumped to the floor. Shaking from my jolt, I caught

Jane just before her head hit the ground. Her eyes were open, but they stared ahead, blank and unmoving.

"Jane?" I said, worried. "Come on back to me. We've still got a lot of arguing to get on with in our lives and I can't have it be all one-sided. C'mon now . . ."

I hugged her to me and felt her gasp in a deep breath. She started to sob.

"Where were ya just now?" I said, laughing a little with relief. "You were looking a little Voldemort around the gills there for a minute. We should probably talk about that."

"I'm sorry," Jane said, repeating it over and over, rocking back and forth in my arms as we sat there on the floor. "I couldn't stop myself. I'm sorry . . . I'm sorry . . . I didn't kill her, did I?"

I turned to check on Mina, but was surprised to see she wasn't lying there anymore. And once again *The Scream* was gone also.

"I think she's going to be just fine," I said.

35

The sun was just starting to set as the two of us, shaken, exited through the back-alley door that had led to the underground section of the Guggenheim. I was having trouble just walking. With so much raw electricity in that last blast, I was kitten-weak and had to rely on Jane to help me walk, making this quite possibly the slowest escape ever.

"I think we need to call downtown and let the Department in on what happened here today," I said. "Connor's going to go ballistic, but at least I can report that I wasn't wholly wrong about there being vampires, or rather *a* vampire, in New York City. That should ease a little of the tension between the two of us."

I reached for my cell phone in the inside pocket of my jacket, but when I pulled it out, it was melted, the same as the last one.

"Fuck," I said, dropping it. The now-hardened plastic blob of my ex-phone shattered as it hit the sidewalk.

"Use mine," Jane said. She reached into her pocket, but

hers had also melted. "Looks like we'll have to tell the Department in person."

"Just let me catch my breath for a second," I said. "Okay?"

Jane nodded and led me to safety across Fifth Avenue, headed for one of the entrances to Central Park. I thought about Connor's warning about the park at dark, recalling the odd lights I had seen while running through the trees. It took all of my remaining strength to plant my feet firmly on the ground to stop Jane from walking me into the park.

"Simon?" she said, still looking a little evil around the gills. "What the hell?"

"I'm not going in there," I said. "There's just too many paranormal thingies in there, stuff that I don't want to encounter in this state, thank you very much. Strange lights in the forest, bronze attack crabs, ghost scientists . . ."

"Suit yourself," Jane said. Her voice was short, and with little gentility she dropped me onto a bench along the exterior wall of the park. "You'll have to tell me all about those sometime."

I hissed in a breath of air from the impact of my body on the bench. Jane started walking off.

"Jane," I shouted. "Where are you going?"

She stopped, but didn't turn around.

"I have to go," she said, her voice cracking and uneven.

"You're just going to leave me here?" I said, incredulous.

Jane spun around, a conflicted look on her face.

"Do you want to end up dead?" she said. "Did you not see me in there? Then let me go. I almost killed you. I almost killed both of us."

I waved her over and patted the empty spot on the bench next to me. With some reluctance, Jane came over and sat down.

"You were trying to save me and yourself. You were fighting for your life."

"I'm so not used to that sort of thing from my days working for the Sectarian Defense League," Jane said. "We had minions to do our fighting for us."

"Yeah, well, doing good means that you have to get your hands a little dirtier and not put other people in harm's way as much."

Jane shook her head. "I don't think that was good I was doing," she said, very somber. "I was out of control. I tried something like that before when I barely even knew what technomancy was, and all it caused was little more than an electric spark."

"Well, that one was a lot more than a spark, Jane," I said, holding up my wrists. The Mummy Fingers that had been wrapped around them were crisped up from the last blast of her power. When I flexed my hands, what remained of the bandages crackled apart and fell to the sidewalk in a shower of burnt flakes.

"I know," she said. "I've just been feeling strange lately."

"How?"

"All this misguided jealousy of yours and the fights we've been having . . . When I've been working in the Black Stacks in the bookstore, it feels like somehow the books have been talking to me, whispering about all my fears. Then when I showed up and saw Mina there with you, something snapped inside me. It's like all of it just fed into that spell I cast. I was electrocuting her and I couldn't stop myself. The horrible part is that I didn't want to."

"You *have* been acting a little season-six Willow on me lately," I said, hoping to lessen the gravity of her words.

Jane's mood didn't lighten.

"I almost killed her," she said, "and you."

"But you *didn't*," I said. "That's the difference."

"What's wrong with me?" she said. She balled her fists up and started pounding them on her knees. "Is this what I left Kansas for? To become this?"

"There's nothing wrong with you," I said, taking her

hands in mine. "Nothing that can't be handled with a little time off from the Black Stacks, anyway. There's a lot we don't know about them, and from what you just said, I don't think they play fair when they have access to someone nice like you. If there's anything wrong, it's with us, our relationship, but I want to fix that."

Jane nodded, unable to speak. I pulled her to me and hugged her while people passed us by, staring. I didn't care.

When Jane finally pulled away, she spoke. "Simon, I hate that I even have to say this so bluntly, but it should be pretty obvious by now. I'm not interested in Thaddeus Wesker. He's my boss. That's it."

I stiffened a little at the change in conversation.

"But the night you met Mina, she said you acted like you had something of your own to hide. She had me convinced that maybe something *was* going on."

"She was *playing you*, Simon," Jane said, putting her hand on my forehead in the universal symbol of *duh*. "The reason I didn't start acting all jealous was because I'm not clingy like that and I *trust you*. God knows why, given all this . . ."

I welcomed the coolness of Jane's hand against my forehead. Just her touch was enough to calm me. After several seconds that I wished could have lasted forever, Jane pulled her hand off my head and stood, then paced away before turning back to me. Her face was too calm.

"I don't know what you want me to make of all this, Simon," Jane said, her voice a whisper. "I really don't."

"What does that mean?"

"You get all jealous because I'm around Director Wesker, you know, just doing my job, when *I'm* the one who has every right to be jealous."

"Of what?"

Jane looked at me, tears finally forming at the corners of her eyes and she shook her head at me.

"Of Mina, you idiot," she said, her voice cracking. Tears

started flowing down her face. "Are you really that dense? Your little hot redheaded friend shows up in town and suddenly you start acting funny: sneaking around, picking fights with me, and just the other night you actually hung up on me when I clearly heard her in the background. How do you think all that makes a girl feel?"

"There were zombies coming! I had to hang up!" I said, hoping that covered any further need for explanation.

"But why couldn't you tell me that?" Jane shouted, her face a mask of disbelief. "If anyone in this town would have understood zombies as an explanation, don't you think it would be me? For heaven's sake, did you forget that I used to temp around dozens of them?"

"I wasn't keeping it from you because there was something going on with Mina," I said. "I mean, there was something going on, but not anything pervy between the two of us."

Jane gave me a give-me-a-break kind of look. If the roles were reversed, would I have believed *her* right away if a hot male friend of Jane's showed up in town and she started acting funny? Probably not.

"Look," I said, taking my time and trying to be clear. "Mina's from a part of my past, a part I'm not terribly proud of. When she showed up out of nowhere, I didn't know what to do. It looked like all she wanted was my help with something and then she'd be back out of my life for good. I didn't want her to know anything about my life now, because Mina's the type of person who'd taint it, who'd use it to her advantage if she could. So I tried to hide all the great things in my life from her . . . namely you, Jane. I figured if I just did what she asked before she caused any real trouble, I'd be done with her."

Jane softened and then gave a wry smile. "Well, *that* really seems to have worked out for you."

I nodded, smiling back. "I forgot that no matter what, Mina has a way of corrupting things," I said. "I'm sorry it took near death and zombies to bring it out. I'm sorry I didn't come clean sooner."

"Maybe I have been spending a little too much time with Wesker," Jane offered, "and the Stacks. Probably not the best idea to be working there right now until I learn to control my deep-frying."

"Why don't you talk to the Enchancellors about reassigning you," I said, "for now? At least until you get more control over your technomancy."

Jane nodded in acceptance and I felt a tremendous weight lift off my shoulders.

"So what about us?" she asked.

I thought about it a minute before I said anything. It was too important to just rush into an answer. "Honestly, I think we make shitty single people, and I think when you suggested some time apart, it was the worst idea you've ever had," I said.

Jane looked surprised. "Really?"

"Really," I said, nodding. "I think we should be closer, more open and honest. I know I don't have a lot of experience with that or with relationships that last more than a few weeks, but I know I want to work on it with you. Look how we both get when we're apart. I make stupid mistakes that get me captured by Cyrus and Mina, and you get all Black Magic Woman."

"We balance each other out," Jane said. "I like the sound of that."

"It's very Zen of us," I said. "We're cool like that."

"Look," Jane said. "I don't know if we're really good together at this point."

"We are—" I started to say, but she stopped me.

"*But* I do know that with all these outside influences tugging at us, if we keep ourselves together as a core, we'll be okay."

I pulled her close to me again, and this time I kissed her. A shock of electricity jumped between us as we touched, and she jumped, laughing nervously through the kiss.

"So, what now?" she said when we pulled apart. "Back to the Department?"

I nodded.

Jane got up to hail a cab, but my ear caught a distant but familiar sound and I stopped her.

"Easy," I said, making a pained effort to stand. My body ached with the events of the last hour. "I'm in no condition to rush, and I doubt Cyrus will come out of hiding to pack that freak show up before we get back here with the cavalry."

"True enough," she said. "What do you suggest?"

"Well," I said, "I'd love nothing more than to go home and catch a Buffy marathon, but let's face it: the paperwork for both of us on this incident is already filling me with dread. I think we should treat ourselves to a little us time while heading back downtown."

The familiar sound was closer now and Jane heard it, too. She turned toward the clip-clop of a horse as one of the carriages from Central Park approached.

Her eyes lit up.

"I do believe there's hope for quelling the dark bits in you yet," I said, and fished out my wallet. "Seems like not everything got destroyed in our encounter."

The carriage pulled up beside us. The driver didn't even bat an eye when he saw me, beaten, bruised, and half-charred. All he seemed to see was my wallet.

I helped Jane into the carriage before hoisting myself up, my bones popping and creaking.

"This carriage smells like burnt food," I whispered in Jane's ear.

She laughed quietly.

"That would be you, actually."

"Right," I said. "Just for that, I'm going to expense this to your department."

The sun was setting over the trees somewhere far over on the west side, I had my girl by my side, and a slow ride down to the Village to look forward to. It would have been a perfectly romantic night, if it hadn't been for Mina, the vampire, the toasted zombies, the electrocution, and the return of the old cultist leader spoiling it all.

36

I awoke to the incessant poking of the carriage driver jabbing at my shoulder. Jane was asleep also, curled up under my arm. I woke her and lowered her to the street, tipped the driver handsomely, and struggled off the carriage. As the sound of hooves faded off into the distance, Jane and I headed into the Lovecraft Café, drawing stares.

"Do I really look that bad?" I asked her.

"Your jacket is still smoking," she said, "and yeah, you do kinda look like hell."

We arrived at the door at the back of the theater that led to the offices, and I stopped. "Maybe you should go in first."

"Why?" she asked.

"If I go in ahead of you and they see me first, they might think there's a zombie infestation."

Jane reached over and ruffled her fingers through my hair, which I only then realized was standing on end, full of static. "Smart boy," she said.

She swiped her plastic keycard at the door and we entered the main bull pen of the Department. A few of my fellow agents eyed me with suspicion, but none of them got up to cave my skull in.

I turned to Jane and hugged her.

"You should go talk to Wesker. Tell him what's going on, find out if he knows anything about this. Cyrus did collaborate with the Sectarians, so maybe Wesker's heard something, even though he's high on their artistic-torture list. I have to go deal with Connor."

"Don't let him punish you too bad," she said. "That's my job." She winked.

Jane started off toward one of the doors that led off to Greater & Lesser Arcana Division.

"I'm holding you to that," I called out after her, feeling the first bit of real hope I had felt in several days. After taking a moment to let it sink in, I headed back toward the set of desks I shared with Connor.

I expected him to still be pissed at me but when he looked up at my approach, his eyes widened like those of an anime character.

"Jesus, kid, what happened to you?" he said.

I explained what had gone on from the moment I had discovered Mina searching through the museum crates to Jane and me finally escaping. I did, however, leave out taking Godfrey with me. When I was done telling him *almost* everything, Connor seemed less concerned and shrugged.

"I guess that's what you get," he said, and turned to his phone. "I'll call the Inspectre and get a containment team to secure the scene."

I stared at him. "I'm sorry?"

"Did I stutter, kid?" he said, not looking back. "I said I guess that's what you get."

"I heard you, but what are *you* getting at?"

Connor turned back to me, slamming the phone down. "Answer me this," he said. "A simple question: How did you know how to look beneath the Guggenheim?"

"What?"

"Well, you couldn't have been just meandering the streets of Manhattan and gotten lucky. I'd like to know what clued you in so you knew to go straight to the Guggenheim?"

I paused as I thought how best to answer him. I really didn't want to get Godfrey in trouble, and I certainly didn't want to get myself in it either. Things were already strained enough.

"It was the map," I said, fishing the crumpled and smoky piece of paper from the pocket inside my jacket. I pointed at the dots I had connected earlier with Godfrey's help. "When I charted out the path from the massacre on the booze cruise to the death of Dr. Kolb, I simply followed the trajectory. It led straight in that direction, toward the Guge, and I guess I got lucky finding the door."

"I see," he said.

I peeled my jacket off, careful to avoid rubbing it against my burnt wrists, and put it over the back of my chair. It had finally stopped smoking. I lowered myself at a snail's pace and tried to collect my thoughts, only to have them interrupted.

"So Godfrey Candella has nothing to do with this?" Connor said.

"Argh," I moaned. "I told him not to tell you."

"Yeah, well, he doesn't do deception quite the way you do," Connor said. "The second he left the art museum, he came back here and info-dumped it all on me."

Once again, I felt trapped. "I would have found the place eventually without him," I said in my defense. "He just sped up the process."

"Do you have any idea how screwed you'll be if any one of the Enchancellors finds out about you putting an archivist in the line of danger out in the field? On top of what you already did at MoMA with this mysterious Mina of yours? The whole point of having archivists is to keep them out of harm's way so that our records don't come into question."

"You should have seen him," I said. "He was so excited to be out in the field."

"That may be, but this isn't a free-for-all here, kid," Connor said. "There are rules for a reason."

"But as part of F.O.G.," I said, "I work outside of—"

"Stop hiding behind the goddamned F.O.G. excuse," he said. "Even if you are one of their chosen few, that doesn't put everyone in this place at your disposal."

Connor stood up and headed off toward the stairs.

"Where are you going?"

"To talk to Inspectre Quimbley in person," he said, and I felt my heart leap to my throat.

"Don't."

Connor looked back and sighed. "Don't worry, kid. I'm not going to rat you out, although I should."

"You're not?"

"No," Connor said. "There are bigger things on our plate than getting into a pissing contest with you over this. I mean, look at you . . . You're burnt, your wrists are gross, and your hair . . . Well, I probably won't be able to watch *Edward Scissorhands* ever again without thinking of you."

"Then why'd you get so pissed at me?"

"I don't feel like breaking in another partner," he said. "Even as dumb as you are sometimes. Besides, you look like you've suffered enough for one night."

"Well, thanks," I said, feeling all warm and fuzzy but kind of confused.

"Don't get too comfy there. The night's not over yet. Get yourself cleaned up while I tell the Inspectre about this, minus some of the details."

Connor started walking off.

"Oh," I said, "I almost forgot. You'll be thrilled to hear that there may actually be vampires involved. I'm pretty sure I ran into one this time, no question."

Connor sighed, shook his head, and pointed over toward the incident sign. I started heading for the ladder.

"We're gonna discuss protocol when we're done with all this," he said. "If we live through it all, of course."

Returning to the scene of Para-lyzed felt much safer with half of the Department crawling all over the subterranean exhibit. A change of clothes and new wrapping on my wrists had also helped to change my spirits for the better. The smell of roasted zombies, however, did not.

The investigation was already in full swing by the time Connor and I got there, and I was surprised when Wesker appeared from behind a stack of crates with three familiar faces in tow.

"Well, well, well," Connor said. "If it isn't the Illinois gypsies."

The Brothers Heron looked somewhat panicked. Marten was in yet another hideous tweed suit and Lanford looked a little more sickly than usual—the result of being on the run, I guess. Julius looked just as healthy and robust as ever, towering over us all.

"Returning to the scene of the crime, eh?" I said. "Or just a follow-up sales call?"

Marten shook his head. "Sorry we had to run out on you at the convention," he said, all manners now, "but the look on your face told us you weren't willing to be reasonable."

"You're right," I said. "I wasn't willing to be. Not much has changed on that front."

"He said he was sorry," Julius's voice boomed out.

Wesker stepped out from behind them. "I caught these three attempting to liberate those two chupacabras from one of the glass cases where they were being stored. It looked like some sort of art exhibit in progress, but damned if I could tell what Cyrus was going to do with them."

"Something that tied in to Will Wegman," I said. Everyone turned to stare at me. "Hey, I don't know what the hell that means; it's just what he said."

Marten nodded. "We tracked them here after Lanford followed you to the park to where that unfortunate jogger met his demise," he said. "If we had any idea that splitting them up would have caused such a string of tragedies, believe me, we never would have sold one of them to that guy dressed as an undead pirate in the first place."

"Your sincerity is underwhelming," Connor fired back. "You were still trafficking paranormal livestock. That's a crime in the tristate area."

"How could you even think to bring something so heinous into this city?" I asked.

Marten looked shocked, like I had slapped him in the face.

"What did we do wrong?" Lanford asked, turning to Julius.

"Heinous?" Marten said, talking to me directly now. "How can you say that? Would you say the same thing about a shark for simply doing what it was meant to do?"

"I say," the Inspectre's voice called out. "Is that the analogy you're going with?" He was standing by the entrance to the exhibit proper, but came over to join the conversation. "When a shark attacks a person, it's only when we've entered its natural environment. Last I checked, gentlemen, the chupacabra is not native to New York City. It's an introduced creature, and as the introducers, you are accountable for its crimes."

Marten looked at me strangely, squinting not just at me but into me.

"Stop that," I said, feeling uncomfortable. "What are you doing?"

"I see the curse wore off," he said. He looked concerned. "So soon. I didn't expect that."

"Yeah, well, you'd be surprised what a little bit of panic does to help a guy take charge of his life again," I said. "So how are you involved with Cyrus, exactly?"

"I take it he's the pirate-looking gentleman?" Marten said.

"I think 'gentleman' is too kind a word for him," I said, "but yes."

"Wait," Connor said. "You're telling me you didn't even know the name of a person you were selling those . . . those . . . *things* to?"

Marten gave a sheepish grin. "In our business, it's sometimes better if we don't ask too many questions. Not if we want to make enough to support our little clan back in Illinois."

"How very familial of you," Connor said, "but where you're headed, I think they're going to have to fend for themselves for a while."

"I'm afraid that won't be happening," said Marten, and he flourished his arms in a grandiose and arcane gesture. Lanford and Julius joined in, too. I braced myself for whatever was about to happen.

But when the gesturing stopped there was nothing but silence and the three of them still standing there.

Lanford looked at both of his hands, then turned to his shorter, balding brother.

"Marten . . . ?"

Director Wesker stepped toward them. "Did you really think that when we found this little exhibit, we would be stupid enough to just let you run rampant with your feeble brand of folk magic? The first thing any agent of Greater and Lesser Arcana worth his salt does is create a nullification field."

I was impressed, despite all my recent misgivings about the man.

Connor stepped forward and got in Marten's face. "I'll ask you again," Connor said. "How do you know Cyrus?"

All the life and theatrics fell from Marten's face. Now he just looked like a tired, middle-aged man with a failing head of hair and a paunch.

"We had never met before," he said with a slow shake of his head, "and until you told us his name, we had no idea who he was."

Connor kicked one of the nearby crates and stormed off. I followed him as Wesker dragged the gypsies away.

Connor moved from the crowd and sat down on top of one of the crates. I hoisted myself up onto the one next to him.

"So these guys are useless to us," I said.

Connor nodded. "Other than getting them off the street for being a menace all their own, I don't think they can help us out."

"There's got to be something here in all this evidence around us to help," I said. "Something that will give us some kind of clue as to just what the hell Cyrus has been up to these past few months."

"You said your friend Mina was caught up in all this?" Connor said, perking up.

"I wouldn't exactly call her a friend," I said. "More of an old psychopath I used to work with. One that had been serving time in the same facility as—"

"Faisal Bane," Connor said, getting up from the crate he was on. He headed off past the Inspectre in the direction of the little colored candy trail that led back to the exit. Connor already had his phone out and was dialing. "Thaniel Graydon, please."

The name sounded vaguely familiar, but I couldn't remember why. After the day I had been through, though, I was surprised I could remember my own name. I limped off after him.

37

"Since when do you own a boat?" Connor said as we walked down one of the west side docks toward the silhouette of a thirty-foot motorboat. Empty, it looked like a creepy little ghost ship. I expected to see spectral figures floating around inside the small cabin on its deck, but was relieved to see nothing of the sort.

"Well," I said, "technically I don't own a boat, but the Fraternal Order of Goodness does. You said you needed one, so I got us one."

"And if I said I needed a supermodel?" Connor said. He undid the knot cleating the boat to the dock without an ounce of difficulty.

"I'd have to check the supply room for one of those," I said.

Connor crossed down to the far end of the boat, undid the cleat there, and stepped onto the deck with one foot while pushing it away from the dock with the other.

He waved to me like he was leaving on the *Love Boat.* "You coming, kid?"

I hesitated as the boat floated away, but jumped over onto it before the gap spread too wide.

"I take it you've done this before?" I said, searching for the ladder leading up to the steering on top of the darkened cabin. "'Cause I don't know how to drive one of these things . . ."

"A couple of times," Connor said. "Not with this boat, mind you. I usually had to rent one, then expense it and wait to be reimbursed months later. Nice of you to save me the trouble this time. Maybe you F.O.G.gies aren't worthless after all."

I found the ladder and climbed up. I fished out the keys the Inspectre had given me and moved to the controls, but Connor held his hand out. "Keys, kid."

I gave them over and Connor fired up the boat, leaving only the bare minimum of running lights on. He pulled away from the dock and out into the Hudson River at a good speed, heading north. "Boating isn't that hard," he confided. "The secret is not to hit the land or other boats."

A fine mist rose around us as we sped toward the distant lit-up structure of the George Washington Bridge. I rode along for several minutes in silence, simply enjoying the disconnect from the city and the feel of the open water, but eventually my curiosity got the better of me.

"You want to tell me who this Thaniel Graydon is now?" I asked.

"Not who," Connor shouted over the sound of the engine, "*what*."

"Sorry," I said. "It sounded like a proper name."

"It is, or rather was. You should know him; he's part of your old-boys network. Thaniel Graydon was a F.O.G.gie. What I know about him is limited to his involvement with the early years of the D.E.A., but I think he had something to do with one of our founding fathers being a necromancer."

This all felt oddly familiar, and then it hit me. "Benjamin Franklin," I said.

Connor turned and looked at me. "How do you know that?"

"I think I *was* Thaniel Graydon," I said. "For only for a few seconds. Back when we were working on Irene's case, I accidentally triggered off this book that Wesker was carrying around and I got the most horrific flashes of this rotting creature . . ."

I shuddered, not sure if it was from the cold on the water or the ancient necromancer's image that once again filled my head. "So I doubt we're going to see someone well over two hundred years old," I said. "Umm . . . are we?"

"Given our chosen profession, it isn't out of the realm of possibility, I suppose," Connor said.

"True," I admitted, "but where are we going?"

"The Thaniel Graydon Center is a special annex to the Rikers Island facility."

"Rikers?" I said, confused. "Isn't that in the East River, closer to Queens? We're going to have to circle Manhattan. Not that I mind. It's a nice night and all . . ."

"Rikers Island *is* in the East River, yes," Connor said, "but the Thaniel Graydon Center isn't attached to it. It's free-floating. It's a prison barge where they keep a lot of their special cases."

Connor took one hand from the wheel and pointed forward at a speck that looked like a giant, floating Lego that grew larger with every second we sped toward it.

I wondered if this was the prison where Mina had first heard my name again and met Faisal. Although she possessed no special powers that I knew of, she definitely qualified as "special" in a lot of ways, and given her somewhat dangerous and erratic behavior, she had probably earned a quick place within the prison community.

Up close, the barge was impressive, a miniature four-story city crammed onto the deck of an immense boat. Blocky white buildings were guarded by tall searchlight towers at the four corners of the barge. Even if you were able to escape the confines of your cell and avoid the lights, there was still the open water to contend with. It seemed a perfect place to house someone like Faisal Bane.

A searchlight picked up our approach and we docked. Men bearing shotguns came from a small workstation hut to help us board, and without a moment's hesitation checked our Departmental IDs. Not much for small talk, two of them escorted us to one of the larger buildings on deck before turning us over to a single officer, also not terribly talkative. He signed us in to a large room filled with rows of tables and benches.

"Looks like a slow night for visitors," I said to Connor. The guard laughed.

"These aren't the type of people who get visitors," he said, speaking up for the first time, "and if they do, they come in ones or twos, usually late at night." He thought about this for a moment. "Kind of like you two," he continued, sounding almost philosophical. The guard held his hand out, and I wondered if I was supposed to tip him. As I reached for my wallet, Connor reached into the pocket of his trench coat and pulled out a folded piece of paper.

The guard snatched it from him and looked down at what was written there. His eyes widened.

"This one might take me a while," he said. He reached up and pressed the button on his communication device. "We're going to need three men to Level C. I repeat, three to Level C. Make that four . . . and dress for a mess."

He folded the paper back up, handed it to Connor. "You two wait here," he said, then started off toward another door at the far end of the room. He rapped on it, and then there was a short buzz. He let himself out before slamming it back shut.

"'You two wait here'?" I said. "Where the hell does he think we would go?"

While Connor and I waited, the clanging and buzzing of doors opening got closer and closer until the door nearest us buzzed. It slid aside to reveal the imposing figure of Faisal Bane strapped to a tall cart with wheels on it. He was in a straightjacket with his arms lashed around him, and tight straps ran up and down the length of his outfit. The only part of him exposed was his head of dark hair. His sharp European features were a little more drawn out than usual, bordering on the side of sickly. Incarceration wasn't treating him well, even though his face was a stone mask of indifference as the guards wheeled him into the room and deposited him in front of us.

The sway of the barge caught all of them off balance, and the cart Faisal was on tipped forward, putting him in danger of slamming down on his face with no way to break his fall. All five men strained to upright the cart and luckily stopped it before it fell all the way over. They set it firmly on the ground and backed away from it with caution.

"Jesus," I said. "Do you keep him all Hannibaled up like this all the time?"

The guard shook his head.

"Why do you think it took me so long?" he said, with a laugh. "Nah, we usually let the prisoners roam free among themselves . . . No one really cares if one prisoner goes after another out here, you know? But, well, we can't really have him running free around you outties."

I refrained from joking that I was an innie and instead gave a respectful nod. This seemed to satisfy the guard. He walked over to Faisal and looked him in the eyes. Faisal stared back at him, impassive.

"Now, I'm gonna be right over there," he said, pointing to an enclosed surveillance room with windows along one wall, "while you conversate with your little friends here. You do or say anything out of line and we're gonna have a problem. You know, the kind of problem that only a stun baton can solve. Alright?"

There was no reaction from Faisal whatsoever, unless you counted blinking.

The guard and his four companions headed off toward the surveillance room, talking amongst themselves, their laughter giving me the creeps as it echoed in this dreary and depressing place.

"Hello, Faisal," Connor said. "Not quite as nice as your old office at the Empire State Building, is it?"

Faisal ignored Connor the same way he ignored the guard, choosing to change his stare to me. "I wondered when you might show up," he said, the traces of something Slavic running through his accent.

Seeing Faisal again brought back all the fear and intimidation I had felt when we first met, but there was a new fire of hate in his eyes. And why not? I had driven Jane to betray him, depriving him of her. Thanks to Wesker, we had even thwarted his assassination attempt on her with his corporate "headhunter."

"I get the impression you're not too excited to see me," I said.

"Relax, kid," Connor said. "I doubt he's ever excited to see anybody."

This seemed to grab Faisal's attention, and he finally looked at Connor.

"Oh, no," Faisal said. "On the contrary. I'm quite thrilled to see Mr. Canderous."

"Why's that?" I asked.

"Because it means you've been in contact with your little crimson-haired friend, doesn't it?"

My face went red when he said it.

"Is that Mina?" Connor asked, quietly. "I thought she was a blonde on the surveillance tapes from MoMA?"

"So was I, if you remember," I said. "But she's actually a redhead. Dye job."

"What's this?" Faisal said, smiling now. "Sounds like Connor's a little out of the loop. You haven't told your partner all about your little blast from the past? Is this lack of trust some new part of defining your precious 'goodness' that I'm not aware of?"

"I can explain more about Mina later," I said, glancing at Connor.

Connor had been leaning back against one of the tables. Out of nowhere he stood up and lunged for Faisal. It was uncharacteristic of him and it freaked me out. I grabbed a piece of the tail of his trench coat before he could make it across the table, hoping it would hold. I pulled him back toward me.

"Connor! What are you doing? Stop it."

Connor continued to struggle, trying to strip himself out of his coat to get free.

"Why, kid?" he said, one arm free. "So assholes like him can continue to work people like you over with their lies? Forcing you to make stupid choices, jeopardizing other agents . . ."

"He's baiting you," I yelled, but Connor wouldn't stop struggling, and my arms were getting tired. I let go of him and slapped him across the face.

Before I could pull away, the electric snap of my powers reaching out shocked me. In the anger and desperation of the moment, I forgot how easy it was to lose control of them when my blood was up. I tried to pull the power back into me, but it was no use. I caught the briefest of glimpses into Connor's life. In my vision, Connor was in his apartment, reading that invisible letter again, this time through tear-filled eyes. The momentum of my slap broke the connection between the two of us and I was back on the prison boat, slightly disoriented.

"You okay, kid?" Connor said, looking shocked as well. "What the hell just happened?"

"Nothing," I lied. "My power almost went off, but I stopped it in time."

"Sorry to interrupt your little slap fight," Faisal said, "but did you come here for some sort of purpose?"

It was my turn to ignore him for a change.

"He's baiting you," I said to Connor again. "Outside of being pure evil, the guy is all about the head games. If you want to be mad at someone for the stupid choices I've made or for the things I've kept from you, then be mad at me."

Connor looked like he was shaking it off. "The student becomes the master, grasshopper. You're right, kid. I know that. I never would have snapped, but this whole situation has my mind messed up."

I stood there in silence for a moment.

"Can I get in on this Hallmark TV moment, too?" Faisal said, and now there was real venom in his voice and frustration. His attempt at toying with us had failed him. When we didn't rise to it once again, he said, "I'll assume you're not here simply because you miss my winning personality?"

"Finally something we can agree on," Connor said. "Kid?"

I recounted the mad state I had found Cyrus in below the Guggenheim, how creepy and phantomlike he had become . . . all this on top of being a cultist.

When I was done, all humor had left Faisal's face.

"I hadn't realized Cyrus had gone this far off the deep end," he said. "It's bad for business."

"I'm surprised you care," Connor said. "I thought you two were together on this one. I'd think this type of fucked-up scheme would be right up your alley."

"Not when it interferes with my grander schemes, it isn't."

I raised my eyebrows.

"*Your* schemes?" I said. "You want to elaborate on that?"

Faisal smiled. "I'd rather not."

"Fine," I said. I looked at Connor. "This is getting us nowhere." I started walking off toward the guards in their surveillance room. It looked like they were playing cards.

But the sound of Faisal's voice stopped me in my tracks. "I hate being on this barge," Faisal said loudly. I detected a hint of desperation in his voice.

"What's the matter?" I called over my shoulder. "Incarceration not as fun as you expected?"

"Being cast adrift at sea is hardly fitting for a man of my stature," Faisal said. "That, and I get a bit seasick. The once and future master of evil, and a little boat rocking does me in. There's some irony for you."

I stopped and turned back to him.

"You know, I had thought my Ghostsniffing operation had been where the real money was, but it wasn't. It's in government. Did you know that this floating prison was built at a cost of one hundred and seventy million dollars? You wouldn't know it by the looks of it. But that kind of money . . . that's enough to put every last inmate here through Harvard, easily. They built this nausea-inducing place to handle the overcrowding of the regular Rikers facility, but, oh, what I wouldn't give to be serving my time on dry land."

I could hear the false sense of melodrama in Faisal's voice. Connor glanced at me and I read the look in his eyes. This might be the only chance we were going to get for any real information. I walked back over to the two of them.

"Do you know what I miss most about the mainland?" Faisal said. "The comforts of home. There's nothing here. At least Rikers Island has educational facilities, medical clinics, ball fields, chapels, workout equipment, grocery stores, a decent barber, a bakery, a laundromat, its own power plant, a runner's track, a tailor shop, a print shop, even a car wash. Amenities. The little things that make life livable . . . you know, things befitting a man of my stature."

"Why don't you paint us a little picture, then?" I asked. "I'm sure we can arrange a transfer or something, depending on how valuable what you have to say is. That *is* why you gave us your little laundry list, isn't it?"

Faisal remained silent.

"But let's make one thing clear," Connor added. "You're not getting free. We can put in a good word for you with the administration, but you'll still be serving your time, either here or there."

"I wouldn't *dream* of trying to escape," Faisal said with mock sincerity. He smiled. "Okay, well, maybe I would dream of trying to escape, but I would never try it." He sighed. "Very well," he said. "Where to begin?"

"If you say 'at the beginning, a very good place to start' or start singing *The Sound of Music*, I'm going to have them put you in solitary," I said.

He thought for a moment, then turned to Connor.

"You know what I love about your new recruits? The naiveté."

"Meaning what, exactly?" I asked. I snapped my fingers to get his attention back to me.

"Here I am, in jail . . ."

"We caught you," I interrupted. "We put you out of business."

"Oh, yes," Faisal said, smiling like the cat that got the canary. "I forgot. Of course you did. That's what I'm talking about. Here I am, in jail, and you think because I'm on this floating hellhole that you've put me out of the evil business?"

"What is Cyrus up to?"

Faisal's eyes narrowed and he stared at me. "When you crashed our party at the museum, literally, you merely set back the course of the Sectarian cause. You didn't stop it. Yes, you put me in here, but you forget Cyrus was the one who had been heading up the Surrealist Underground, the other, more artistic arm of our fund-raising. And he's the one that got away. He's been running things on the outside. I didn't know about all this necromancy of his, though. I'm pleased to hear he's taken up a hobby."

I ignored Faisal's happiness about Cyrus's Zombie-palooza. "So this whole Para-lyzed thing is just an extension of your original plan?" I asked.

"A reboot of sorts," Faisal said. "It was Cyrus's idea to go with this more artistic/sadistic route where art would turn into revenge against our enemies, all at a profit to our evil little patrons. That all seemed a bit over the top to me. I'm more subtle. But once I met your old friend Mina in here and saw how obsessed she was with you, well, I couldn't help but get on the vengeance bandwagon. I had told Cyrus to have you killed *after* you had helped Mina with the heist, not before. Apparently, in his demented state, he couldn't wait to try, could he?"

"Meaning what?" I asked.

"The Oubliette," Faisal said. "When he told me he had sabotaged it, I was furious. Still, I would have thought Mina could have finished the job. Very disappointing."

"I'm glad to see that I can bring like-minded psychos together," I said, glum.

"Cheer up," Faisal said. "You're still alive, aren't you? Despite my best efforts. If anyone's got a reason to be depressed, it's me. Seems you can't send a homicidal redhead off to do a man's work these days. So much for equal opportunity."

"Even with her freedom at stake, Mina couldn't make herself kill me for you," I said with pride, even though I could still feel the ache in my jaw from my last pistol-whipping.

"Cyrus and Mina were only the beginning. I'll have every cultist at my disposal gunning for you. Only a matter of time before someone gets to you, my boy," Faisal said. "Only a matter of time."

"Could we stick to the madness at hand?" Connor said. "You were saying how Cyrus's plan didn't really jive with your worldview or something."

Faisal nodded. "I understand what goes in to turning a person to our purpose, and that type of thing takes time and subtlety. I know the wheels of change are going to grind slowly for the world to fully embrace evil openly, but Cyrus is out there, and being in here, my choices on how we went about what's best for the Sectarians in the long run were somewhat limited. So I encouraged Cyrus to go forward with Para-lyzed. All that mattered was that it would raise cultist-rights awareness and keep revenue coming in while I planned out what to do next."

"But we've put a stop to that," I said. "Cyrus knows we're on to his little paranormal freak show. He won't dare return there. That phase is over. So the real question is: Do you have any idea where we can find Cyrus *now*?"

"You could ask a little nicer," Faisal said. "You catch more flies with honey . . ."

Faisal went quiet for several minutes and the two of us waited him out.

"Let me get this straight," he said. "First, you took away the Sectarian Defense League, which I had worked so hard to build . . ."

"On the blood of others," Connor added, but Faisal just kept talking.

"Then you took away my freedom by incarcerating me, and you took away my right-hand woman, Jane . . . I've given you the bulk of our plans, and you're still not satisfied?"

"Not without handing us Cyrus," Connor said. "With the art show shut down, we would have figured out most of what you've told us once we went through all the evidence. All you've done so far is save us some time. I hardly think that's grounds for transfer."

Faisal looked pained.

"Well, there was one thing Cyrus had been talking about," Faisal offered, "but I can't promise you it will lead to anything. Either way, I want your word that you'll attempt to get me transferred. My word may be sketchy, but I know you do-gooders. You keep to what you say."

"Help us out," I said. The idea that there might be something out there larger than this Para-lyzed madness filled me with a sense of dread. "I promise we'll do what we can."

"I'd also like to be clear on something here," he said, "because I do have a reputation to uphold. I'm only telling you this because if Cyrus does what I think he's going to do, it'll be even worse for business. While we share the same cause, we do *not* share the same ideology. I'm a pragmatist. I understand that for every little cause, there is an effect. But Cyrus? He's an idealist. He'd rather get caught up in the doing of things, the means of it, to get to an end. I've never agreed with it, but people like him can prove quite useful in their own way. There was a time when he could be reigned in, controlled, but he's just kept marching forward, reckless with his ideology, fucking up everything I worked so hard to put in motion." Faisal cleared his throat. "You see, boys, timing . . . is everything. All these grandiose displays will be too much exposure too soon, and instead of winning people to our cause, we'll be condemned. He's so driven that he wants the world to know about us now, by any means necessary. I can only imagine he's feeling a bit desperate right now, and desperate men are not to be trusted."

"Then tell us what he's going to do," I said.

Faisal cocked his head and looked at me.

"How do you feel about reality television?"

38

"Do you ever get the feeling Faisal was bullshitting us about Cyrus going off the deep end, even by cultist standards?" I asked. Twenty-four hours later, Connor and I stood outside the big white tent that covered the entirety of Bryant Park just behind the main branch of the New York Public Library. He was still dressed in his usual trench coat, but I was busy tugging at the lengthy coat of my tuxedo, making sure it concealed my bat.

"You mean are we really supposed to believe that Cyrus is planning a very public attack during Fashion Week?" Connor asked back.

I nodded.

"Well," he continued, "it does mix together a lot of what we know of him—his madness, his greed, his artistic desires for taking their message public with as much damage as possible . . ."

"I can't really imagine anything going down here during Fashion Week," I said. "Other than some best- and worst-dressed lists."

"Sounds like a perfect place to get some notice, kid,"

Connor said. He grabbed my arms and brushed them down. "Stop fidgeting. It's fine. Think about what's going on here tonight. Every year the park gets converted into the home of all the biggest fashion releases for the year. The surrounding streets are mobbed with people dressed in outfits more valuable than your apartment."

"And there will be cameras everywhere," I added.

Connor nodded. "Besides, why would Faisal Bane be lying at this point, aside from being a filthy lying cultist? He's got too much to gain by being honest with us. You saw how sick he looked at sea. He desperately wants to be on land. He knows that if he's bullshitting us, we'll pull the plug on them moving him to the mainland facility. Right now, it's a win-win situation for him if he's honest. I only wish he knew exactly what kind of spectacle Cyrus is going to try to pull here."

We had brought the entire situation to the attention of Inspectre Quimbley. He and as many people available from every other department had been gathered to surround the nexus of activity in front of us. No matter what went down, we were prepared. At least, I hoped we were prepared.

"You ready?" I heard from behind me, and I turned around. Jane was standing there and she looked gorgeous. I was used to her hair being up in a ponytail, but tonight it cascaded over her shoulders in delicious blond waves. Her long black dress sparkled like crazy and was slit up one leg. I stood there speechless.

Jane mimed bending to scoop something up. She held her hand out to me like she was holding something.

"I believe this jaw belongs to you," she said.

I grabbed it and pretended to shove it back into place.

"Don't mess your tie up," she said. She reached over and pushed my arms out of the way as she straightened it. I smiled as I watched her concentrating on getting it just right.

Connor coughed beside us and the two of us snapped out of our moment.

"Are you two ready for prom?"

Jane thwapped him on the arm with her handbag. "Don't hate."

"Now listen. There're going to be television cameras and photographers everywhere in there, so we need to keep this low-key," Connor said. "You two call at the slightest hint of something funny going on in there, alright?"

Jane and I nodded.

"Yes, Dad," we said in unison.

Connor sighed, then shook his head. "I can't believe the fate of the Big Apple lies in the hands of the world's cutest and most nauseating couple. You'd better get going. If you need me, I'll be along the south side of the tent outside with the rest of the White Stripes."

I motioned for Jane to give me a moment alone with Connor. After kissing me on the cheek, she stepped out of earshot.

"You sure you don't want to come inside instead of Jane?" I asked. "I'm sure no one in New York would bat an eye at two men walking into a runway show together. It *is* Fashion Week, after all."

Connor shook his head.

"After all the juvenile jealous crap you've put her through to alleviate your own guilt over working with Mina? I think you two need the on-the-job bonding time more than you and I do."

"Thanks," I said. "You're a pal."

I walked over to Jane and took her arm on mine.

"Hey, kid," Connor called out behind us. We turned. His face was deadpan. "Try not to die on any of the gowns, okay?"

"Will do," I said.

"That goes for both of you," he shouted as we crossed the street and left him behind.

The line to get in snailed along forever, but it gave us time to locate mayoral office liaison David Davidson in the crowd. Camera flashes were going off left and right. I waved him over to us.

"Nice to see you under more pleasant circumstances," he said, flashing that winning smile of his. His tuxedo was impeccable, but then again, he always was.

I thought back. The last time I had seen David Davidson was over the body of late Dr. Kolb in Central Park.

"Well, more pleasant for now," I said, shaking his hand. "You remember Jane?"

Davidson took Jane's hand, raised it to his lips, and kissed it. "Of course I do," he said. "Charmed. May I say you look lovely tonight?"

"Thank you," Jane said with a toothy smile. "And, yes, you may."

Davidson reached inside his suit coat and pulled out a handful of identical envelopes. He thumbed through them. "Mr. . . . Canderous, there you are . . . annnnd . . . Ms. Clayton-Forrester."

He held them out and I took both of them.

"I just want you to know," he said, lowering his voice to a whisper, "tickets to this were harder to arrange than setting up a visit for the president to the United Nations."

"We appreciate it," I said. "The whole Department does."

"Should anything actually happen here, though," Davidson continued, "the mayor would appreciate your discretion in handling the matter. He would prefer there not be as public a display as that last one back at the Met, especially given the media coverage here."

"We'll do our best," Jane said, surprising me with the return of that boundless optimism and cheer that had been lacking these past few days.

"Exactly," I said, "but I don't know how subtle we'll be. It's hard to deal with extraordinary affairs by ordinary means. But like the lady said, we'll try our best."

Davidson gave a nervous smile. "I guess that's as good as we can hope for," he said, pulling out his cell phone. "I suppose I'd better have emergency services at the ready just in case . . ."

With that, he wandered off into the crowd, his cell phone already at his ear.

I looked over at Jane, only to find her looking back at me, smiling. Dressed as we were, it was hard not to relish in the strange fantasy of it all. I could feel the electricity in the air, and for once it wasn't my power . . . or Jane casting spells through a junction box. It almost made me wish we were a normal couple out for a night on the town, rather than out to stomp the forces of evil.

The fashion plate bouncers manning the entrance to the giant tent stopped us when we arrived. After having our tickets examined to the nth degree, we were finally allowed inside. The interior of the tent was lit with a wash of cool colors that complemented the clean, crisp look of the whole Fashion Week affair. A white runner stretched down the center of the main aisle, presumably the catwalk for the show. It was flanked by hundreds of black wooden folding chairs that were quickly filling with the cream of the New York fashionista crop.

As we made our way across the transformed park, more of the staff checked our tickets and led us to our seats. We sat in two of the four unoccupied seats at the end of our row, and I looked over at Jane, who was still beaming. She squeezed my arm, and for a split second it felt like an actual date.

After a moment, I turned and looked out over the arriving crowd.

"Let me know if you see anything," I said.

The two of us looked around the tent, which was filling up. I recognized a few of the faces in the crowd from television or film, but I was more interested in the camera crews that were busy setting up their equipment. I pointed them out to Jane.

"So it looks like tonight's going to be televised," she said. "Good thing I spent some time on my makeup."

"You look beautiful," I said without hesitation, "no question about that, but with those cameras here, it pretty much means that if anything paranormal goes down, we're screwed. That's not just local news. It's *national* television. And Cyrus Mandalay wants to go large scale with evil."

Jane's eyes danced as the lights went down and the music rose. The fashion show started, and all we could do was keep vigilant while ignoring the pageantry before us. My head pounded from all the lights and from peering into the darkened crowd for signs of anything paranormal. My phone, my third one in as many days, vibrated to life in my pocket. I discreetly pulled it out and checked the display.

The Inspectre.

I tapped Jane on the shoulder before flipping it open. I held the phone up between the two of us and we leaned our heads in.

"Anything out there yet, sir?" I whispered into it.

"Negative," he said. "There's been nothing reported on our end. How are things in there, boy? Anything out of the ordinary?"

"Other than anorexics walking up and down the runway in flamboyant outfits? No, sir."

"Damn and blast," the Inspectre swore. "If Cyrus was going to do something, I would have expected him to make his move by now. There's simply no activity out here, so keep your eyes sharp . . . and keep an eye on the girl, too, my boy."

The fatherly concern in his voice nearly broke my heart.

"Will do, Inspectre."

As I flipped my phone shut, a couple approached and I assumed it was for the two unoccupied seats next to us. I rose to let them in.

"I'm sorry . . ." I started, but stopped when I saw who it was. "Godfrey?"

It was Godfrey and he nodded curtly, shushing me.

Gone were his pristine suit and tie. He was dressed in a tuxedo far more fashionable than mine, and he looked nervous. When I saw the woman on his arm, I could see why.

She was dark-haired and gorgeous. I definitely knew her from somewhere, but I couldn't place her.

"Hello, Simon," he said. "Hello, Jane."

The two of us were speechless and all we could do was nod hello.

Godfrey seated the woman with him and then sat down next to me, the nervous look still on his face.

"Godfrey," I said. "Are you okay?"

He looked a little breathless, but gave me a thumbs-up. "Just . . . nerves . . ." he said between breaths.

"What are you doing here?" I whispered. "You shouldn't be here."

I had already gotten myself into a little bit of heat with Connor over the poor guy, and now he was here in potential harm's way.

Godfrey pulled off his glasses and cleaned them. This seemed to calm him a little. He slid them back on his nose. "It's funny. The other day in the café, there was a *Village Voice* open on one of the coffee tables when I sat down. This one personal ad caught my eye and I responded to it, and well, turns out that Mandi here was looking for an escort to this event at Fashion Week. She was in last year's show but her modeling shoot in Thailand conflicted with the week leading up to it so she couldn't participate this year."

"So you answered a personal ad in the *Voice* and you ended up with a *supermodel* on your arm?" I said. No wonder she looked familiar. I had probably seen her on a cover somewhere.

Godfrey nodded, smiling. "What are the odds on that?"

Pretty good, actually, I thought, considering what I knew about his power. He truly was the luckiest man in the world.

"Excuse us," I said to his date, and grabbed Godfrey and Jane, dragging them off behind our seating area.

"Godfrey, you've got to get you and your date out of here now," I said. "The Inspectre will kill me if he finds

you in here. They don't want you anywhere near this type
of field work. Something weird's going down."

"What? Tell me."

"We don't know," Jane chimed in.

"Maybe I can help," he offered. He looked like a big
sad-eyed puppy who just wanted to do good.

Realizing that arguing with Godfrey wasn't going to
work, I caved. Maybe if I threw him a bone it would get
him out of here faster. "Fine. Um, can you think of anything supernatural about Bryant Park?"

Godfrey's eyes rolled back into his head as he searched
through his vast array of mental records. Twenty seconds
later, the pupils rolled back into place. Godfrey shook his
head.

"Nothing supernatural," he said. "Sorry."

"Dammit," I said.

"I *do* remember something creepy, though," Godfrey
said.

"I'm sorry?" Jane said.

"There's this one fact about Bryant Park . . . like I just
said, it's actually a bit more creepy than anything. Nothing
supernatural has been documented about Bryant Park."

"But . . . ?" I said, urging him on. Somewhere off behind me the tone of the room shifted and a low murmur
began to spread through the crowd. "But what?"

"Well, before the Crystal Palace fire that happened here
around 1858, the park had actually been used as a potter's
field from 1823 to 1840."

"Potter's field . . . ?" Jane said. "Is that some sort of
quidditch thing?"

Godfrey shook his head.

"No," he said. "You know. A potter's field . . . a graveyard for the indigent, the poor."

I was already redialing the Inspectre. From across the
tent, several screams erupted from the crowd.

"You mean to tell me," I said to Godfrey, "that we've
been looking all over the place for a psychotic necromancer

and *we're sitting on top of a graveyard full of bodies*?"

"Well, when you put it like that . . ." Godfrey started. "Still, we're talking seventeen years of that mass grave filling up. So that puts the number in the thousands, but you have to figure there's only about a ten percent viability of corpses in any shape to be reanimated."

Godfrey whistled.

"Still," he continued, "that's going to be an impressive number of raised undead."

When the Inspectre answered his phone, I held up my hand for Godfrey to stop.

"Cyrus isn't going to be attacking from the outside," I shouted into the phone. "His army is already in here, inside. The tent is set up over a *graveyard*!"

"Damn and blast," the Inspectre shouted, and I could already hear him moving away from the phone. "Everyone move in."

My line went dead as Inspectre Quimbley disconnected, still shouting out orders.

I slipped my phone back into my pocket as the inside of the tent erupted into chaos, and I turned to inspect all the sudden shouting and screaming. People were jumping up from their seats everywhere, pushing and shoving one another as they tried to run from an unseen enemy for the exits at the far end of the runway. Fear filled the air.

"Simon," Jane screamed. "Look out!"

What felt like a leather glove wrapped itself around my leg, and I looked down. A corpse was pulling its body up from under the ground with one free hand and digging into my leg with the other. The skin was dry and taut like scratchy leather but hung in strips from the body through its tattered remains of clothing.

I reached inside my tuxedo coat and pulled out the retractable bat, extending it. "Good thing I brought my dress bat," I said, and swung it down at the poor reanimated soul clawing at me. The head came free with a dry snap and the body slumped over, releasing me. I shook my leg to get the hand free and resisted the willies in front of my girlfriend.

"C'mon, Jane," I said. I grabbed her arm and started dragging her toward the highest concentration of people freaking out in the crowd.

"Wait," she pleaded. "Simon, what about Godfrey?"

I stopped and looked back. Godfrey had frozen in his tracks because two zombies covered in fresh dirt had him pressed up against the side of the tent.

"Shit," I said, angry with myself for leaving him. Connor was right. I had already put Godfrey in harm's way more than once so far, and his life and safety were my responsibility now. I ran over to him with Jane hot on my heels.

Godfrey looked on at the creatures with fascination, studying them and making no move to get away. Maybe it was the archivist in him, but if I didn't do something, he'd die with that same curious look on his face.

I sped up to a run, raising my bat up over my head and swinging it down hard on one of the zombies. I heard its skull crack and split, and then my bat continued down into the area between its shoulders. And stuck.

I tugged to get my bat out of the remains of the still-twitching creature as Godfrey's face finally fell to horror, but my bat wouldn't come free. The bony fingers of the other zombie started clawing at me while I was still struggling with the first, but I needed my weapon if I was going to stop it.

"Watch your head, sweetie," Jane called out from behind me, and I turned, then ducked, as I saw her swinging one of the wooden chairs at the other zombie. The chair hit the creature with surprising force and shattered, all of it falling away except for one lone, jagged piece that stuck out of the creature's head like it was some kind of zombified unicorn. "See, I did learn something from your little "Shufflers and Shamblers" talk at the bookstore!"

The jagged point swung dangerously close to my cheek and I spun myself away while still holding on to the bat lodged in the other one, causing the second creature to swing into the protrusion's path. Something inside the impaled zombie popped, and the air was filled with a mixture of mold and the rotten stench of ancient putrification.

Holding my breath so I wouldn't throw up on my tuxedo, I finally pulled my bat free and knocked the creatures to the floor, where they both stopped moving.

"Go take care of your date," I said. Godfrey nodded, but when we spotted her, she was already long gone from her seat and safely pushing her way out of one of the tent flaps. If anyone was capable of making a hasty escape in high heels, it was definitely a supermodel. "Fine, then. You and Jane stick with me."

Jane put her hand on my arm. "I love it when you get all authoritative, but maybe we should hold up a second before we go leaping into action? Mind if I take a look around?"

I smiled and followed Jane as she pushed her way through the crowd and ran over to the nearest camera. She took a deep breath and raised both hands up to it.

"Oh," she said, and turned suddenly back to me. "You might want to catch me if this knocks me out or something."

She leaned toward me and I kissed her, our mouths pressing hard together.

Jane put her hands on the side of the camera and started muttering in that technobabble sound that I didn't understand. Godfrey stepped closer to me.

"What is she doing?"

"Not really sure," I said with a shrug. "She's cute when she gets all magical, though."

"I can still hear you," she said. "Just because I'm patching into the camera feed doesn't mean I'm not still here in front of you."

"Sorry," I said.

"Don't be sorry," Jane said. "Just wanted to give you a heads-up before you said something about my butt in front of Godfrey."

Godfrey looked shocked.

I took a swipe at a zombie chasing after a passing B-list celebrity. "Don't think about the crazy shit going on around you."

"Guys," Jane called out after several seconds, and I turned back to see if she needed help. She looked a little drained, but she was able to stand by leaning against the camera rig. "I checked the entire room by patching into all the camera feeds. I don't see any signs of Cyrus in the crowd, but he *has* to be here, right?"

Godfrey nodded. "According to Gauntlet research, a raising like this requires the close proximity of the necromancer responsible for it."

"Well, if he's not here," Jane said, "how is he doing this?"

"He *is* here," I said, "we're just not looking in the right place."

I looked above the crowd, and there was my answer. The one spot that overlooked the whole interior of the tent from the far end of the room, a well-concealed slit that gave the perfect view into the tent from the New York Public Library.

I glanced around the room. The cavalry had arrived and a dozen or so D.E.A. agents were working their way through the crowd now. I spied Director Wesker and Inspectre Quimbley pulling a zombie off one of the stick-thin models and throwing it to the ground. It was nice to see the divisions getting along for once. Zombies always brought people together.

"He must be in the library. The Fashion Week tent is in good hands," I said. "Let's go."

"Where are we going?" Jane said. She had Godfrey by the arm and dragged him along behind us as we picked our way through the crowd.

"We can stay here doing damage control," I said, "or we can get to the root of the problem and take care of it."

"No more making with the squishy brains?" Jane said.

"Please don't talk about that right now," Godfrey said, his voice weaker than usual. "Trying not to throw up here."

I looked behind me, and sure enough, Godfrey looked a little gray in the face. Not as gray as some of the leathery corpses shambling through the crowd, but close enough that I stopped talking about it.

"Fine," I said, leading the two of them off toward the main branch of the New York Public Library. "Let's go check out some books."

39

Jane held her own, weaving through the crowd, but Godfrey was more or less stunned by the chaos erupting around us and Jane pulled him along behind. When we emerged from the tent, she let go.

"Go on, Godfrey, get out of here," I said, and looked up at the architectural marvel that was the library.

"I can help," he said, all meek, still looking rather shell-shocked.

"You can help by not dying," I said. I turned to him and shook him until he looked directly at me. "Don't be a fool. Those things are vicious and there're way too many of them."

"Yes," Jane added, "and they're icky."

"That, too," I said, nodding. "Go across the street and keep an eye out for the Inspectre until the police arrive."

Godfrey nodded, adjusted his glasses, and headed off across the street through traffic. Several cars slammed on their brakes and honked, but by then Godfrey had made it across safely.

"Come on," I said to Jane, and set off in search of a way into the library.

As long as I had lived in New York, I had never really taken stock of the library, but running around the foot of it while we searched for an entrance, I was impressed by its old-world grandeur and the sheer size of it. The library ran an entire two blocks from Fortieth to Forty-second streets, and was massive. We circled the building hand in hand and came around to the main entrance on Fifth Avenue, its many stairs and two stone lions gated off from the regular sidewalk.

"If those lions come to life or anything," Jane said, "I may just pee on myself."

"Sexy," I said. I started climbing over one of the police barriers. I held my hand out to help her over. "It's okay. I think I already did earlier."

"And that's why we make such a perfect couple," she said.

Since Jane was still in her full-length evening gown, she sat sidesaddle on top of the barrier as I steadied her and threw her legs over it. Taking our time, we made our way up the steps, looking for any sign of movement, especially from those menacing-looking lions.

"You know, this would be terribly romantic if it weren't for all the undead stuff," she said.

Most of the doors to the library were revolving ones, but all the way toward the right side was a set of standard doors. I retracted my bat, reholstered it at my side, and fished around inside my tuxedo pocket for my lock picks.

I hesitated as I recalled pulling them out to use for Mina's break-in. Then I looked Jane square in the eyes and pulled the leather case out. I unrolled it, exposing the pick sets.

I gulped. Though things had been much better between us lately, the stuff Jane had said about being more open in our relationship was something I really needed to work on. "Jane," I said. "You're not the only one with a dark past around here. I haven't been honest about everything lately . . ."

She glanced down at the lock picks, eyebrows raised, then stopped me by putting her hand on my arm.

"There will be time for all that later," she said, "but right now, I think we have a problem."

"That's the understatement of the evening," I said, almost laughing and feeling relieved just for having opened up and owning a small part of my past.

Jane rolled her eyes, then pointed toward the door. "A more immediate one," she said. "Are you sure those picks are going to work?"

I looked where she was pointing, only to realize that the door had an electronic lock. I slid the lock picks back into my pocket and started feeling around in my jacket.

"Crap," I said.

"What's wrong?"

"I can't pick it, but I can use my power on it." I thought about the last time I had done this. Mina had put a gun to my head that time at the Museum of Modern Art, but I figured I could read the lock the same way, and without that kind of pressure on me this time. "Thing is, I'm out of Life Savers, and if I use my power, I don't want to pass out once we get in there."

"You're out?" she asked. "You *always* have them on you!"

"They're in my regular jacket," I said. "Sheesh, when you switch out purses, haven't you ever left something in the old one by mistake?"

Jane turned away and looked toward the street. I thought she was pissed at me. We really didn't have time for this.

"Will a pretzel do?"

"What?" I said. I turned and looked. One of New York's thousands of street vendors was set up at the corner of Fifth and Forty-second.

I nodded and knelt down in front of the lock. "Umm, sure. The carbs in it should convert to sugar. I'll get working on the lock if you go get me one."

I handed her a five.

"Keep the change," I said. "And thanks."

"What change?" she said. "When's the last time you bought street food?"

Jane hiked up her dress and ran down the steps toward the vendor cart. I turned back to the door and grabbed the electronic keypad in both hands. This time I felt an immediate connection with it, and my mind slipped into the psychometric past of the object.

It was nighttime in my vision, and I was in the head of a guard. He was at the door, punching his code in, and quick as that, I had what I needed. I pulled myself out of the vision to find that Jane had returned and was holding out a pretzel.

"You look kinda creepy when you do that whole thing, hon," she said.

Feeling shaky, I stayed on my knees and took the pretzel from her.

"Your face kinda glazes over and your eyes go all dull."

"Sorry," I said. "I'll work on that."

Jane shrugged. "No big. Just thought you might want to know."

I wolfed down the pretzel and waited several minutes until I started to feel better before pulling on my gloves and punching in the code for the door. Anything I could do to keep my power in check under the craziness that was tonight helped. The little light on the electronic lock turned green. I pushed the door open and stepped into the spooky darkness of the library.

I eased in, my eyes taking a moment to adjust to the darkness. Jane followed right behind me, clutching my hand.

"You sure this is where Cyrus is?" she whispered.

I spied something off to the left of the interior doors. It

was the unconscious body of the guard I had just seen in my psychometric flash.

"Pretty sure," I said.

We had to be brief, but we took the time to check him to see how badly he was injured. Aside from a lump on the back of his head, the guard looked like he was in good enough condition to leave there for now.

"Well, if we just follow the trail of bodies, we'll be okay," I said. I grabbed Jane by the hand and the two of us headed farther into the library.

The sound of the battle outside in Bryant Park was hard to miss as we entered the library's main room. Books ringed the room behind rails that led down to a sunken research area filled with long wooden tables and hooded lamps. The ceiling rose several stories above us, marble walls and vaulted windows to either side. Four-tiered chandeliers hung from a faux blue sky with fluffy white clouds on it. It was a calming scene, given the circumstances. I thought maybe I should start using my library card after all this was over.

Jane and I stopped when we reached the center of the cavernous room.

"Where do you think he is?" Jane whispered, continuing to look around.

"I'm not sure," I said. I listened for any sign of him, but all I could hear was the sound of continuing chaos outside the library in the big Fashion Week tent. "But we've got to start somewhere. Any suggestions?"

Jane thought a minute. "How about we start with the *N*'s?"

"Why there?" I asked.

"Well, that's where I'd keep a necromancer," Jane said, giving a wan smile. "Under the *N*'s."

Her logic made as much sense as anything else tonight, so we set off toward the shelves around the edge of the room.

The *N*'s turned out to be along the wall facing Bryant Park and, lo and behold, when I entered the aisle, I could make out the silhouette of Cyrus Mandalay standing on the ledge of one of the high-arched windows up ahead. His attention was focused outside, and given the noise, we didn't need to be especially careful in sneaking up on him.

About two-thirds of the way down the aisle, I motioned for Jane to stop and wait while I continued ahead. All I needed was to get close enough to knock his legs out from under him with my bat as he stood on the window ledge. The backs of his calves were about eye level, perfect for my natural swing.

Winding up behind Cyrus's back, I caught his face in the reflection of the glass. It was a mask of concentration as he stared down into the park. The thought occurred to me that if I could see Cyrus's face in the reflection, then he could probably see mine, which explained why his reflection shifted from the park to me in that instant. Before I could swing, his foot lashed out and caught me in my temple. A flash of blinding whiteness hit my eyes and I couldn't help but drop my bat and clutch my head as I reeled backward.

Cyrus jumped down from the window ledge and landed in front of me. Even without the added height, he still towered above me at well over six feet. He grinned, his facial tattoos warping as his sharklike smile spread wide.

"See?" Jane cried out from behind me. "I *told* you he'd be under *N* for necromancer!"

Cyrus grabbed me by the hair, wrapped his arm across my throat, and held me there. "What?" he said. "Is this really the *N* section?"

I nodded, my chin digging into the taut muscles in Cyrus's arm.

Cyrus chuckled, and the sound echoed throughout the quiet hush of the library. "Nice detective work, Ms. Clayton-Forrester, but I'm afraid you're wrong. It's just a coincidence that you found me in this section of the library. It simply had the best view that I needed for today's theatrics."

I pushed against Cyrus's arm, but it was no use. He had been an imposing fellow when he had been the owner of Tome, Sweet Tome, but cultish crazy had pushed him into the realm of unearthly strength, and there was no way I was breaking free.

"Jane, run," I shouted.

Part of me half hoped she had some kind of ace up her sleeve, but she smartly turned back and ran up the aisle, which was impressive given the heels she was wearing.

That was, she ran for about ten feet, before a new obstacle presented itself. A column of zombies had started working its way down the aisle toward us and Jane ran smack-dab into them. She spun swiftly to escape, but decaying hands latched on to her and held her in place. In a last-ditch effort, she dug into her sequined clutch and pulled her phone free, but Cyrus made a gesture and one of the zombies knocked it free from her hand. The rest of them grabbed both her arms and pressed her up against one side of the shelves.

"Bad girl, Jane." Cyrus *tsk*ed. "You were such a promising Sectarian, too. I saw you when you went all Tesla coil on that double-crosser Mina back at the Guggenheim, my dear. We won't have any repeats of that. I think we'll just keep you pinned right there against those books like a butterfly on a specimen board, far from anything electrical."

Cyrus grabbed my head like he was palming a basketball and turned me so I looked up at him. "And as for you," he said, "I think I have an exciting little surprise to share with you."

Holding me in his viselike grip, Cyrus helped himself back onto the window ledge and then lifted me up to join him, my bat still lying useless on the library floor.

With his free hand, he pointed down into the crowd through the hidden slit in the roof of the tent. He was pointing at Argyle Quimbley, who was earnestly protecting a pack of supermodels from a horde of zombies using a folding chair, quite adeptly, I thought. No wonder F.O.G. had appointed him to teach me Unorthodox Fighting Techniques. Still, the odds were against him. Zombies never tired.

"Lucky you," Cyrus said. "For all the trouble you've caused me, you're getting ringside seats to watch as I tear your precious Inspectre apart, limb by limb."

"For all the trouble I've caused *you*?" I said, laughing. "Are you kidding me? I've just been trying to protect my city."

"What with you foiling my plans twice, I'm a pariah with every cultist in the tristate area," Cyrus shouted, his anger increasing along with the pressure of his arm around my neck. "You and that partner of yours made a laughingstock out of my grand plans that night at the Met. Now you've ruined Para-lyzed."

"Sorry . . .'bout . . . that . . ." I said, gasping for breath.

"So first you get to watch the old man die," Cyrus said, delighted with himself, "and then the girl."

At the mention of the Inspectre and Jane, I started to panic. Well, panic more than I already was. Unfortunately, the more I struggled to free myself, the more air I used. Stars began to pop and burst before my eyes as darkness started to take over.

"Um, excuse me," a familiar voice called out. It was meek and nervous and 100 percent Godfrey's. Cyrus relaxed his grip a little and turned us toward where it had come from. Godfrey stood farther along the bank of windows. He looked fantastic in his tux, yet nervous as hell, but he stood there, unmoving. "I think you should let go of him . . . now."

The nerves in his voice kept his threat from seeming anything more than silly, and even I wanted to join Cyrus when he laughed out loud. He jumped down from the windowsill and started walking us toward Godfrey.

I was worried about slipping on my bat, but I didn't have the best lines of sight from my chokehold position, and I couldn't see it anywhere.

Cyrus gestured and a few zombies broke from the pack and also headed toward Godfrey. Godfrey started backing away, but Cyrus closed the distance in a flash and smashed him in the face, breaking his glasses. They tumbled to the floor and Godfrey clutched his face, blood running through his fingers.

"Oh, God," he said. "I think I'm about to throw up."

"I've got it from here, Godfrey," another familiar voice said from behind me. Connor. "Thanks."

There was the unmistakable dull, metallic thud of my bat, and I felt Cyrus's arm release me as he toppled over and hit the floor hard. I spun around and, sure enough, there was Connor, holding my bat. He was covered head to toe in bits of rotting flesh, and he twirled my bat around in his hands.

"That felt good, kid," he said. "Maybe I oughta get me one of these."

"Oh, boys," Jane called out. "A little help here?"

The zombies still had her, but with Cyrus unconscious, they seemed a little less focused on holding her now. In fact, they looked far more intent on trying to eat her.

"I thought if we neutralized the necromancer, the zombies would drop," I said to Connor.

"That seemed like the likeliest of scenarios," he said, handing my bat back to me. "This is the other, I guess. The dead have been raised, but now they're just not in anyone's control anymore. Let's have at 'em, kid."

Connor dashed off into the sea of undead. Already many of them were just wandering around aimlessly, while others suddenly became focused on the two of us as we joined the fray.

Jane had already broken free of her captors and backed to the other side of the book aisle. Her hands flew like lightning as she reached onto the shelves, pulling book after book free and tossing them right between the eyes of every zombie she targeted. She was cool, calculated, and unremorseful—all things that for once made me thankful for her bouts with the dark side of herself. It meant she could do something like this in survival mode without really scarring all that was good in her at the same time.

Connor and I made short work of the rest. Slow and unfocused zombies were much easier to contend with than when Cyrus had been controlling them. Godfrey had already pulled out a pocket-sized notebook that was covered in his own blood and was taking notes, although he had to hold the notebook an inch from his face to do so without his glasses.

"Jesus, Jane," Connor said with a whistle. "That was some impressive book throwing."

Jane curtsied in her evening gown, which had remained relatively intact despite our fight.

"I've got mad shelving skillz," she said. "All that time in the Black Stacks at Tome, Sweet Tome. A book doesn't have to be all dark and arcane to do some damage, you know."

"How did you know to come here?" I said to Connor.

"Ah," Godfrey said, looking up from his notebook. "That would be my doing."

"Godfrey?" I said, turning to him.

He nodded, then gave his nonexistent glasses a phantom push up onto his nose. "After you dragged me out of the tent, I didn't know what to do with myself, but I had to do *something*. So I sought out Mr. Christos here because I thought you might need backup."

"And you did, kid," Connor added. "And this is why we don't leave our partners out of our lives, understand?"

I nodded.

"Good," he said, reaching into his own coat pocket. He pulled out a short length of rope and knelt down. He flipped Cyrus over and the rope sprung to life, tying itself tight around Cyrus's wrists.

"Godfrey here finds me and drags me in after you, convinced you were on to something. So I get him to play decoy while I secured your bat." Connor slapped Godfrey on the back. "Sorry I didn't get my swing in sooner. You feel okay after that punch of his?"

Godfrey nodded with a big smile on his face, the blood forming an evil clown smile on his lips. "I believe that might be my first Departmental injury, unless you count paper cuts down in the Gauntlet. Or the time I twisted my ankle on the stone steps down there."

I waggled a finger at Connor. "Whatever happened to what you said about keeping Godfrey out of all this?" I asked.

Connor shrugged. "Jesus, kid, did you see the way things were going down there? We needed every man we could get our hands on. Don't take everything I say to heart, okay?"

I paused for a minute, kicking myself for being so literal-minded at times. I was so focused on my own issues that I had not really paid attention to the rest of the things around me.

"If you hadn't shown up to save the day . . ." I started, then stopped with a shiver. Jane put her arm around me.

"That's the great thing about being me, kid," Connor said. "Even if you haven't been looking out for me, I'm *still* always looking out for you. I'm a good partner like that."

"I'm sorry," I said.

"Don't be sorry," Connor said. "Just be a better partner."

This softer side of Connor confused me. What was going on in his life that suddenly gave him this deeper appreciation of me? Just the other day he was ready to cut me loose if I didn't get my act together. Now he was all Walton's Mountain.

Now was not the time to think about it. Zombieriffic things were still happening out in the tent, and then there was the matter of keeping this whole incident contained. Since a good portion of this evening's events was taped for television, we'd have to secure all the equipment and pray that none of the footage had been broadcast live. First, we had to clear the library of Cyrus Mandalay, then the zombies.

It took all four of us to carry Cyrus out of there, but by the time we regrouped with the rest of the Department, it was like we were one big, happy family in an ocean of undead body parts.

And now we had another prison barge friend for Faisal Bane to play with.

40

No one escaped cleanup duty later that night. Some Other Division and Greater & Lesser Arcana employees headed back uptown to take on the bulk of the workload under the Guggenheim while several other divisions stayed to work on cleaning up Bryant Park. I was thankful that we hadn't been stuck with that task—sure, the zombie menace had been quelled, but there were bodies all over the inside of the tent. The Guggenheim was just fine with me. Even Godfrey Candella had come along, still in his fashion show outfit, furiously taking notes on the remains of the Paralyzed exhibit.

Worn down as I was, the powers that be took mercy on me and I was spared the task of zombie body removal. Instead, I concentrated my efforts on going through boxes and boxes of invites Cyrus has stashed into one of the crates for his freak show when David Davidson arrived. Everyone looked up from what they were doing.

Davidson looked a little rough around the edges after all the spin he must have had to work tonight, and he loosened his tie.

"Well?" the Inspectre said. "How stands the situation?"

Davidson said, "Well, the good news is that most of what happened was contained to the big tent behind the library. The bad part is that there were a lot of celebrities who witnessed it, and part of it was being broadcast live."

I crossed over to him.

"So the cat's out of the bag," I said, pissed off that we had done so poorly at containment. "We're public."

Connor came over to me and patted me on the shoulder. "Easy, kid. Let's hear what the man has to say."

Davidson gave me a stern look, then turned to Connor and smiled. "Thank you, Connor. The last thing Cyrus said before the people from the Thaniel Graydon took him away was a resounding "Even if you arrest me, you're still going to have to deal with all the media." A pretty weak parting threat, if you ask me."

"But what about all the media?"

David Davidson actually let out a chuckle. "If there's one thing that's easy to do, it's spin something in the fashion industry," he said. "With all the witnesses and footage leaking out, to deny what was going on would be foolish. So why not play into it?"

Despite his confidence in Davidson, the Inspectre looked worried. "Meaning what, exactly, my boy?" he said.

Jane came up to me and put her hand in mine, squeezing it. The pain in my wrists from earlier still rang out, but I continued holding her hand.

"Ladies and gentlemen," Davidson said with a flourish. "I give you the fashion industry's newest marketing stunt— a high-fashion zombie walk!"

"Zombie walk?" Jane asked.

Davidson nodded. "Yeah, I hadn't really heard of it either, but there's an underground movement on the Internet of these flash mobs that show up costumed as zombies. Mostly they're fans of zombie movies and the like, but they get together, usually in urban areas, and wander around in character for several hours. Anyway, we had a few down by NYU a while back, and I thought it might be a good idea to start funding some of their events . . . you know, so they'd gain more popularity and just in case I ever needed a plausible cover story for a real zombie outbreak. Like, say, at Bryant Park."

"And you expect people to buy this?" I asked.

Davidson nodded again. "People will believe almost anything they can Google. You should look it up. Besides, who can tell the difference between brainless, emaciated supermodels and gaunt, brain-hungry zombies? It's fashion . . . People are far more likely to buy into a flash zombie walk than they are the harsh supernatural reality that the dead were rising and walking the land, consuming the living."

All of the agents erupted into applause.

"That's what passes for genius?" Jane whispered to me.

"I guess," I said, joining in the applause. "Seems to be working."

I turned to look for Connor, only to see him standing alone over by the invitation boxes I had been working on, stock-still as everyone around him clapped. I went over to him, but he took no notice.

His face was stoic and his hand was clutching one of the invitation envelopes. He reached in his pocket and pulled out the letter I had seen in my psychometric flash of his desk. He clutched it in his other hand.

"Connor," I said, "you okay?"

"You know how I've been a little distant lately? Wanting you to keep out of my business?"

I nodded.

He unfolded the letter from his pocket and handed it to me. The page was blank except for one single message in the center of it. No address, no signature, nothing.

It read: AIDAN CHRISTOS IS OURS. STOP LOOKING OR HE DIES.

"Aidan?" I asked. "Your brother?"

"How many Aidan Christoses do you know of? Someone sent it to me a little while ago, kid."

"I accidentally got a psychometric reading off your desk," I said, sheepish. "I know. I'm sorry. But whoever sent it to you knew I might see it, and they somehow blocked it from my power. It knocked me out. But why now? Why send something after all this time?"

Connor was silent, assessing the information I'd given him. "Because whoever they are, they must know I work with you. And now that your control over your power is growing, they know it's only a matter of time before I use you to help me track him down."

"But if you were going to keep that letter from me to keep him safe, why tell me now?"

He held up one of the invitations. The name on it read only Aidan, and it had an address. Right here. In New York City.

"What are the odds, kid?"

"I'm not sure," I said, "but I think it's time to find out."

Connor nodded. "Let's find him."

The two of us headed back toward the exit. When the Inspectre saw us leaving, he must have seen our determination, and didn't say a word. And I knew why: You could never get away with stopping people with the kind of hope we had on our faces.

ABOUT THE AUTHOR

ANTON STROUT was born in the Berkshire Hills mere miles from writing heavyweights Nathaniel Hawthorne and Herman Melville. He currently lives in historic Jackson Heights, New York (where nothing paranormal ever really happens, he assures you).

His short story "The Lady in Red" can be found in the DAW Books anthology *Pandora's Closet*, and a tie-in story to *Dead to Me* entitled "The Fourteenth Virtue" can be found in DAW's *The Dimension Next Door*.

He is the cocreator of the faux folk musical *Sneezin' Jeff & Blue Raccoon: The Loose Gravel Tour*, winner of the Best Storytelling Award at the first annual New York International Fringe Festival.

In his scant spare time, he is an always writer, sometimes actor, sometimes musician, occasional RPGer, and the world's most casual and controller-smashing video gamer. He now works in the exciting world of publishing, and yes, it is as glamorous as it sounds.

He is currently hard at work on the next book featuring Simon Canderous and can be found lurking the darkened hallways of www.antonstrout.com.

For this paranormal investigator,
it's business as unusual…

DEAD TO ME

by Anton Strout

psy·chom·e·try (si-kom'i-tre) n.

1. The power to touch an object and divine information about its history
2. For Simon Canderous: not as cool as it sounds

Possessing the power of psychometry never did much for Simon Canderous, until it landed him a job with New York City's Department of Extraordinary Affairs. But he's not at all prepared for the strange case that unfolds before him—one involving politically correct cultists, a homicidal bookcase, and the forces of Darkness, which kind of have a crush on him…

"Following Simon's adventures is like being the pinball in an especially antic game, but it's well worth the wear and tear."
—Charlaine Harris, *New York Times* bestselling author

penguin.com